Everyday Magic

Charlie Laidlaw

RINGWOOD PUBLISHING
GLASGOW

First published in Great Britain in 2021
by
Ringwood Publishing, Glasgow.
www.ringwoodpublishing.com
mail@ringwoodpublishing.com

ISBN 978-1-901514-77-3

British Library Cataloguing-in-Publication Data
A catalogue record for this book is available from the British
Library

Printed and bound in the UK
by
Lonsdale Direct Solutions

Dedication

Dedicated to my children, who aren't children any more.

Best wishes

Best wishes

'No space of regret can make amends for one life's opportunity misused.'

Charles Dickens

One

When Carole was little, she found a magic clearing in the woods near her home. She had been exploring, surrounded by oak, birch, and hazel trees, picking her way carefully between bramble and nettle. There was birdsong, squirrels darting across branches, and patterns of sunlight on the woodland floor. She had been looking for bilberries, and her hands were full of the small black fruit. She stopped to sit on an outcrop of rock by a wide stream that, in winter, could quickly become a torrent of brown water. In summer, it was comforting; in winter, treacherous. She ate her bilberries, the stream cascading over a small waterfall; the sound of water in her ears. It was summer and the stream bubbled crystal clear. The woodland rose in folds from the stream, and she climbed steadily upwards. Here, the trees crammed in on her; it was darker. When she looked up, she could only see sunlight trapped on leaves far above. It was a part of the old woodland that she'd never been to before, but she pushed on; she had a feeling that she was on an adventure and might suddenly come across a gingerbread house or wizard's cottage.

At the top of the hill she found herself in a small clearing. It was only a few yards across, framed with oak trees, and perfectly round. Sunlight from directly above made the clearing warm, and she stood at its centre, wondering if she was the first person to have ever discovered it. Each of the oak trees around the clearing seemed precisely set, each one a perfect distance from the next, and she walked around them, touching each one, wondering if someone had planted

1

the oak trees, or if the clearing really was a magic place. She still believed in magic. Then she stood again at its centre, wondering at its symmetry and why a long-dead sorcerer might have planted the oak trees. Then, realising that the sorcerer might not be dead and that she had walked uninvited into his private domain, she hurried away, not sure whether to be frightened or excited. But it was a place she often went back to that summer, and on following summers, sometimes alone and sometimes with her little brother. They would sit in the centre of the woodland circle, eating bilberries, hoping to meet the sorcerer who had built the clearing. She wasn't frightened of him anymore; the clearing was too peaceful to have been made by a bad wizard. It was their secret place, but mainly Carole's, because she had found it. It was a comforting place: it was somewhere she would go if she was sad or angry about something, because the woodland circle and its shifting half-shadows offered calm and new perspectives. She could almost hear the trees speak to her, the wind in their branches making the leaves whisper, but so softly that she couldn't understand. She would listen, eyes closed, the leaves rustling, but she never understood what they were saying. The circle of trees stood solid and immovable, dark and stoic, old and wise, each one the colour of stone.

Two

There may be traffic disruptions en route.

The grown-up Carole (with an 'e' because she's punctilious about it) Gunn looks to be in her mid-thirties but, at the risk of offending her, is probably older, and who is taking her reluctant daughter to a piano lesson. In a good light, Carole might still be considered beautiful, with large oval green eyes, button nose, full red lips and short brown hair, but not today because she's frowning. Frowning rearranges her features: purses her lips, makes her eyes smaller. It's a pity that she frowns so much. She knows it too, mainly because her mother keeps telling her, and also says that Carole didn't always frown so much. Her mother, bluntly forthright, is a source of much unwelcome advice.

The daughter, Iona, is slumped in the passenger seat of Carole's Honda, arms petulantly folded, and wordlessly staring out the window on her side. She's called Iona because it was on that small Scottish island she was conceived, possibly. This is something of an embarrassment to Iona, because her name is a constant reminder that her parents actually had sex, and had the affrontery to name her after the place where it happened. She has repeatedly said that when she's older she'll change her name to something like Madonna or Gaga. It can also safely be assumed that Iona doesn't want to go to her piano lesson with Dr Orlando Cruz, whom her mother chose because of his rather exotic name and his rather well-crafted website, promising expert tuition of the *highest quality* and which is guaranteed to instil *a great love for music*. Carole hasn't actually bothered to meet

3

Dr Orlando Cruz, and so therefore doesn't know that he can't play the piano very well and is a worse teacher.

This is Iona's second piano lesson and, if it's anything like the first, will be spent listening to rock music and communicating in sign language because Dr Orlando Cruz doesn't understand much English. (The website was actually the creation of his half-brother who is a website designer in Slough and can speak English). Quite why she is being subjected to piano lessons has not been explained to her, although her mother is prone to random and enthusiastic ideas. Hopefully, this one will pass, as have others in the past.

At the next roundabout, take the second exit.

It's a stop-start journey with lots of hold-ups at traffic lights, so Carole is able to discreetly place her mobile phone on her lap and with practised dexterity compose and send emails. She does this while staring straight ahead and, at the next roundabout, remembers to take the second exit.

From: carole.gunn1499@gmail.com
To: mary.day@bespokearts.co.uk
Subject: Granny

Dear Mum

Just dropping you an email to say that Granny died today. It's all very sad, particularly for Iona who is understandably distraught. But it was mercifully quick, so that's a blessing. Graeme Worrell from across the road simply couldn't do anything about it. She just walked out in front of his car. Well, she was old and probably didn't hear him. He has one of those Toyota electric things, which are very quiet, and supposed to be good for the planet, if not for the hard-of-hearing. He was on his way back from Tesco's. They have leg of lamb on special offer, by the way. I know how much you like roast lamb ...

The traffic inches forward and Carole is now obliged to pay

more attention to the road ahead, if only briefly, as they are once again stopped in a line of cars at temporary traffic lights. A big yellow lorry is surrounded by large men in high-vis jackets who don't seem to be doing anything. Two of them haven't actually bothered to get out of the big yellow lorry and are reading newspapers. One of them seems to be eating a sandwich although the lorry is some distance ahead and Carole can't be sure what he's eating. She sighs, still frowning.

... The funeral will no doubt be a grisly affair, but at least Ray will be back for it. As you know, he's in New York this week, doing something-or-other, although it's hard to know what bankers do these days. I didn't think that the banks had any money, although I could be wrong. He's supposed to be back on Friday.

We'll have the funeral on Sunday morning, even though it's my birthday, so if you and Dad could come down a little earlier than usual that would be great, although I know you didn't much like Granny. I appreciate that she could be difficult, and she did pee on your dress last Christmas. I'm sure she didn't mean it. Just over-excitement, I expect, and too much turkey.

Love to you and Dad.

Carole

'Mum! For God's sake!'

'What?'

'Stop texting.'

In two hundred yards prepare to turn left.

'I wasn't texting,' says Carole to Iona, who is now a teenager, and therefore fiercely grown-up. 'I don't really do texting. Only when I have to.'

'You were tapping away on your phone!'

'I was sending my mother an email.'

Iona, all big blue eyes and sullen face, snorts loudly. 'Whatever,' she says, looking out the side window. 'It's still illegal.'

'Sending my mother an email?'

'Using your phone while driving. God, Mum!'

Carole knows better than to reply to her daughter who now knows everything about everything. Was she the same at Iona's age, she wonders? Do teenagers really have the key to all of life's secrets? If so, what happens to that key? Does it get lost somewhere? Carole sometimes feels that she doesn't know anything about anything anymore and that, perhaps, her daughter could teach her about life's little mysteries. Like, for example, her bloody husband. Like, for example, is he in New York by himself? Or if not alone, who with? Or like, for example, is he *actually* in New York? Carole had only the month before caught him looking at an online brochure for a luxury spa hotel in the Cotswolds. She didn't say anything just in case he was planning an anniversary surprise for them both. Inevitably, it hadn't been mentioned by him, and his anniversary present to her had been a jokey card (from Tesco, she recognised it!), a bottle of Cava (not even champagne!) and a peck on the cheek (not even both cheeks!).

But deep inside, Carole has never been a suspicious person, and Ray has never given her any reason to be suspicious, although the spa hotel has been playing on her mind. Maybe he was innocent of bad intentions, but he was guilty of something. Nobody looks at hotel websites unless they're planning *something*. Perhaps she should confront him about it, she thinks again; perhaps she should have *already* confronted him about it. But Carole doesn't much like confrontations or raised voices, and once more sweeps the spa hotel under a mental carpet. There are quite a lot of things under Carole's mental carpet which she's usually careful to step around.

'Actually, Iona, I did know that it was illegal. That's why I was doing it discreetly.'

'Doing it discreetly doesn't make it legal, Mum.'

'Doesn't it, darling?' replies Carole absently, thinking about spa hotels in the Cotswolds, gastronomic meals in front of log fires, and why *had* her husband been looking at online hotel brochures? She would, in due course and in her own way, find out where the balance between innocence and guilt lay. She grips the steering wheel a little harder, her phone still balanced on her lap.

'Anyway, I should be in school.'

Iona has never complained about missing school before. 'You're only missing a cooking lesson,' Carole reminds her.

'Domestic science, Mum. It's not just about just cooking.'

'Isn't it, darling? Anyway, learning the piano is much more important.'

'Why?'

'Because it's a skill that may be useful when you're older, that's why.'

'Useful? How exactly?'

'Useful in all sorts of ways,' says Carole, without actually answering the question.

'Mum, can you play the piano?'

'No, but that's not the point.'

'Whatever,' says Iona, rather triumphantly.

From: carole.gunn1499@gmail.com
To: ray.gunn@unitybankinggroup.com

Subject: Granny

Ray

How much longer are you going to be away? Because the kitchen tap is dripping (again)!!!

I tried to tell you that this morning when I phoned, but you put the phone down.

What I was also going to tell you is that Granny has died and it would be nice if you could be back for the funeral which will be on Sunday, before lunch with my parents. Iona is very upset ...

But Iona doesn't seem remotely upset, her mouth now framed in a similar frown to her mother's. She seems merely irritated, no doubt at having to attend her piano lesson, listen to loud music, and hold intermittent conversations with Dr Cruz in broken English. Unless, of course, he's managed to learn English *and* the piano in the intervening week, which seems doubtful. But it's an unfortunate genetic inheritance, this frown, and lends Iona, Carole's only child, an air of permanent disappointment.

Up ahead, the men on the road in high-vis jackets appear to be in an argument with a man in a white van. The man in the van has his head out the window and is gesticulating with both hands. The two men in the yellow lorry's cab continue reading their newspapers and both now seem to be eating, ignoring the man in the white van. They're probably well used to being shouted at. It would appear that the man in the white van is speaking for everyone who is stuck in this queue of cars, alternately gesturing to the road and to the yellow lorry, and making it clear – even to Carole, some distance back – that the high-vis road workers should be doing something.

... Mr Worrell was so apologetic about running her over. I could see tears in his eyes. I tried to tell him that it wasn't his fault, but he didn't seem to be listening. He invited me and Iona over for rabbit stew, which is nice of him. By way of apology, so he kept telling me. Of course, I declined. We've never had anything to do with him before and Iona doesn't like the idea of eating bunny rabbits. Mr Worrell's eyesight might not be that good, but I'm sure it was an accident, although I know that he didn't like Granny very much, not since she used his garden as a loo. But she was very old, and it was probably an emergency. Anyway, I don't think he would intentionally run her over, although his car only makes a thin whine, which doesn't sound like a car at all ...

'It's how accidents happen, Mum,' says Iona wisely. 'Anyway, who are you emailing now?' Iona's voice has an accusatory tone to it.

'Your father. He's in New York, maybe.'

Iona casts a quick sideways glance at her mother who is still staring straight ahead. 'Only maybe?'

'It's where he says he is,' replies Carole.

A smile puckers at the edge of Iona's mouth. 'Well, you married him. Therefore, you must love him.'

'Do I?' Carole is mystified, as she is about many things.

'You probably love him more than you love me.'

'Don't be ridiculous, darling. I dislike you both equally.'

In one hundred yards prepare to turn left.

Of course, Carole doesn't mean this. She loves her daughter unreservedly, but likes to cover it up; Carole isn't one to wear her emotions on her sleeve. She supposes that she feels the same about Ray, although she also feels that she's in an emotional rut. Perhaps it's just the familiarity of marriage, she thinks: the routines and mannerisms, the same things they say to one another, the same TV programmes they like to watch (when Iona allows), the same rituals that every married couple falls into. Her love has perhaps become an assumption rather than a fact. Then again, how do you verify an assumption? Or can love be a simple fact?

Prepare to turn left.

Carole likes the companionship of the sat nav; she likes the woman's certainty about when to turn left or right, and which exit to take off the roundabout. She likes it when she sometimes takes a wrong turn, or the wrong exit off a roundabout, and how the sat nav lady simply and patiently suggests that she do a U-turn and, if Carole can't do that, how the lady kindly calculates another route, without shouting at her.

Sometimes Carole deliberately takes the wrong exit off roundabouts, or turns right instead of left, for the simple pleasure of listening to the sat nav lady tell her that it was all going to be okay, and that she wasn't *a fucking imbecile*, which Ray once called her when she by mistake drove onto the exit lane of a motorway and nearly collided head-on with a lorry. (She hadn't adopted a sat nav lady back then and, to be fair, Ray had been rather shaken by the incident.)

'If he says he's in New York, maybe he is in New York,' says Iona.

'Or maybe he isn't,' replies Carole, frowning eloquently.

'Why would he lie?' her daughter asks, with just the right amount of innocence.

'Lying is a terrible thing, Iona. Never ever tell lies, okay?'

'Pot, kettle, black,' mutters the daughter.

It's only recently that she's discovered that blackbirds aren't baby crows, an avian lie told to her by her mother. She also remembers watching the TV while her mother typed on her laptop. *There's a unicorn in the garden*, her mother had remarked. The younger Iona had dutifully got up and looked out the window. The only wildlife she could see was a sparrow in a tree and a squirrel bounding across the lawn. *But while you're there, darling, could you shut the window?*

Please turn left.

The sat nav lady sounds as if she smokes a lot of cigarettes and has just woken up from a night of sleepless passion. Carole imagines her as tall and voluptuous with lustrous long dark hair. Carole isn't tall and couldn't be described as voluptuous or having much of any hair. Having short hair was a decision she took years before; back then, her life involved scrabbling around in mud, and mud and long hair were incompatible. Now, having short hair has become a habit, like the sat nav lady's cigarettes, and Carole wouldn't know what to do with long, lustrous hair. The sat nav lady sounds particularly husky and Carole imagines her sitting up in bed, hair dishevelled, a cigarette held daintily between two fingers, an ashtray balanced on her knees and beside her, still asleep, someone devilishly handsome who looks nothing like Ray. She momentarily feels guilty about this uncharitable thought, remembering passionate nights with Ray, although neither of them ever smoked, and Carole doesn't much like the smell of cigarette smoke and has banned her mother from smoking in their house, an edict her mother reluctantly agrees to.

Prepare to turn right soon.

The sat nav lady is still speaking in her husky voice, perhaps trying not to wake her lover, or perhaps trying to do the opposite, kissing the nape of his neck and running a finger down his spine. Carole feels momentarily guilty for distracting her when she could have found her way to Dr Cruz perfectly easily.

Carole's phone vibrates.

From: mary.day@bespokearts.co.uk
To: carole.gunn1499@gmail.com

Subject: Granny

Caro

Sorry to hear your sad news, if it is sad news. I had to give that dress to a charity shop, so I do hope it's gone to a nice home, or to someone with a poor sense of smell.

We'll see you on Sunday, same as always, and will try to arrive a little earlier to fit in with your arrangements. Have you given any thought to what you'd like for your birthday? But please don't expect me to cry at the funeral. Did anyone actually *like* Granny?

Roast lamb would be wonderful!

Love

Mum

Suddenly Carole brakes as a dark shape leaps across the road and disappears into trees on her right.

'Christ, Mum! What was that?'

'A doe, I think.'

'A deer?'

'A female deer.'

She accelerates away, thinking about Ray for no reason; how happy they'd once been, when their futures were ahead of them, full of the promise of golden sun. Or does everything seem better in retrospect? She often thinks about that. This week, she has concluded, has been shit, although quite why it's been shit she hasn't decided. Maybe because she hasn't actually *done* anything. She's dusted and cleaned, washed clothes and bought food but, beyond the mundane and humdrum, hasn't achieved a single thing. It's a feeling that's been gnawing at her, slowly nibbling away. Her life seems mapped out in dirty clothes, trips to the supermarket and an endless round of dusting and cooking. Beyond that, she has lost a sense of purpose, of being useful: the family fulcrum around whom only tedious necessities revolve. She sometimes wonders if anybody, husband or Iona, would notice if she suddenly walked out. Would they only notice when they got hungry or ran out of clean shirts? Would they really care, once Ray had mastered the microwave and washing machine? But where would she go? Friends couldn't be expected to put her up indefinitely. She also loves her husband, she supposes, although that might be out of habit, like cigarettes, but less harmful. The fact is, as she acknowledges, she's become enveloped in a life of dull routine, and all she can see ahead is more of the same. But lately, for no reason, she feels hemmed in by it all. Her daily routines no longer offer any kind of contentment, if they ever did; their repetition has become an affront to her sense of self-worth. Her life, without her noticing, has become ordered and methodical and, she admits, Iona's piano lessons are her way of breaking from the mould she's made for herself.

Prepare to turn left.

Carole wishes that she could be the sat nav lady. Someone in control, but never judgmental; someone quietly-spoken, but who is listened to; someone able to reach back in time, and reach down the side of the settee, and find the golden key of wisdom that her daughter seems to possess. She tries not to compare herself with the sat nav lady, but sometimes can't help it. Carole doesn't think that the sat nav lady would have washed a dirty dish in her life, or mopped a floor, or hoovered a carpet. Sometimes, Carole has to remind herself that the sat nav lady is just some clever wiring and lives somewhere under her car bonnet, or in the glove box, or somewhere else entirely. (Carole isn't very mechanical.)

Her phone vibrates again.

From: ray.gunn@unitybankinggroup.com
To: carole.gunn1499@gmail.com

Subject: Granny

Carole
Back Friday, I think. Call a plumber. Please don't call me in the middle of the night.
Anyway, it was a useless, old cat.
Ray X

Carole runs an irritated hand through her sensibly-cut hair, despite him putting an X after his name. One keystroke, either denoting something or nothing at all. He can be so inconsiderate sometimes, she thinks; jetting off to exotic places, without ever suggesting that she come too. Not that she would ever go with him, of course; she doesn't much like flying and Overseas makes her queasy, what with their strange languages and stranger food. This whole business with the cat sums everything up neatly. Not one word of sympathy for Iona. Just a loud admonishment from Overseas telling her not to phone him in the middle of the night.

At the roundabout, take the second exit. In three hundred yards, please turn left.

She remembers Granny in better times, back when she was a better cat (whatever that is!), when they got her from the cattery. She was a rescue cat and had gone through God-knows-what with her previous owners, or so Carole was told by a cheerful cattery-person in Barbour jacket and wellington boots. Carole saw it as the duty of the Gunn family to give the cat a good home, even though it tried to bite her when she made to pick it up and hissed loudly when she hurriedly put it down again. The cattery-person said that the cat was probably still a little traumatised by its previous owners and that temporary bad behaviour was only to be expected. *We wouldn't like to be picked up by a stranger, would we?* the cattery-person asked, to which Carole made no reply as, before she'd married, she had been picked up by quite a few strangers. The cattery-person emphasised the word *temporary* and, on a brighter note, said that cats were God's favourite creation. Carole had immediately wanted to know how she knew this. Was it specifically mentioned in the Bible? *Had God saith*, said Carole, *that cats are my favourite animal and, incidentally, you must not eat them*?

The cattery-person had got flustered and said that cats were sacred to the ancient Egyptians. Carole told her that the ancient Egyptians worshipped many gods including Ra and Osiris and that they also had a god of cats called Bastet, commonly known as Bast, who was the warrior daughter and defender of Ra, god of the sun, who had the head of a falcon.

Bastet, Carole went on, warming to her animal theme, originally had the head of a lioness and, later, that of a domestic cat. However, that didn't make cats sacred to a Christian god, unless the cattery-person held to ancient Egyptian beliefs. The cattery-person had looked upset and her bottom lip had wobbled, and Carole immediately felt

14

sorry for her, and also sorry for showing off her knowledge of old gods, and immediately offered to buy the cat. She had once been an archaeologist, a fact she then shared with the cattery-person by way of explanation or apology, back before mostly everything had been discovered.

Thinking back, they'd called the cat Granny because it was already an elderly cat. The cattery-person looked utterly astonished that Carole would want an old cat when there were so many adorable kittens, and gave Carole £9 off the price. Carole dutifully handed over £1, thinking that she didn't often get to do financial deals. Even Ray was impressed, until he worked out that Granny was about eighty-four in cat's years.

'Tell me,' says Carole to her daughter, 'which one would you prefer? An iPhone or a Samsung?'

'God, Mum, thanks! An iPhone obviously!'

'Just thinking what I should upgrade to,' replies Carole, oblivious to her daughter slumping back into her seat with a loud sigh. The eloquent frown is also back in place, on both their faces.

Prepare to turn left.

They're now in a broad and familiar Georgian avenue, and Carole can hear loud music from a nearby flat and she hopes that it won't disturb Iona's piano lesson. Underneath her car are cobbles which makes the car's suspension rattle.

You have reached your destination.

Miraculously, there is a parking place right in front of the house, and Iona is already out of the passenger door before Carole has even said *goodbye* and *see you in an hour.*

Three

Carole and Ray live in a small village in East Lothian, or what used to be a small village before house builders decided that small villages should all aspire to be small towns, in a conspiracy with county planners which Carole doesn't understand. Has Edinburgh's population suddenly skyrocketed without her noticing? If it has, why can't new houses be built closer to the city, without added road congestion, and without her having to meet new people? Carole already knows enough people, some she likes, and doesn't need to be on speaking terms with the new people she's constantly bumping into in local shops. But all those new houses mean that Carole has no need to drive into Edinburgh to deposit her daughter with a piano teacher. There are now a great many piano teachers who live much closer to the Gunns, many of whom speak fluent English and can actually play the piano.

But Carole, of course, has another reason for travelling into the city, and it's all to do with her gnawing unhappiness. She feels tethered to her home and family, and their reasonable and unreasonable demands, but now also wants to be tethered to something else. Like a horse, she thinks: an old nag still dreaming of adventure. She doesn't know what this *something else* could be – maybe something to bring back purpose to her life – and, almost by default, it's made her nostalgic, but of quite what she doesn't know: maybe a sense that her past was full of unfulfilled promises, a confusing vista of possibilities that, somehow, have eluded her. She had chosen Ray and, for some reason, or no reason, drifted into

16

motherhood. She hadn't chosen to give up work; she had simply chosen to be a mother and, all too soon, motherhood had become her job. It's a conundrum that Carole wants to solve, but in her own way. The dull monotony of her life has made her question; she doesn't quite understand how her life is now defined by drudgery, and she wants to know if this lack of contentment is a temporary aberration or if something fundamental has shifted. She has friends exactly like her, women who have made career sacrifices to raise families. They seem happy enough, or so they tell Carole. Some go out of their way to tell her how happy they are, as if they are also trying to convince themselves. Nor does she understand why she so suddenly feels unhappy. She was okay last month. Maybe she will be again next month, she tells herself. Maybe it's just a hormonal thing that will sort itself out.

At the time of Iona's birth, Carole was a junior lecturer in archaeology at the University of Edinburgh and had led digs to ancient sites on Shetland and Orkney. She was a good teacher, a valued member of the faculty team, and something of an expert on stone circles and the mysterious people who once inhabited Scotland. It was a job that she loved, instilling her passion in her students, and was forever ecstatic when her young team uncovered even a fragment of pottery. It was a job that was all about making sense of the past, reaching back into history and piecing the fragments of long-dead lives together. It was a job that fulfilled her, gave her purpose, and which she had all too easily cast aside.

This strange nostalgia, if that's what it is, that seems to have materialised out of nowhere, has taken her completely by surprise. Just a few weeks ago, she thought that she was content, or as content as she deserved to be, and more content than many of her friends who, between telling her how happy they were, would also confess their unhappiness over coffee and biscuits or white wine and more white wine. Now, in just a matter of weeks, semi-contentment has been replaced by something else. But *what* exactly? Carole doesn't know, but it's bound up in her past and the choices she's made. But that simple analysis only explains some of her angst. Nor does it tell her how to rekindle a new contentment, because that's the prize she's looking for.

Being rational about it, and Carole is generally rational, it's probably no more than early-onset middle age, if there is such a thing; or maybe just a temporary period of introspection: something normal and usually healthy: the mind's way of rearranging its in-tray so that everything, eventually, is happily sorted out.

But Carole, between being rational, is also querulous and questioning; it's the personality quirk that made her such a valued member of her faculty. If something was told to her as established fact, she would want to see evidence. To her way of thinking, the past is simply a jigsaw of bits and pieces and, sometimes, it's the smallest bits that are the most important. Others in her faculty were content to look at the big bits – the largest fragment of pottery, a swathe of ancient clothing. Carole, to her professors' amusement or grudging respect, would concentrate on the small stuff and, along the way, finding a fingerprint on a piece of Neolithic pottery or a bloodstain on a small woven square. It was sometimes the small things that helped tell the real story or, at least, populate the past with real people.

Carole has therefore decided to look for small things in her own life. It may be a waste of time, and probably will be, but she wants to understand how she could so completely have given up her old life; searching out fragments of who she had once been, and wondering how her life could have been different. She was happy back then and, by and large, has been happy since. But the balance of her life has shifted; the cargo of her past has moved. She has become a little unbalanced, and she needs to find the reasons for that shift in order to find a new balance. Or does everything simply go back to finding her husband looking at a Cotswolds hotel online? The rational Carole knows that her husband always goes to high-powered conferences in exotic places. While other sectors may have reined in excess, the banks seem to have lots of other people's money to throw around. Maybe he was simply checking out possible venues.

But maybe it was more than that; something clandestine and possibly unforgiveable. If so, has she somehow contributed to his wayward glance? Worse, maybe it's not just a glance. She supposes that life is full of forks in the road; go left or go right? Is Ray looking right, left and right again and deciding which seems the most attractive route, without being run over?

Or her? What forks in the road has she encountered over the years? None that she can immediately recall, because her road has been boringly straight, merely meandering from the utility room to the kitchen, to the supermarket, to the hairdresser. No, the forks in the road were encountered years and years before. But can you go back the way you came, back to a past fork in the road, and take a different route? The sat nav lady would know, with her quiet certainty about left or right turns, and her precise knowledge of every roundabout, motorway or minor road in the country, and in probably a lot of other countries.

After some prevarication, Carole is embarking on a quest and, like many things that she does, is going about it both methodically and haphazardly. She now intends to randomly search out places from her past and revisit them.

But to what purpose? Well, Carole does concede that there is probably little purpose to it. The past has been and gone, and she knows that. But she still retains the archaeologist's optimism that, somewhere, she might find the fragment of pottery that completes an ornate beaker or vessel and makes everything make sense. It's what Carole used to do, in her undergraduate years, fitting things together like an ancient jigsaw. She isn't looking for a Tutankhamun's tomb – a complete flash of understanding. She's just looking to find small clues to how and why she's become who she is, and why she frowns so much because, through her mother's repeated admonishments, she's started to notice it herself.

That's the reason for Iona's piano lessons, and why she chose a piano teacher in Edinburgh. It forces her to drive into the city and to actually get started on her quest, if that's what it is, although she has little idea what her quest will involve or what she's looking for.

*

The previous week, Iona's first piano lesson, Carole had driven around the city without real purpose, simply trying to decide which places or landmarks held significance for her. This week's quest, she's already decided, will be to visit the street she first lived in as a first-year undergraduate, always keen to impress her tutors and professor, and volunteering to take part in every dig the university organised, mostly to the far north of Scotland. Back then she lived in a shared flat in a fairly run-down block of tenement flats near Tollcross, a small area of relative neglect between the city centre and the rich inhabitants of the suburbs. It's an area hemmed in by other people's wealth, but an area she'd always liked, filled with real people. It wasn't Morningside glamour, where famous authors or heart surgeons lived; it was an area where working men actually worked with their hands and then, after work, used their hands to hold pints of beer. Carole used to watch them in their local pub, although she's always preferred white wine and, being somewhat ladylike, has never actually drunk a pint of beer, or not that she can remember.

Back then, of course, it was a kind of paradise. She'd

never lived away from home before, and it offered a freedom she had never experienced: of being able to go to bed when she chose, eat whatever she wanted or could afford, and wear whatever clothes looked cleanest, or least dirty. (Carole is only *somewhat* ladylike.) It was her first taste of what the future could hold; all those possibilities jostling for attention, a world of options to choose from; a long path ahead of her with lots of exciting forks on it. Carole never frowned back then; her features always radiated optimism, even when she had to walk to university in the pouring rain which, living in Scotland, was a regular occurrence. But she never minded the rain, and it was a monsoon downpour that brought Ray and her together.

She shared the flat with Kaitlin, Bernice and Joe. All were students like her, although Kaitlin was studying French, Bernice was studying geography (when she could be bothered, which wasn't often) and Joe was studying biology. That made him the responsible student among them because, someday, he would find a cure for all diseases and therefore do something useful with his life. Her flatmates couldn't decide whether archaeology was a useful subject or not, because the past was the past and, anyway, there were lots of books and the History Channel if anyone was interested in old stuff, which they weren't.

For a few months it was the best time of her life; an antithesis of everything that had gone before: a realisation that she was now an adult and, presumably, able to make grown-up decisions. Weekdays were all about freedom although, at weekends, she would make the short journey to her parents' home in Morningside, despite neither being authors or heart surgeons, and have her clothes washed and ironed and eat a healthy Sunday lunch. Sunday lunch has always been a tradition in her family. She can just remember her maternal grandmother, and her gargantuan Sunday lunches, and it's a tradition that's been passed to Carole's

21

mother and, presumably, to Carole. She always looked forward to escaping back home for Sunday lunch and, often for the only time that week, actually eating real vegetables. It's also a tradition she's maintained, although with a bit of role reversal: her parents now come to her for Sunday lunch, but the roast beef or roast lamb is still the same. Carole hopes that Iona will one day inherit the mantle of Sunday lunch, maybe inviting Ray and her to share it, although Iona only seems interested in eating food, rather than preparing it.

At the next junction turn left.

Carole stops at traffic lights and looks around her. Over there, the Italian restaurant they would sometimes go to. On the menu was cheap pizza and even cheaper wine, and it was therefore a favourite haunt of Carole and her flatmates. Around the corner, the pub that was their Saturday night hangout, with fiddlers and guitarists playing folk music. Just up the road, the supermarket where they would go on Sunday evenings to pick up whatever was on the Bargains shelf, which sometimes yielded all they needed for the coming week or, often enough, nothing at all. The Bargains shelf could not be relied on. You had to be there at precisely the right moment; a minute too early and the shelf would be empty; a minute too late and other impoverished students would have been there first. But while the restaurant, bar and supermarket are still there, the supermarket has changed its name and the pub is now advertising Saturday night karaoke. The other shops, bars and coffee houses she no longer recognises. She supposes that it's progress. The cheap café she sometimes went to is now an up-market replica, with a chalk board on the pavement advertising varieties of coffee that Carole has never heard of.

Carole finds a parking space and switches off the engine. The street is how she remembers it, but is also unfamiliar. She would have walked down this street thousands of times but, somehow, it feels different. Maybe it has changed, or maybe she's changed. She remembers walking to the bakery on sunny mornings and bringing back warm croissants; she remembers (with some shame) tottering back from the pub, and the night when she met Ray.

Ray used to boast that he'd sown a lot of wild oats in his time. Why he thought Carole would want to know this is anybody's guess. Now, mostly, Ray consumes wild oats with fruit chunks and honey. Ray is slightly overweight, knows it, and constantly tries to calculate portion sizes and calorie intake. It's a genetic flaw, this tendency for flab, that Iona has unfortunately inherited from her father, although Iona doesn't see herself as overweight, and most certainly would never say no to a second serving of chips. It's the reason why Carole chose Iona's afternoon of domestic science for her piano lesson. She doesn't want her daughter to learn how to cook chips, pizza or full-fat ice cream, despite her daughter protesting that domestic science is about more than just cooking.

The pub that she remembers is just across the road, the place where Carole met her husband, and she now approaches it with some trepidation. The last time she was there, years after her first flat-share, was as a new graduate about to embark on a doctorate on the purposes and symbolism of stone circles. She hadn't been looking for love. She had only recently been in love, and her heart hadn't yet quite mended. But in an evening of gin and tonics, that's what she found. They'd both gone to the pub to shelter from the rain, which had steadily worsened and become torrential. Even Carole, acclimatised to wind and rain, had felt the need to seek shelter. She'd arrived first, him a little later, and both of them were cold and wet. They'd chatted at the bar and, when the rain eased, she'd thanked him for his company and left. Phone numbers hadn't been exchanged. Quite why they hadn't been exchanged, Carole can no longer remember. But she'd been charmed by him, by his easy smile and had later cursed herself for letting him slip through her fingers. She should have asked for his number, or simply given him hers. But to do either would have seemed presumptuous or demanding or merely desperate, and she'd slipped into the night with little chance of ever seeing him again. But they did get together again, but quite when and how she can't remember.

Inside the pub, she orders a small glass of white wine and looks around and is surprised by how little has changed. The area outside may have gone a little up-market, but the pub's interior remains caught in a time warp. The large mirror behind the island bar is the same; so too the hideous red wallpaper. Strung out above the bar are twinkly lights, the pub either celebrating Christmas months early or not bothering to take them down after last Christmas. The twinkly lights are therefore a result of unnecessary forward planning, or sheer laziness. They are, however, perhaps the least depressing thing in the pub, and she struggles to remember why she was such a frequent visitor, before remembering that it was just around the corner from their flat and therefore convenient. Apart from the twinkly lights, nothing appears to have much changed from her last visit, including the drunk at the end of the bar. Carole remembers him with brown hair and clean-shaved cheeks. Now he's unshaven with white hair. This momentarily depresses her, the passage of years, and she wonders if he's achieved anything between then and now. She rather thinks not, and momentarily wants to ask him, to remind him that she also used to drink in this pub, but doesn't. They don't know one another, and never did, and she's not looking for depressing life stories, even if he wanted to tell her his. As she discreetly watches, he finishes his pint and whisky and simply gestures to the barman for a refill. No words are exchanged, and two new glasses are swiftly placed in front of him. Money is also wordlessly exchanged. The drunk drinks half of his pint of beer, wipes a hand over his mouth, and stares intently at the wall opposite. Carole watches him, wondering what he sees, when he would have stared at the same piece of wall for many years. He's on the same barstool that he used to sit on. But maybe he's not really admiring the wallpaper, she thinks, but staring at something inside himself; perhaps also trying to find a missing piece of jigsaw. Perhaps, he's thinking that he could have been an astronaut or world-renowned scientist. Perhaps that he *should* have been one, or both, of those things, except that he came to a fork in the road and, without benefit of a sat nav lady, had chosen the wrong turn. However we end up, she thinks, the fault always lies in the past.

Carole supposes that she's also looking for an affirmation of her past; to find connections between who she was and who she is, and whether they are both the same person, divided simply by time and experience. She's therefore on an enigmatic quest, like searching for the end of a rainbow, but knowing that there's no pot of gold and that searching for one is a waste of time. But is her quest a waste of time? Carole doesn't yet know.

She finishes her drink, puts on her coat, nods to the barman, and takes a last look at the drunk who is still staring at the wall opposite him. His face is expressionless. She then walks round the corner to the street she once lived in; the street where she'd first found adult freedom, and the ability to do what she wanted, without having to fit in with what her parents wanted. Eating when she wanted to; not eating when she didn't feel like it; and not having to set the table every evening *because that's Carole's job*, her mother would regularly say. Years later, it's still Carole's job because it's not a task that Carole has ever given to Iona. Iona doesn't have jobs because all of them belong to Carole. Carole's job is to make sure that nobody else has any domestic jobs.

The street hasn't changed in the slightest. The tenement

blocks are the same, and it smells the same. Carole has an acute nose; she can smell what others can't. She can smell cigarette smoke on her mother's breath from across a room; sometimes, if she has to travel by bus, the smell of other peoples' perfume and aftershave can be overpowering. Ray once said that she could retrain as a sniffer dog, perhaps crawling on all fours at airports and smelling out suspicious packages. At the time Carole thought it was funny, but she's not so sure now, as she is about most things. Certainties have been replaced with uncertainties; she now doesn't know what to think about anything anymore. It's an unsettling feeling; to feel slightly lost inside; an equilibrium disturbed.

Like the pub, the small Italian restaurant at the corner is also much the same, but in a reassuring way, with nicely-painted walls on which hang tasteful pictures of Rome and Florence. Looking in, Carole can't remember if these are the same pictures from years before but, also reassuringly, she sees a waiter she remembers who is behind the counter and polishing glasses. Luigi now has grey hair and has put on weight. Back then, he was thin and possessed of supreme vanity, always preening and flirting with the female customers. He would wield the restaurant's over-sized pepper grinder with exaggerated suggestion, winking at the girls and ignoring everyone else. Carole also remembers that one of Luigi's never-ending tasks was to polish glasses, which he's still doing, and she wonders if Luigi ever gets tired of his polishing duties; whether he hates it, or loves making each glass sparkle because he truly believes cleaning glasses is his purpose in life. Does it matter to him that he'll just have to clean them all again tomorrow, and the day after that, and every day next week? Does he ever think that, perhaps, patrons should bring their own glasses, or otherwise be obliged to drink straight from the bottle? In other words, is Luigi ever plagued by the same thoughts that now occupy Carole's mind? Feeling nostalgic, she briefly considers going in and introducing herself as one of his old customers. But why would he remember her? And what would she say to him anyway? Maybe only to apologise for stealing one of his loo rolls from the ladies' toilets because they'd run out, and none of her flatmates (including her) could be bothered walking to the nearest shop. Worse, if she went in and ordered some food, would he still wield his pepper grinder with the same swagger, or wink suggestively at her? Even worse, would he simply offer her pepper, but then wink at someone younger? Or maybe, she thinks, noticing again his grey hair, his winking days are over.

There's a tenement block to her left with scaffolding and workers in red hard hats leaning out from the second storey. Their arms are draped over the scaffolded balustrade, and they're all smoking, looking down into the street. Then one of them wolf whistles and immediately Carole is black affronted. Despite still wanting, slightly, to be winked at by waiters, she is also a profound feminist and sexist behaviour she cannot tolerate. She looks up angrily only to see they're not looking at her but at a pretty young woman in tight jeans on the other side of the street. The young woman seems to be blushing and is keeping her head down, long dark hair partly covering her face, quickening her pace. Carole feels sorry for her, at the unwanted intrusion into her privacy, at being objectified, and at the insensitivity of building workers who are now all laughing, between puffs on their cigarettes, seemingly finding their offensive behaviour hugely amusing. Carole wonders whether to shout up at them, but can't immediately think of anything to shout, and so takes several deep breaths and also quickens her pace.

Then she's safely past the scaffolding and now, slowing down, approaches the tenement where she once lived. It was a bohemian time in her life; a shared existence of carry-out curry and long nights drinking cheap wine and listening to loud music. Although she didn't much like curry, and still

27

doesn't, it tasted of freedom. (But she does still make curry because it's a favourite of both her husband and daughter.)

She looks up at the third-floor window which had once been her bedroom window. She had red curtains; now, they are cream. Her window frame had been rotten, with the glass threatening to fall out – an aesthetic and safety issue that they raised several times with their landlord, who wasn't much interested. Now, the window frame looks newly painted. She wonders who lives there now, and whether they exist on curry, cheap wine and loud music. Maybe a new but different version of Kaitlin, Bernice, Joe and, of course, Carole. Maybe the flat has new wallpaper, rather than their peeling and tattered wallpaper; maybe the bathroom has a clean bath and doesn't smell of bad drains; maybe it has a new kitchen instead of Victorian decrepitude.

But more than anything she remembers an evening when she, Kaitlin and Bernice were in the living room. It was cold; the small bar heater in the boarded-up fireplace barely kept the room warm, and the flat didn't have central heating. They were therefore drinking large quantities of white wine to keep warm, although whether this was a scientifically-proven way of keeping warm nobody knew. Joe was somewhere else, which he often was.

It was Kaitlin, the beauty of the flat, who was the most drunk and always the most voluble, however much she'd had to drink. Someone who had an opinion about anything and, for some reason, always wanted to share it, however banal. It might be the price of bananas in the local HappyMart, what one of her lecturers had said that morning, or the fate of the Amazonian rainforest. Each seemed to be of equal importance in her mind, and all communicated with the same flat intonation.

'I actually wish that I hadn't,' she now said in her nasal Birmingham accent and then, unusually for her, closed her mouth. It was clear to Carole and Bernice that Kaitlin was now regretting opening it in the first place.

'Hadn't done what?' asked Carole.

'Slept with him,' said Kaitlin after a pause, looking at the floor which, frankly, wasn't worth looking at, being a mixture of drinks slops and cigarette burns, although in a bad light it did make interesting if random patterns. They often joked that it could win the Turner prize.

'Get to the point,' suggested Bernice, who, from a posh part of south England, had a commanding voice that even Kaitlin couldn't ignore.

'Joe,' admitted Kaitlin, after a pause. 'It was a mistake.'

'So why tell us now?' asked Carole, visibly surprised.

'He said it would ruin the dynamic of the flat if anyone else found out,' Kaitlin now burst out. 'But I now feel that I've got to tell you guys. We're all friends, right? Suddenly, I want you both to know.'

'A mistake?' echoed Bernice. 'Ruining the dynamic of the flat?'

'That's what he said.'

Bernice took a deep breath. 'When?' she demanded.

'In the summer. July, maybe. Just a couple of times, when you guys were out.'

Bernice took an even deeper breath. 'That's what the bastard said to me as well. Dynamics, secrecy, all that shit.'

'When?'

'September. But a lot more than *just* a couple of times.' Bernice was competitive in everything including, it seemed, sex with a flatmate.

Carole looked between them. Both seemed to be angry, but whether at Joe or each other was harder to tell. Then they both looked at Carole.

'Well?' demanded Bernice.

'Well what?' asked Carole.

'You know fine well,' said Kaitlin. 'When did you sleep with him?'

29

'Actually, I haven't,' said Carole. 'He's not my type.'

'Really?'

'Really.'

It was clear that neither of them believed her. Kaitlin snorted, and Bernice rolled her eyes. There was a lengthy, awkward silence in which the three girls alternately looked at the floor or glanced furtively at one another.

It was then that Carole first experienced self-doubt. Kaitlin was the flat beauty, no doubt about that, and therefore someone who most men fancied. Luigi's pepper grinder always seemed more erect when it hovered over Kaitlin's plate, his eye winking even more rapidly. Joe and Kaitlin didn't therefore seem unnatural, except that they were flatmates and hanky-panky, by unspoken agreement, not allowed. But Bernice? Therein lay the conundrum because Bernice was no glittering princess. On a scale between Bernice and Kaitlin, Carole was certainly well above dumpy Bernice. So why hadn't Joe made a pass at her? He'd even caught her naked in the bathroom one morning when she'd forgotten to lock the door. Hadn't he found her naked body alluring? Why choose Bernice over her?

'Are you sure?' Kaitlin asked her.

The silence had been long enough for Carole to forget what she was supposed to be sure about. 'About what exactly?' she replied.

'About sleeping with Joe.'

'I have not slept with Joe! It's something I would remember,' replied Carole, still looking at Bernice and wondering if, perhaps, she was so far below Kaitlin on the scale of attraction to be actually below Bernice. It wasn't a comforting thought. Not, of course, that she would have slept with Joe, for all his boyish charm and good looks although, coming to think about it, she might have. But he'd never shown any interest, not one iota, even averting his eyes from her naked body in the bathroom, even though – she also now admitted – she'd left the bathroom door unlocked on purpose.

Neither of the other two girls seemed to believe her, but neither made a fuss about it. Maybe Carole had, maybe she hadn't, and it didn't seem to matter anyway because the dynamic of the flat had been altered. Joe was right about that, and for the rest of that evening there were competing frissons of jealousy and anger. When Joe returned later that night, there was a heated argument, and several days of frosty silence. Everyone moved around one another as one would an unexploded bomb. It was soon agreed that they should go their separate ways. The other two girls now seemed to hate each other and, of course, Joe was the personification of evil. What had tasted of freedom to Carole now tasted of disappointment, or a dawning realisation that freedom came with consequences, not all of them pleasant. It was, in retrospect, a step toward adulthood and an understanding that life, inevitably, has its ups and downs. She moved out to share with a couple of other female archaeology students in her year, and stayed living with them for the rest of her time as an undergraduate. Maybe, Carole thinks, I will go and visit that flat, although it doesn't hold strong or affectionate memories. It was just a place to live, and Carole was never close friends with the other two girls, who both chose to avoid university expeditions, and who were eternally curious about Carole's passion for scrambling around in mud. Carole sometimes used to wonder why they'd chosen to study archaeology, because digging in dirt was integral to it, but can't remember ever asking them.

But there were good times in that first flat, lots of them, and Carole now tries to focus on them, rather than the end of their flat-share, as she slowly retraces her steps back to her car. The building workers are still leaning against the outer scaffolding and still smoking. Carole wonders if they ever manage to get any work done, or if this is their way of eking out a contract indefinitely, so that they can retire in thirty years' time without having finished whatever they were supposed to be doing now.

But it's not until she's past the scaffolded building that she realises that nobody has wolf whistled at her. Just to be sure, she looks up. The three builders are looking down, vaguely in her direction, but simply seem bored. Carole is at first grateful that no sexist behaviour has been aimed at her, then outraged that none of them feel she's worth a catcall.

Carole pivots on her heels and walks back to her old flat and looks up again at her old room with its new curtains. Then she brushes a hand through her hair, willing it to become long and lustrous, mentally flicks it over her shoulders and walks more slowly past the scaffolded building. Inevitably, the hard-working builders are still leaning against the outside balustrade and this time, she sees, all of them have spotted her and are looking down at her. But, again, no wolf whistle, which now seems to Carole to be an affront of the worst kind.

Now in a bad mood, she drives back to pick up Iona from the clutches of Dr Cruz. Iona is waiting on the pavement, tapping a foot in irritation, and frowning.

Iona climbs in and fastens her seatbelt. 'Thank God that's over,' she says.

'What's over?' asks Carole, easing the car from its parking space.

'Mum, in case you've forgotten, Dr Cruz is going back to his family in Portugal. I told you last week, remember? An *extended* holiday because his mother is *extremely* sick.' Iona emphasises *extended* and *extremely*, hoping that Carole will have forgotten all about piano lessons by the time Dr Cruz arrives back in Edinburgh, if he ever does.

Carole does, of course, remember, although she had temporarily forgotten, and she's also remembered that it's her birthday in a few days, and wonders if anybody else has remembered. It's not a particularly important birthday, not one with a zero after the first number, and so can be temporarily forgotten about as well. 'Do you want me to find another piano teacher?' she asks.

'No, Mum, I do not.'

'Are you sure?'

'Mum, I'm learning stuff from Dr Cruz. If I went to someone else, I'd have to learn different stuff.'

'Is that important?' Carole asks.

'Very important,' replies Iona, nodding her head firmly, but not looking at her mother. 'It simply wouldn't be fair on Dr Cruz and everything he's taught me.'

Carole doesn't remind her daughter that she's only had two lessons and couldn't therefore have learned very much but, perhaps wisely, doesn't say anything.

She drives home slowly, feeling unloved by builders or anyone else, but guided all the way by the kindly sat nav lady, who now seems to be speaking in a less husky voice, having smoked fewer cigarettes and said a temporary, and no doubt tearful, farewell to her demanding lover. Carole is experiencing conflicting emotions, but doesn't quite know which emotion is uppermost. She is, maybe, a good mother (whatever that is), she is, maybe, a good wife (whatever that is), but she isn't who she is, and whether she still wants to be who she is. Was she a better person back when she flat-shared with Kaitlin, Joe and Bernice, or is she a better person now? On their journey home, Carole keeps her phone tucked in her handbag; she has nothing to say to anyone. Her phone doesn't even beep once; nobody, it would seem, has anything to say to her either.

You have reached your destination.

It's late afternoon by the time Carole swings her car into their small driveway, past the house sign that reads NAVARONE, etched in black lettering onto dark wood, and switches off the engine. She doesn't know whether

33

it's been a good day or a bad day, but it has been a day of remembering times past, good and bad, and, perhaps, that makes it a good day – except for the builders, or maybe because of the builders. The drunk in the pub and Luigi's grey hair have also been reminders that people grow older – imperceptibly if you see that person every day, but in great leaps if you meet them after years of separation or look at old photographs. She supposes that the drunk or Luigi might also have noticed her, if only a brief glimpse between drinking or polishing, and remembered vaguely that they'd seen someone like her before. She's not therefore sure whether today's journey back to her old flat has been worth it, or the memories it has dredged up. It has simply reminded her, if she needed reminding, that time passes equally for everyone.

Still feeling unsure about herself and her place in the world, Carole consoles herself with the thought that Iona has no doubt learned something useful.

Four

Carole's fascination with the past possibly came from a random discovery in the back garden of their new house near North Berwick, a coastal town on Scotland's south-east coast. She'd been allowed a small patch of flowerbed at the bottom of the garden, and had chosen seeds from the local garden centre. Not wanting to know the names of the plants, she simply looked at the pictures on the front of each packet, and imagined the nice flowers that they would no doubt have all year round, including in the middle of winter. Her mother then sifted through her choices, and put several packets back on the rack, explaining to Carole why certain species wouldn't grow in their garden. Back home, Carole planted her seeds and watered them, carefully following her mother's instructions, and then sat on the grass and watched the patch of earth for signs of life. Disappointingly, despite sitting there for at least thirty minutes, nothing seemed to be happening. Then she saw something glint at the edge of her eye and, following the glint, found a half-buried glass bottle. She was sure that it hadn't been there the day before.

She carried it into the kitchen where her mother was chopping vegetables and handed it over. Her mother took it to the sink and washed it. It was just an old milk bottle her mother told her, and pointed to some lettering which, her mother explained, was the name of the dairy. But to Carole, it was more than a discarded milk bottle (and *why* discard it in a garden?); it was a tangible link with the people who had once lived in their small house, and it offered small clues about them – although, apart from liking milk and throwing empty milk bottles into the garden, Carole could discern nothing more. But it was a small piece of someone else's history; a tangible link into a family's past – something more solid than an old photograph: something that they would once have held, pouring milk into tea or bowls of cereals if, that is, they had invented cereals back in the Middle Ages. It inspired her to make more archaeological expeditions to the bottom of the garden, turning up some broken glass (from another milk bottle) and the remains of a flowerpot. She often wondered if, in another part of their garden, she might find gold and diamonds and, perhaps, a pirate's treasure chest, but she wasn't allowed to dig in other parts of the garden. Her mother didn't think there would be buried treasure and, after Carole cut her finger for the second time digging up broken glass, put her foot down. No more digging, full stop. By then, she'd also dug up her seeds, so nothing ever came from their trip to the garden centre.

It was that summer when she discovered the clearing in the woods, perfectly round and perfectly fringed with oak trees. It was therefore the ideal place to search for hidden treasure, although it was a couple of miles from the sea and even Carole couldn't imagine pirates carrying a treasure chest that far from their ship. But, she reasoned, maybe they had a horse and cart and lots of lowly sailors to carry the treasure chest up to the clearing. But, maybe, it was the sorcerer who had buried the treasure, and she wasn't sure whether the sorcerer who owned the clearing would be happy if she started digging in it. She did ask him, of course, on a day when the leaves were loudly whispering, but she couldn't understand what they were saying and, maybe, they couldn't understand her either. But she took that as the sorcerer's permission, if indeed there *was* actually a sorcerer. She was at an age when the idea of magic was both logical and ridiculous; it existed, she was sure about that, but always somewhere else, in enchanted kingdoms filled with dragons and castles. Her part of Scotland was certainly filled with castles, some in better condition than others but, scanning the horizons with fierce concentration, she had yet to see a dragon or a witch riding a broomstick. One day she took a trowel with her to the clearing.

The first thing was to decide where to dig, and she took a long time thinking about this. The obvious place would be the precise centre of the clearing but, even to her, that was maybe a bit obvious. If something was to be hidden in the circle, then it wouldn't be where everybody was bound to look first. Then again, if the circle was a magical and secret place, somewhere that wasn't supposed to be found, then what she was looking for could be at its centre. Carole twirled her trowel in her hand and faced each of the oaks in turn. Each of them was whispering something, but softly, without words she could understand.

She set to work, digging beside each oak tree in turn. It was hard work with a blunt trowel, first cutting out a square of grass that had to be prised away from the earth underneath, and then exploring deeper into the hole. After an hour of digging, her knees green and brown from grass and earth, she had uncovered absolutely nothing. While frustrating, it was also exciting: the constant thrill of anticipation that the next hole she dug would unearth ancient treasures. But, after a long time digging, with holes dug beside each oak, she had to concede that, maybe, she was looking in the wrong place. Perhaps the clearing wasn't where jewels and diamonds would be buried; maybe the clearing was too obvious a place to hide away a pirate chest. If so, then maybe the clearing was a clue to where the treasure was *actually* buried but, try as she might, she couldn't find anything that might point her in the right direction. It was simply a symmetric circle of trees and grass, lit from above by the midday sun. That left only the centre of the circle to explore and Carole got busy again with her trowel, cutting out a square of grass, and digging underneath. Like her other holes, all she unearthed were bits of wood and small stones, which she would carefully examine to see if they were diamonds or emeralds, and then put back in the hole.

It was hot and thirsty work, and Carole hadn't brought anything to drink with her. She decided that she had been on a big enough adventure for one day and set to filling in her hole, first scraping earth from each of the stones and bits of wood, before discarding them back into the hole. One stone seemed flat on one side, so she put that in her pocket. Another stone seemed to be oddly shaped, so she put that into her pocket. She filled in the rest of the hole and hurried off home.

Later, once she'd drunk two cans of Coke and had a bath, on her mother's orders, she remembered the contents of her pocket and put them in a water-filled bowl in the kitchen and added in washing-up liquid. A little later, when she went back to check, earth had fallen away revealing a small blue stone and a rather crude heart-shaped brooch. Carole couldn't think what else it could be.

With mounting excitement, Carole carefully scrubbed off the remaining grime with a nailbrush, and shouted for her mother. The two of them looked at Carole's treasures, now laid out on a square of kitchen towel.

'You really do have a knack of finding things, don't you,' said her mother, picking up the heart-shaped object and peering at it from all sides.

Her mother made a few phone calls and the next day they travelled into Edinburgh to see an ancient man at the university. Quite who this ancient person was, and what he was good at, wasn't explained to Carole. She explained that she'd found the brooch in a wood near her house. She didn't want to give away a precise location, thinking that the sorcerer might not be happy that she'd taken away his treasure without asking permission.

The professor (Carole still didn't know what he was a professor of) made all sorts of nice noises, but without actually saying anything, at least for a while. He had white hair that stuck out sideways from his head, so that Carole thought that he must either be a genius or completely mad. He had a small microscope that he put in one eye and looked at Carole's treasures through it.

Then he put down the heart-shaped brooch and said that what they were looking at was called a Luckenbooth. It was a symbol of love, he said, pointing carefully, and Carole could see for the first time that it was actually two hearts intertwined. The professor explained that Carole's brooch was made from silver, which was once mined in Scotland, and probably dated back to the seventeenth century, although it was hard to put a precise date on it. He then picked up the blue stone and slotted it into the centre of the Luckenbooth. Carole hadn't noticed that the stone could fit into the brooch. He said that the stone was a sapphire, once mined on the Isle of Harris, and was regarded as the *divine stone*, because the blue of the stone was thought to mirror Heaven. It also symbolised purity, wisdom and chastity, he said, although Carole didn't know what chastity meant, and her mother evaded her question later. 'What you have, young lady,' he said, 'is quite an exciting object. A token of love, bought by a young man to, perhaps, give to his new wife.'

This gave the brooch new meaning for Carole. No longer was it just a bit of lost jewellery; it was something made from love and given from love, crafted from silver and with a precious stone at its centre. It would have meant something to the giver and the person receiving it. It wasn't of much value, said the professor, but it must once have held great value to the young people who last held it.

When Carole got home, she went to her room, holding the brooch and sapphire in one hand, sat on her bed, and cried. She was upset by it now. It was no longer just something that had been lost, and which she had happened to find. It now held levels of love and loss that she could only guess at. She tried to imagine the two people it had belonged to, and how it became lost. Was she wearing it as she walked through the wood? Was she holding hands with him? Did it brush up against a tree branch and become dislodged? Did they search for it? Did the young lady cry, as she was now crying?

Or was the young man called away to war, never to return, and leaving his young wife with nothing to remember him by? Or were they together for the rest of their lives, sometimes remembering with a laugh their walk in the woods and losing her keepsake? Carole hoped for the latter, deciding that they must have lived nearby because, back then, cars hadn't been invented and she was a little unsure when bicycles were invented. Maybe they had once lived in their small house. Maybe they had gone on to have a big family, with small sons and daughters who also explored the wood and found the clearing. They would probably not have stayed in the circle for long, she thought; back then, almost everyone believed in sorcerers and witches. It was a crime not to believe in witches, so Carole had learned in school only a few months before. Her local town had been famous, or infamous, for witchcraft. The witch fires on Edinburgh Castle's esplanade had burned bright with North Berwick witches. She didn't like to think about that. Instead, more than anything, she wanted to know how a token of love from centuries ago could have become buried at the very centre of a remote clearing in a wood.

She knew, of course, that these were questions that would never find answers. Whatever love the brooch had once symbolised was now lost in time. She put the brooch and sapphire into her treasures box (mostly photographs and small stones from nearby beaches) and put the box back in her wardrobe. She hoped that the young man who bought it and the young lady who received it had lived happily ever after and that maybe, just maybe, the sorcerer of her clearing had kept it safe for them.

Her mother phoned the *East Lothian Courier*, and a photographer and reporter came to talk to her and take a picture of her holding the brooch. A small story appeared the next week, with Carole holding the two pieces of her brooch to the camera like an offering, with a big toothy grin pasted to her face. Quite why her mother wanted her to be famous, if only for a few days, she didn't explain, but Carole put the newspaper cutting into her treasures box along with the brooch.

She also now knew what she wanted to do when she grew up.

*

Her first morning at university was a strange one because it was the same building which she'd come to with her sapphire brooch. Then, her mother had held her hand; now, there was nobody to hold her hand and, in any case, she was carrying books in one hand and a bag of books in the other. The corridors were the same as she remembered, although painted now in more vibrant colours. The crusty old professor with the mad hair had, of course, long retired, but she remembered the long corridors and the views onto other university buildings. It felt like a small affirmation; a personal vindication that she'd made the right decision: that finding old milk bottles and even older brooches had led her to this place.

At first, for a few weeks, she lived at home, and Carole didn't feel like a proper student. Real students came in late, looking as if they'd just come from a party, and said things like *see you in the wine bar later* or *see you in the pub later* or *see you in the flat later for a few drinks*. Carole couldn't

41

say those things to anybody and, in a way, those early weeks felt like an extension of school, being still expected to take her shoes off at the front door and do the washing-up every night. Then she saw a flat-share note pinned on the Student Information board: FLATMATE WANTED. HUMAN, IF POSSIBLE. PREFERABLY FEMALE, ALTHOUGH WILL CONSIDER OTHER. Carole, who met both criteria, arranged to go and look at it and was rather formally interviewed by the other three inhabitants of the flat. The two girls did ask some sensible questions *(Was she a psychopath? Did she mind a bit of mess?)* interspersed with some irrelevant ones. *(What was her favourite children's TV character? What was her bra size?)* The third of her potential flatmates, Joe, didn't ask any questions, simply looked her up and down, and then went off to the kitchen to play loud music. Interrogation over, Bernice took her to her potential room, and had the good grace to apologise for the state it was in. She also explained that the room had become free because the fourth inhabitant had decided that university wasn't for her, and had gone off to drama school. (Although Carole never met her, she became rather famous for a while, married an A-List superstar, and moved to Los Angeles.) Bernice explained that they would have a flat meeting and decide which applicant they would choose, although Carole shouldn't be disappointed if they didn't choose her. Carole hadn't reached the main road before Bernice was on the phone to offer her the room. She later found out that she was the only applicant who, having seen the room, had actually wanted it.

She moved in the next week, helped by her father, who carried her heaviest bags up the three flights of stairs to her new flat. She could tell that her dad was less than impressed, although she had emphasised repeatedly to him that it wasn't a palace. Being forewarned had not, however, made him expect the run-down state of Carole's new home. He made indistinct noises, looking around, frowning at the carpets, drawing in breath at the state of the kitchen, and holding his nose when he peered into the bathroom. On the way up the stairs he'd asked if he could use her loo but, on closer inspection, clearly decided that he could wait. He then made more indistinct noises, nodding at some unspoken thought, kissed her on the cheek, and quickly escaped back to his car and to a disease-free toilet. But, despite her flat being decrepit, it was immediately home. It was home, simply because it *wasn't* home.

The university course was everything she'd been hoping for, and more, because on this course she was positively encouraged to dig. It immediately inspired her. For Carole, ever since that first milk bottle, digging up the past was important; to stitch together the lives of long-dead people from fragments of artefacts. It was like making sense of a ragged tapestry, she sometimes thought; examining each stitch in time and eventually finding patterns that made sense. Carole had always felt an affinity to those who had gone before; they would have had the same hopes and dreams, experienced the same moments of happiness or disappointment. They would have been no different from us now and she was always wondering about them; what their names might have been, what children they had, what kind of lives they would have lived. She always felt that their stories should be told, or at least understood, in fragments of pottery or delicate pieces of jewellery. It was, in her way, about honouring the past, and of those who had gone before, so that she, Carole, could have her brief moment on planet Earth.

*

The first great love in Carole's life was Rob Thomson. He was in her class and perhaps as passionate about archaeology as she was although, for the first few months of their course, she never actually talked to him. But she did coyly smile at him once or twice, feeling her pulse quicken.

But Rob, it turned out, didn't have her single-minded enthusiasm. Rob was more practical, seeing university as a stepping stone, although a stepping stone to quite what he couldn't explain, and perhaps not to himself. Most people who went to university as a stepping stone chose neutral subjects like law or business studies: courses that might have wider use in the worlds of business or commerce. Archaeology didn't have wider applications: it was only a stepping stone to more archaeology. Rob was from Aberdeen, to her Edinburgh; and they properly met at a party at her shared flat, before the extent of Joe's libido became common knowledge.

It wasn't a very good party because it was close to Christmas and most of their friends had already departed for home and family. Some were looking forward to Christmas; others saw it as an opportunity to have their clothes cleaned for them, as Carole did every Sunday. It was somewhere between Pink Floyd and The Beatles when Carole first really saw him. She'd seen him in class, of course, but not really noticed him, not *properly* noticed him, despite her pulse. She sat at the front of lecture halls, not wanting to miss anything that the lecturer said; he sat at the back and, as he told her, had acute hearing which meant that he never missed anything that was said either. She was never sure about Rob's hearing; he was often capable of not hearing what she was saying. He was standing in profile to Carole, talking animatedly to another girl in their class. He was making extravagant gestures with one hand, and prodding the girl repeatedly in the shoulder with a finger. Clarissa was barely tolerated by the other girls in Carole's class. It was rumoured that she *put it about a bit*, although evidence of this was scant. She was, however, regarded as a threat to their boyfriends' fidelity, being someone well used, allegedly, to being prodded by a lot of things, and not just fingers. But Clarissa was, everyone grudgingly admitted, the class beauty, although how she got into university was beyond anybody's understanding. Clarissa might have been model-beautiful, but was dim beyond redemption. Her long hair was tied in a ponytail and her long legs were encased in skin-tight black leather trousers. Her generous bosom was also wrapped in something clingy and flimsy, so that she looked, at least to Carole, like a Barbie prostitute doll. She was nodding at something that Rob was saying, but not saying anything back. That suggested that Rob was saying something intelligent, and that she therefore had nothing to say.

Carole decided to join them and Clarissa, after a few polite words, drifted off to join another group. To Carole's surprise, he didn't drift off with her. In the next few minutes, she discovered that Rob hated eggs, drank neat whisky and disliked both Pink Floyd and The Beatles, who were now playing loudly from their loudspeakers. Rob, it seemed, liked talking about his dislikes. Carole had to admit that she liked eggs, Pink Floyd and The Beatles, but not whisky. From the outset, therefore, they had nothing in common.

'But why do you hate Pink Floyd?' she asked.

'Because they're dinosaurs,' he replied.

This made no sense because they were forever studying fossils. 'Okay, dinosaurs, but still nice dinosaurs.'

He shrugged. 'I just don't like them, that's all.'

To Carole's surprise, despite disagreeing about everything, they got on well. The lovely Clarissa walked past several times, and Carole could see men's heads turning but, strangely, not Rob's. Carole wondered uncharitably if Clarissa kept walking past intentionally, and then decided that she didn't care.

Much later, after several more drinks, Rob suggested that

they leave.

'But it's our flat party,' protested Carole. 'I should be here, if only to help clear up afterwards.'

'That seems like a very good reason to leave,' said Rob. 'Anyway, I live just around the corner.'

For no good reason, she said yes. Leaving the bathroom door unlocked hadn't worked with Joe, although she'd never particularly fancied him, and at that moment she felt vulnerable and unwanted. Quite why she couldn't fathom because she was generally bright and optimistic. Rob's curly brown hair and blue eyes seemed to offer an antidote, although to what she didn't know. Carole also didn't quite know what they would do when they reached his flat, or what she would allow him to do, but decided that she'd cross that bridge, or several bridges, when she got to them.

'By the way, thanks for inviting me,' Rob said.

'No thanks required. I invited everybody who was still around.'

Rob really did live around the corner, above the Italian restaurant. She looked inside and, behind the counter, Luigi was polishing glasses. He looked up as they passed, and Carole waved. He waved his dishcloth back and winked. The proximity of her flat to Rob's was a surprise, and she wondered why they'd never bumped into each other in the street, or in local shops or the pub. His flat, on the third floor, had the same layout as hers, although his was more tastefully decorated in pastel colours, with furniture that wasn't from a bygone era or pillaged from down-market charity shops. Carole's flat, it would seem, had a meaner landlord. It was cold, and Rob sat her on a comfy sofa near the fireplace in which there was a modern electric heater which actually worked properly. Rob switched on all the bars, then asked what she would like to drink.

'Surprise me,' said Carole, 'but nothing too surprising,' she added, just in case he brought her a large glass of whisky.

'Something surprising, but not too surprising, coming up,' he said, returning a few minutes later with a glass of whisky for him, and a glass of white wine for her. They clinked glasses, with Rob settling himself beside her.

'My fellow inhabitants have left for Christmas,' he informed her, in a tone that suggested that, whatever they got up to, there was nobody around to barge in. The world only beats a path to your door when you're in the bathroom, thought Carole, for no reason thinking about Joe. She swallowed the thought along with a swig of white wine.

'And when do you leave?' she asked. 'If you are leaving, that is.'

'Tomorrow.' He kicked off his shoes and Carole saw, with approval, that his socks didn't have holes in them.

'To Aberdeen?'

'To the bosom of my family,' he said. 'Actually, it'll be fun. I have two brothers, and two sisters. All older than me, so that makes me the family baby. But, strangely, we all like each other. I'm getting a train tomorrow afternoon.'

Carole sipped at her drink, looking at him over the rim of the glass. He was, she had to concede, rather handsome and, without thought, kissed him on the cheek. 'That's for being nice to me,' she said.

'Have I been nice to you?'

'You talked to me, when you could have been talking to Clarissa.'

'She doesn't really do talking,' he replied, looking into the electric fire. His eyes burned red in the subdued light. 'I'm not actually sure that she speaks English very well. Anyway, what are your plans?'

'Like you, home tomorrow. A short hop across town, so a quicker journey than yours. But no brothers or sisters, so a much smaller family gathering.'

'Did you ever want brothers or sisters?'

Carole bit her lip. 'I did once have a brother.'

'Oh.'

'He died,' said Carole. 'One minute he had a headache, and a few days later he was dead.'

'Carole, I'm so sorry. I didn't know.'

'No reason why you should have known,' she said, trying to sound bright and cheerful, but probably not succeeding. 'He was very little, and very young. Anyway, it's nice to properly meet you.'

He smiled and put an arm around her, because Carole had started to cry, which wasn't something that she did often, and possibly not since Tim's death years and years previously. She rested her head against his shoulder, feeling warm and, despite the tears, strangely peaceful.

The first bridge that she had to cross, or not cross, now loomed on the horizon. She turned her face to his and they kissed. He tasted of whisky, which wasn't as unpleasant as she'd imagined, although she hoped that he possessed either toothpaste or mouthwash, and preferably both.

'You don't have to go,' he said softly. 'Stay the night. I'll behave, if you want me to,' he added quickly, smiling his lopsided smile, and electric firelight burning in his eyes. He looked both nervous and expectant.

'If I go back to my flat, I'll have to help with the clearing up.'

'I'll take that as a yes,' said Rob, as Carole once again put her head on his shoulder and closed her eyes.

'I don't usually sleep with someone on a first date,' she told him, eyes still firmly closed.

'Only usually?' Rob still sounded hopeful.

'Actually, never. It's a strange rule I have.'

'But we've been together lots of times.'

'Being in a lecture theatre doesn't count as a date, Rob.'

'We've also had coffee together,' he said. 'In the canteen.'

Carole remembered. 'You were with a bunch of people, and I was with a different bunch of other people … at a different table,' she added, now squinting up at him. 'So that doesn't count either.'

'No matter,' he said, finally admitting that Carole's defences might be a bridge too far. 'With nobody here, there are spare bedrooms, although I can't guarantee the cleanliness of the sheets. However, if it helps, I wash mine every day, so you'd be guaranteed not to catch a disease.'

'I'll take my chances,' said Carole.

She chose the bedroom that, just around the corner in her flat, was also her room. In Rob's flat, it had a modern chest of drawers, and a fitted wardrobe. In her flat, she had a chest of drawers that was missing handles, and a wardrobe that had probably been made by a first-week joinery student. She crept into bed, feeling suddenly exhausted, and realising that she didn't know who Rob shared his flat with. Her new bedsheets smelled of lavender, so she guessed a girl, but resisted the temptation to look inside the wardrobe for confirmation. She was asleep within seconds.

*

She was woken by a pigeon cooing on the windowsill. She hadn't drawn the curtains, and it was quite light. The pigeon had its head to one side, its feathers ruffled against the morning frost. Somehow, to Carole, pigeons just didn't look right. Whoever made pigeons, faced with the bleak prospect of having to make so many, perhaps cut a few corners. To Carole, they retained an over-stuffed look that other birds have outgrown. Sensing her uncharitable thoughts, it flew away over the rooftops, its wings clapping a solitary applause in the early morning silence.

Without really thinking about it, she found Rob's bedroom, which in her flat was Joe's bedroom. In Rob's flat, he also had a fitted wardrobe and a chest of drawers with all its handles. He even had an unstained carpet that felt deep and luxurious. She slipped into bed beside him, still not sure what she might, or might not, do next.

His body uncurled. 'Good morning,' he said. 'This is a surprise. A pleasant surprise,' he added hurriedly.

'Good morning to you as well.'

'How long have you been awake?'

'I was woken up by a pigeon. Anyway, sorry about last night.'

'Sorry? Why?'

'For crying on your shoulder. Too much to drink, I expect.'

On the ceiling, an insect of some sort was walking about with purpose and getting nowhere. It was caught in a pool of light that had filtered through Rob's curtains which, unlike Carole, he had actually bothered to close. The insect walked round and round in its circle of light, like an actor in a spotlight; then a cloud hid the sun and the spotlight disappeared. The fly, or whatever it was, sensing freedom, then flew off.

Tomorrow, thought Carole, is already today and I have met someone almost for the first time in my life who I could grow to care for. But she also thought, I only really met him yesterday, and know virtually nothing about him. I don't know what his hopes and ambitions are. I don't know his middle name, or if he has one. I don't even know who he shares his flat with. She didn't know what to feel, or whether she had the right to feel anything. Then again, he knew virtually nothing about her either.

More light came in through the curtains, and small rainbows traced themselves on the walls. The insect, which must have been hiding somewhere, now found its spotlight again. Somewhere a baby cried. Carole put her arms around Rob and they lay face to face very close. Carole again felt at peace but also vulnerable.

'What are you thinking?' he asked.

'Random thoughts.'

'Of what species?' he persisted, smiling his lopsided smile.

'Abstract thoughts about abstract things,' Carole replied.

Rob levered himself upright and rubbed sleep from his eyes with both hands. 'Which doesn't actually mean anything.'

'It simply means that I'm glad to be here,' she replied.

'So am I.'

'Technically, you can't be glad to be here, because you actually live here.'

'I meant, I'm glad that you're here.'

She smiled, innocent in the new day. 'This is officially our second date. Yesterday evening was our first date.'

'Which means?'

'Which means anything you want it to mean.'

First, they kissed, then made love with a passion that surprised her. Afterwards, they lay in each other's arms and Carole felt happy, feeling perhaps that she had met someone who could be a friend and soulmate; someone who would keep her safe and be there when she needed somebody's shoulder. Being more practical, they could also help each other with their coursework. They slept for a while, until the new day took on mechanical noises. A lorry ground its gears on the main road, and a car horn blew away the vestiges of sunrise.

She kissed him goodbye outside the Italian restaurant where Luigi was still behind the counter polishing glasses. Carole supposed that he must have actually been home in the interim and hadn't been there all night. Or maybe he had been; maybe the purpose of Luigi's existence was to polish glasses. Rob went one way towards the main road, a small rucksack over his shoulder, heading for the railway station. She went the other way, back to her flat, where she found that nobody had started on the clearing up, and that the place was a complete mess. Then again, because her flat was always a mess, it didn't look much worse than usual.

Five

Back in their driveway, Iona is already out of the car before Carole has switched off the engine, with her piano lesson book under one arm and a frown on her face. Carole sits for a few moments, thinking about builders, and that first night with Rob, with an equally eloquent frown on her face. It was all so long ago, but she can remember it with perfect clarity; all those jumbled-up thoughts, a jumbled-up happiness, and an afternoon of washing dirty glasses and dishes and pouring bleach down the loo.

Carole steps out of her car into a biting wind. Soon, the TV weather forecaster had said with a cheery smile, it would come from the north with the possibility of snow and travel chaos. Christ, she thinks, and this is supposed to be spring! Where Carole lives, it's too near the sea to much worry about snow and, being a housewife, travel chaos isn't something she needs to think about. Where she lives, it's the east wind you have to beware, blowing in from the Russian steppes and freezing everything in its path. But for now, despite the approach of Easter, it's simply cold and wet.

Inside, and Iona is already slumped in front of the TV. She's watching *The Simpsons* and Carole momentarily wonders if she ever watches anything vaguely educational. At her age, Carole was forced to her room, which didn't have a TV, and had to do her homework, even if she didn't have homework to do. Carole worries about Iona a great deal, but assumes that all mothers worry about their daughters. She often wonders if she would have worried so much over a son. She thinks, perhaps, that sons make trouble and daughters get into trouble. Maybe that's the difference, she thinks; daughters are somehow more vulnerable, and therefore need to be protected from other people's sons.

Carole pokes around in cupboards to discover something to eat for supper, then checks in the deep freeze. Granny is still there, she sees, although it would have been odd if Granny hadn't been there, wrapped securely, if incongruously, in a Tesco Bag for Life. She finds chicken kebabs and some oven chips, happily on the shelf above Granny.

Now that she's sorted supper, Carole stands by the kitchen window looking into their garden. It's a small garden, with grass fringed by flower beds, and a couple of small trees with a washing line strung between them. There's a small workshop that juts out into the garden, with a door into the garage, and another door into the garden. The workshop, if that's what it is, because no work actually gets done in it, is mostly used to store their barbeque. Carole can't decide where to bury the cat, or if it matters. Granny had never shown particular affection for any specific spot in their garden, and they'd never had to bury a pet before, because they'd never had a pet before. She thinks, maybe, that near the birch tree at the bottom of the garden might be a good spot, and she could perhaps plant something cat-friendly over her grave. Catmint, maybe. She'd have a look on the internet.

Pleased with this decision, Carole turns the oven on and a few minutes later pops in the kebabs and, a few minutes after that, the chips. She's never been one for looking at labels that tell her how long to cook something for or, indeed, if kebabs need to be defrosted first. If a recipe calls for something to be simmered for twenty minutes, Carole's strategy is to boil it rapidly for ten minutes. She likes to think she has an instinct for cooking, although her family often disagrees.

Supper, as usual, is largely eaten in silence at the kitchen table. Iona would much prefer to have her supper on her lap in front of the TV but Carole is usually adamant that supper should be eaten as a family at a proper table. At least, she's adamant about it when Ray is around. Carole and Iona don't have much to say to one another; Carole is still distracted by an afternoon of memories, and Iona never has much to say anyway.

'Did these kebabs come out of the deep freeze?' Iona suddenly asks, breaking the silence, and putting down her knife and fork for emphasis.

'Yes, darling,' replies Carole.

'The same deep freeze in which we have a dead cat? God, Mum!'

'It's perfectly hygienic,' Carole reassures her, although Iona has pushed her remaining kebab to one side of her plate and is now eating only chips, with her fingers. Iona then remembers that the chips would also have come from the deep freeze and pushes away her plate.

'The cat should have been buried by now,' Iona says. 'It should have been buried the day it died.'

'It's nothing to worry about. It's completely frozen. Solid as a block of ice.'

'So? It's still dead, Mum.'

'If it matters, these came from the shelf above Granny.' She waves a fork over her plate. 'So, perfectly hygienic,' she repeats.

'No, Mum, it doesn't matter what shelf they came from. It most definitely is *un*hygienic. Sorry, Mum, but I can't eat this.'

'We'll bury Granny on Sunday,' says Carole. 'Your grandparents are coming down for the funeral.'

'Funeral!' Iona seems astonished, all big eyes and pursed lips. 'You're not *really* planning a funeral for the cat, are you?'

'Well, why not?' she asks.

'First of all, it's a cat, Mum!' Iona then can't think of

anything that could reasonably constitute *second* or *third*, and simply sighs loudly.

If she's honest, Carole now rather regrets her funeral plan, which was hastily conceived in the car to Iona's piano lesson; but she's also sentimental and wants Granny's passing to be properly marked. It wasn't just a cat, she was *their* cat, and Carole had chosen it herself. 'Well, I just thought it would be nice,' she answers rather defensively.

'It's still just a cat,' Iona reminds her.

'It was one of us.'

Even to Iona, this sounds absurd. 'Mum, you've gone mad!' She scowls at her plate, because she hasn't eaten much and is still hungry.

'Have I, darling?' replies Carole absently.

Instead of replying, Iona goes pillaging in the fridge and finds bread, cheese and ham, which she loudly consumes, wordlessly making the point that food from the freezer will no longer be considered edible.

Carole thinks about her daughter's accusation. Is giving their cat a decent funeral a sign of madness? Surely not, because it's about family bonding and doing the decent thing. But she's also aware of a shift in perspective, as if looking at herself from a different angle; she again needs to find links to her past to explain what she has become. It's a puzzle that Iona could probably answer, having acquired the adolescent key to all wisdom, but perhaps wisely, Carole doesn't ask. Today's excursion into Edinburgh hadn't offered any clues, although she had enjoyed remembering old memories. Well, some of them.

Iona, having eaten the contents of the fridge, goes off to watch a film about a zombie apocalypse while she, Carole, does the washing up. This nightly chore is hers alone to accomplish because Iona believes that her mother should do everything. It's not exactly fair on Carole, but it's something that has become established and immutable. Carole doubts that Iona knows what washing-up liquid is or how to clean a dirty saucepan.

Carole turns from the sink, dries her hands and then sees that a small black and silver object has appeared on the kitchen table. She knows immediately what it is, but not how it got there. It's an open and empty mussel shell, and it usually lives behind a picture on their living room mantlepiece. Frowning, Carole wonders how it could possibly have made its way to the kitchen table. She hadn't moved it, that's for sure, and Iona has been too engrossed in the dead coming back to life to search behind mantlepiece pictures. In any case, she's certain that it hadn't been on the kitchen table before supper. Wordlessly, she takes it back to the living room and puts it back on the mantlepiece.

Usually Carole sleeps well, but not tonight. There seem to be too many things on her mind, although she's not sure what these *things* are. The past, certainly. The present, maybe. The future? But Carole isn't one to worry too much about the future. There are enough niggling worries in the here and now.

*

But if Carole can't understand how the shell could have made its way into her kitchen, she does know precisely how she acquired it in the first place. It was Easter, only a few months after she'd met Rob, and they were taking part in a half-hearted archaeological dig at the Neolithic village of Skara Brae on the Orkney mainland.

By then, Rob was sometimes sleeping at her flat – this was before the Joe bombshell which happened later that year – but mostly she slept at his flat, which was less decrepit and always scrubbed and cleaned to gleaming perfection by Beth, whose bed Carole had slept in that first night. Beth, a rather humourless Divinity student from Inverness had, they all agreed, some form of obsessive-compulsive disorder. She simply hated dust or dirty dishes, and seemed quite happy to spend large chunks of every evening hoovering and dusting, or scrubbing pans or plates, which suited the other occupants of Rob's flat just fine, and who enthusiastically encouraged this odd, but welcome, behaviour. Beth undertook her role as unpaid cleaner with stoic acceptance and, as far as Carole knew, had never complained that nobody else raised a finger. By contrast, Carole's flat was always a total mess and nobody in her flat it seemed, including her, much cared. On the one occasion that Beth came round for a drink, Carole saw that she was visibly shocked. Carole also hoped that Beth might suddenly launch into some manic cleaning episode but, disappointingly, she didn't and soon left.

Apart from Beth, Rob shared with Kate, a business studies student, and Mike, a junior accountant and family friend of Rob's, who was a few years older than the rest of them. Mike was someone to be envied, as he earned money, but also someone to be pitied, because he had to wear a suit and tie every day, and attempt to be at work by nine in the morning when the rest of them were often still asleep. All in all, Rob's flat was much nicer in every way, with windows that didn't rattle, furniture that wasn't falling apart, and a heating system that actually kept the place warm. Carole liked waking up in his arms, feeling secure, listening to the rhythm of his breathing. She liked feeling him wake, stretch, and kiss her good morning. She liked making love in the half-light of dawn.

It's generally accepted that Skara Brae is one of the most remarkable prehistoric settlements in Europe. It was only discovered in 1850 when a storm stripped grass from a large mound, revealing several stone houses underneath. Subsequent excavations revealed others, and the site has since been dated to before Stonehenge or the Egyptian pyramids. Each of the eight houses comprises a large square room with a central fireplace. There are also beds, shelves, seats and dressers, all in a better condition than the contents of Carole's flat. Each house also has a primitive toilet, much like the one in Carole's flat.

But, for her, the beauty of Skara Brae – she had first visited it on a family holiday – was that everything is made of stone. On an island with virtually no trees, everything had to be hewn from rock. No creature comforts for its inhabitants and which, for Carole, really put the stone into Stone Age.

The reason for the archaeology team travelling by minibus north from Edinburgh was that one of their professors had been looking at aerial photographs of the site and concluded that there might be new finds to be made a little distance from the main site. Quite what those finds might be was never fully explained but, with their limited dig set to take place some distance from Skara Brae itself, a UNESCO World Heritage Site, permission was grudgingly obtained.

By arcane university rules, the three male students – including Rob – were put into one B&B, and the three female students into another. It was explained to them that the minibus would pick them up every morning and take them to the site, returning them to their respective B&Bs every evening. Carole's room was small, with a picture of Jesus over her single bed; but at least she didn't have to share with anyone. Being mostly an only child, she'd never had to share a bedroom with anybody, except people that she wanted to, and with her brother for a while. In other parts of the house were other devotional pictures; in the dining room, a picture of the Last Supper; in the shared bathroom, a picture of Jesus walking on water; in the living room, a picture of Jesus, framed with a halo, holding up both hands in blessing. There was a picture of Moses parting the seas in the hall, and Jesus helping someone to their feet, with a pair of rather modern-looking crutches lying on the ground.

It could safely be assumed that Mrs MacIntosh, the B&B's proprietor, had either acquired her artwork as a job lot from a niche charity shop, or was deeply religious. The three girls settled on the latter, despite Mrs MacIntosh simply exuding bleak hostility to each one of them. From the moment that Carole and her two companions stepped from the minibus, it was clear that Mrs MacIntosh believed that students should all be in a special place in Hell rather than in her house. She looked at each one of them intently, perhaps checking for signs of the Devil, her lips pressed together in a thin and unwelcoming white line, before showing them to their rooms. Mrs MacIntosh was dressed completely in black, wore a crucifix around her neck, and possessed a piercing stare. It was a stare of such unnerving and complete hatred that the three girls assumed that something terrible must have happened in her life – perhaps, a storm washing away her children, or her husband being struck down by lightning.

Despite her landlady, Carole was looking forward to the week. It would be her first proper expedition: digging in flowerbeds and woodland clearings didn't count. This was the time when her passion for the past was at its height; a new student on the university course she had always set her heart on – well, ever since discovering an old milk bottle – and she immediately found herself feeling protective of those who had once lived at Skara Brae; secure, if not very comfortable, in their stone houses. Back then, Carole's passion wasn't just about wanting to dig things up; it was about finding tangible links between now and then. Those links might be no more than a fragment of a leather belt, or a piece of pottery; but all would add to their understanding of who these Iron Age people were and, maybe, why they had eventually deserted their little community to go ... *where*? That's one of the unsolved mysteries of Skara Brae. Maybe they succumbed to some infectious illness or maybe they just got bored and decided to move somewhere with comfier beds and warmer toilet seats. Carole wanted to find out.

On their first morning at the site, their team leader – an enthusiastic lecturer who Carole quite liked – took them on a guided tour, explaining how Neolithic people mainly cooked using dried seaweed and existed on a diet rich in fish and seafood, although they did also keep livestock. There is also evidence of crop cultivation, he said, so it could also have been a place of some abundance, except in winter, and, for its time, considerable civilisation.

After an early lunch of bread, ham and tomato, washed down with a tepid mug of mushroom soup, a big yellow digger appeared on the back of a flat-bed truck. By then, the professional members of the team – university staff from the archaeology faculty who presumably knew what they were doing – had pegged out where they wanted trenches to be dug. Within an hour, the digger had done its job and was once again tethered to its flat-bed truck. They all peered expectantly into the trenches, although none of them had any idea what they might see. It was therefore unsurprising that they saw nothing except earth and stone, although the team now had to climb into the trenches with small trowels and brushes and see what treasures might be uncovered. It might be a pathway, or a wall, a gateway to Narnia or, more than likely, nothing at all.

Although this was her first dig, it was a task that Carole relished because this was getting down and dirty in moist soil, with the constant anticipation that she might be on the brink of some major discovery. It was also nice because the person she had teamed up with was Rob. In their little trench they exchanged a furtive kiss and smiled at one another. They hadn't talked since the ferry crossing from the Scottish mainland, and not much then because the sea was rough and Carole had felt sick.

'Hopeful?' asked Rob, a lop-sided grin on his face.

'It would help if we knew what we were looking for,'

replied Carole.

Instead, Rob climbed from the trench and walked over to their minibus. Its back doors were open and the professional staff were looking at a map. Rob returned a minute later. 'We are, apparently, looking for evidence of a ritual site.'

Orkney, of course, is home to many ritual sites, including the standing stones of Stenness and the Ring of Brodgar, making the whole island a place of ritual significance. Carole knew that the entire area had already been scanned with ground-penetrating radar to discover anything under the subsurface, and had found nothing. Quite why their lecturers and professors thought otherwise still wasn't clear. This time it was Carole who climbed out of the trench and marched across to the minibus.

'We still don't know what we're looking for,' she told the young lecturer she quite liked.

He was looking at a detailed map of the immediate area on which were squiggles in yellow marker pen. Without turning from his scrutiny of the map and its squiggles, he replied: 'Evidence that the area we are looking at might have been used for something.'

'Something?' echoed Carole.

'We don't know,' admitted the lecturer and gestured to the map.

'Something ritualistic?' persisted Carole.

'Maybe, maybe not. But look here.' He tapped a pencil against the map. 'There's the faintest of indentations leading from the main Skara Brae site to the place we're digging. That suggests, perhaps, a footpath. If so, where we're digging may be of some significance. Anyway, that's the theory,' he said, finally turning from his map and grinning.

'What about the geophysics? The radar?'

'Inconclusive,' he replied.

Back in her trench, scraping moist soil with her trowel, Carole told Rob about her exchange with the lecturer. 'In

62

other words, they haven't a clue,' she finished, scraping out a small stone and throwing it over the side of her trench.

Rob straightened, stretched and rubbed his back. Above them was an expanse of blue sky, and around them a cold wind blowing in off the sea. Seabirds, like small scraps of paper, bisected the few low clouds.

'Time for a break,' said Rob and dropped his trowel and brush by the side of their trench. Around them, in other trenches, were the hunched backs of other students, and the sound of trowels scraping against stone.

They walked down to the beach and watched small waves suck at sand and pebbles. 'I came to this spot when I was a child,' said Carole, remembering how her dad had taught his two children how to skim stones. Carole could remember Tim's laugh when he finally got the hang of it, skimming a stone for two or three jumps across the still water.

'Is that why you signed up for this dig?'

'No, I would have signed up for it anyway. At heart, Rob, I'm a treasure hunter.'

'An avaricious treasure hunter?'

'No, a nice one, whatever that is.'

She frowned; it was the Easter break and she could have stayed in Edinburgh, sleeping in late, and partying with friends. Signing up for expeditions wasn't compulsory; you could still earn your degree without leaving the confines of the university. But why would you want to, when there was a world outside just waiting to be discovered? Carole did want to make those discoveries; she was determined to be a *proper* archaeologist, on her first expedition, making her course feel *real*, even if that meant digging around in dirt to find things that probably weren't there. 'So why did you come?' she asked, brushing hair from her eyes.

He didn't answer for a moment, looking at the far horizon, the wind also blowing in his hair. 'Maybe to be with you,' he then said.

That evening, a few of them, including Rob and Carole, requisitioned the minibus and headed off to a small hotel in a nearby village. They drove east alongside the Loch of Skaill; water to their right, dark hills to their left. Out to sea there was a flicker of lightning and, a few seconds later, the crackle of distant thunder. The storm was set to pass north of Orkney, so they shouldn't get too wet, or so the forecast said. The minibus was driven by one of the lecturers, although not the one that Carole liked, and it was clear that he'd rather be anywhere else than driving a minibus of chattering students to a pub he didn't want to go to. He said nothing, grunting only to questions, and not looking happy. Carole and Rob sat at the back of the minibus and held hands. When they arrived at the hotel, its small bar was almost empty. The landlord looked pleased to see them.

Drinks were bought and quickly consumed, because their unwilling driver had given them only an hour of freedom before taking them back to their respective B&Bs. Everyone also ordered food from the limited menu which was also quickly consumed, before the next round of drinks was ordered. They were all grouped around a large wooden table near to a log fire, which crackled and spat. Their driver sat at a nearby table by himself and read a book.

On the way back, they stopped first at Carole's B&B and the three girls dutifully climbed out, waving goodbyes to the other students still in the minibus.

'Nice place,' said a voice in Carole's ear.

'What the hell?' It was Rob, with his lop-sided grin, also giving a small wave to the minibus which was already disappearing round a corner. Above them was a clear sky and stars from horizon to horizon. The storm that had been threatening earlier had indeed petered out over the North

Sea. 'Christ, Rob! You'll get us expelled, or something.'

'Expelled? From where?'

'From this place for a start. I'm not allowed male visitors.' Carole frowned. 'Actually, no visitors of any human variety.'

Rob leaned in close. 'Then live dangerously, Carole. It's the only way to live.'

It's not a life choice that Carole had ever considered, being methodical if also a little haphazard, and not much given to taking risks. But what he was suggesting was also an affirmation of his affection and for that, maybe, she should be grateful. 'You'll have to creep past the living room,' Carole told him, now registering that the other two girls were giggling rather loudly. 'Mrs MacIntosh will no doubt be in front of the TV, so creeping *quietly* might be a good idea. Christ, Rob, why didn't you tell me about this little plan?'

'It only came to me in the minibus. I thought you wouldn't mind.'

'Well, I do mind! It isn't fair! Not fair on me. Your libido could get me into trouble!' But she also remembered the beach, and Rob's reason for coming on this dig, and of holding hands on the minibus on the way to the hotel. 'You'd also better wear this,' she said, handing over her parka with its fleece hood.

Carole went first into the B&B and, sure enough, Mrs MacIntosh was in front of the TV and, even better, seemed to be asleep. Jesus beamed down benignly from his place above the fireplace, giving Mrs MacIntosh his blessing, although perhaps not to Carole who was gesturing to the other girls who were still outside. Together they all crept along the downstairs landing and up the stairs, which thankfully didn't creak, the other two girls still giggling. Carole's parka looked ridiculous on Rob, being several sizes too small. One of the other girls gave Carole a thumbs-up, whatever that was supposed to mean.

Safely in her room they lay down on her narrow bed which, being much older than Carole and unused to two occupants, sagged rather alarmingly in the middle. But this did have the advantage of pushing them together so they dutifully took off their clothes and snuggled under the warm duvet. In the night, wedged up against Rob, Carole dreamed of being in her trench and of digging and uncovering great treasure. It was a nice dream, an affirmation that her visit to Orkney hadn't been a waste of time.

She was woken up by a loud scream from the corridor outside her room. For a moment, she didn't know where she was, or why she was in a narrow bed. She blinked herself awake, switched on the bedside light, hurriedly wrapped herself in her dressing gown, and opened her bedroom door. She found that everyone was now standing outside their doors, also wrapped in dressing gowns. The only person not wearing a dressing gown was Rob, who was wearing boxer shorts and looking both sheepish and alarmed.

'This intruder entered my bedroom!' said Mrs MacIntosh in a rather shaken voice who was, inevitably, wearing a black dressing gown that was clutched tight to her chin.

'Sorry, wrong room,' said Rob, trying to be reasonable. Carole hadn't described Mrs MacIntosh in any detail, so he probably assumed her to be normal. 'I'd just been to the loo and got, well, a little disorientated.'

The other two girls were looking on wide-eyed and biting their lips, but also trying not to laugh.

Mrs MacIntosh took a deep breath and turned to Carole, although why she assumed Carole was the other half of this guilty duet was beyond her. 'House rules, young lady. You have just broken the most important one. I will not tolerate sin or fornication under my roof!' Carole momentarily wondered how she knew that fornication had taken place, and had to think back to remember if it had. But of course it had, otherwise Rob would have stayed securely on the minibus, and this unpleasantness could have been avoided. 'I expect both of you to be gone in the morning.'

Back in their room, Rob sat heavily on the side of the bed which squeakily protested. 'I suppose I should apologise,' he says.

'Fat lot of good that'll do,' she replied, also sitting heavily on the bed which again loudly squeaked. 'But how did she know you were in *my* room?'

'Your face rather gave it away.'

'Oh, Christ!'

'Actually, I rather blame him,' said Rob, pointing to the picture of Jesus over her bed. 'He obviously didn't approve either, the bastard.'

The next morning Rob and Carole stayed in their room until the minibus appeared. Mrs MacIntosh was immediately outside and loudly remonstrating with the morose lecturer who had been their driver from the evening before. Carole picked up her rucksack, all neatly packed, and headed down the stairs. Rob clattered down behind her. Mrs MacIntosh didn't say goodbye, and simply stared malevolently at them with her arms crossed.

There was an awkward silence in the minibus, with everyone looking out of different windows, until they pulled onto the grass verge outside the next B&B. Their lecturer switched off the engine and turned round in his seat. 'Sorry, Rob, but you'd also better pack your things.'

After dropping everyone else at Skara Brae, Carole and Rob were driven to the ferry port and had to wait several hours for the next boat to Aberdeen. Neither of them said much. Rob knew how much this curt dismissal from her first expedition had hurt her. On board, they stood at the stern and watched the mainland of Orkney slowly diminish in their wake. Carole thought that living dangerously wasn't something she'd try again, although everyone – including the professional staff – all seemed to find the whole episode greatly amusing. But, it was also explained, there was no more budget to find alternative accommodation, even if there was any nearby, so they would have to leave.

'Sorry,' said Rob, for the hundredth time, which didn't make it any better.

Carole didn't say anything, looking over dark water to the island where her father had once tried, and failed, to teach her how to skim stones.

'But I do have a present for you,' Rob now said. One hand was bunched tight and he took hold of Carole's hand and deposited something onto it.

'It's a mussel shell,' she said.

'But not just any mussel shell. I found it yesterday in our trench.'

Carole feigned outrage. 'You've pillaged an ancient artefact from a World Heritage Site!'

'It's just a shell.'

Carole remembered her dream from the night before, of digging and finding treasure. But she couldn't remember what that treasure was.

'For good luck,' said Rob.

Carole didn't really believe in lucky charms but she looked again at the shell, covered with the grime of millennia, and, despite herself, wondered who had last held it, all those thousands of years ago. Maybe, she thought, real treasure can be something mundane. Once this was food which, on an inhospitable island, would have been more valuable than gold or jewels. Maybe real treasure is more than its intrinsic worth.

Maybe, also, treasure can be something that conjures up a memory, however pleasant or unpleasant, or a mixture of both. An old photograph, perhaps, or an insignificant memento of a doomed trip. She wrapped the shell in a tissue and slipped it into her parka pocket, a small something that she would keep forever to remind her *never* to live dangerously again.

Six

The morning after discovering the mussel shell on the kitchen table, Carole sleeps through her alarm clock and wakes up late. Iona, unusually responsible, appears to have had breakfast and gone to school. There is a dirty plate and cup close to the dishwasher, but not actually in it, and breadcrumbs everywhere. Carole feels a little guilty for sleeping in, then sighs and cleans up her daughter's mess, and goes into the living room to check that the mussel shell is behind the framed picture and hasn't inexplicably gone wandering again. She is relieved to find it still in its place, and picks it up for a few moments, remembering the ferry trip back to the Scottish mainland. Her first proper archaeological dig, a whole day, with nothing to show for it, except a mussel shell. Then again, she reminds herself, nobody else found anything all week.

Carole showers and then heads into Edinburgh. With Dr Orlando Cruz in Portugal, she has decided on one more nostalgic trip to the city. Then, she has promised herself, she will get on with being sensible, whatever being sensible is, until Dr Cruz returns to Scotland. She's not only going to revisit her first flat but this time she'll also look up at Rob's flat and remember the good times, before and after Skara Brae. She could have done so the day before but, somehow, she wants to process one piece of her past at a time.

Carole doesn't like to be rushed. The sat nav lady is her usual self, husky and confident, and Carole is grateful not to have woken her earlier when she could have been in the midst of passion or, worse, fornicating surreptitiously in an

Orkney B&B. But it's not somewhere that she imagines the sat nav lady would ever choose to visit. She imagines her in a London penthouse, with a cigarette in an impossibly-long cigarette holder, or taking long holidays in Jamaica or weekend breaks in northern Italy, sipping cocktails overlooking an Alpine lake. The sat nav lady and Mrs MacIntosh would have had nothing in common, what with the sat nav lady requiring weekly hair appointments, regular visits to the gym, and impossibly-expensive facials in only the most exclusive spas. Mrs MacIntosh would not have approved and Carole momentarily wonders what happened to her. Long dead, she supposes, and runs a hand through her short hair, checks her make-up in the rear-view mirror before remembering that she hasn't applied any. There are more *traffic disruptions en route* and Carole agrees that the sat nav lady should plot an avoiding route, which she obligingly does, taking them into town down unfamiliar streets.

Although Carole should know Edinburgh, she really doesn't. She knows the university and where she's lived, and where friends lived, but much of the city is a mystery. It's something she can't explain. As an archaeologist, the past is her passion, and Edinburgh is full of the past – from the castle, which she has visited, to all its old buildings and streets, which she largely hasn't. Instead, her passion was for digging things up, not looking at old things. Historic streets and old buildings have already been studied and catalogued; Carole's interest was, or is, in the undiscovered; in a flint, discovered near the Callanish Stones on the Isle of Lewis; or an axe-head on another dig on Orkney, this time at Stenness, an incomplete stone circle; or a piece of pottery on the Knap of Howar, some of the oldest stone buildings in north-west Europe, on an island off Orkney. Although she also went on digs on the mainland, her first love has always been the islands, with their huge horizons and brooding vistas of dark water. Carole's interest was, and maybe still is, in the Neolithic past, of settlements by shorelines; and they always remind her of the family holiday she'd had with her parents and brother, who announced on their last day on Orkney that he had a headache.

Although Carole no longer knows where she is, being taken down side roads that she's never been down before, the sat nav lady clearly does know Edinburgh. Her guidance is precise and comforting: *You might not know where the fuck you are*, she also seems to be saying, *so it's lucky that I do, and have the time and inclination to take you to your destination, despite a hair appointment and having invited friends over for a swim and glass of Prosecco. I will also be flying to Barcelona later today with Juan, who is a very dear and special friend.* The route she navigates is circuitous, guiding Carole down some very narrow streets and, once, a one-way alley. Carole marvels at the sat nav lady's skill and knowledge and how she knows not just Edinburgh but the whole of the UK, perhaps the world, telling millions of users to *turn left* or *turn right* or *take the second exit off the roundabout* in, presumably, many different languages. Carole wonders if she could, temporarily, get the sat nav lady to talk in another language on a route that she knows well. That way, she could have the pleasure of marvelling at her talent, while learning the rudiments of a different language. But it's a fanciful thought, quickly forgotten, because Carole is first and foremost a wife and mother. Yes, she's proud of being a mother, but she could have taken the third exit off a roundabout and ended somewhere else. But would that somewhere else be a better place? Would she be happier? That, somehow, is what she has to find out, even if this is going to be her last trip into Edinburgh for a while.

Carole is now in a part of the city which she doesn't remotely recognise. It's in a Georgian area, with fancy mansions and neat front gardens. Every lawn is mowed;

71

every flowerbed weeded. It would appear to be nowhere near where she wants to be; her first flat was in an area of Edinburgh that didn't have Georgian mansions or neat front gardens or, come to think of it, front gardens of any description. She is therefore surprised when the sat nav lady announces:

Your destination is on the left.

Carole pulls into the side of the road and looks about her, but can see nothing familiar. She wants to revisit her old street and Rob's flat and make new connections with old memories. But this place has no memories; she has no idea where she is except that she must be in a posh suburb with all those big houses and manicured gardens. She looks around for a signpost that might tell her which area of the city she's in, but can't see one. She then checks the postcode she entered into the sat nav's innards to discover that she's nowhere near her old street. Well, she knows that. Sighing, she once again enters the correct postcode and pulls out into the road. As always, she listens attentively to the sat nav lady as she plots a new course to where she wanted to go in the first place. Again, it's a circuitous route, taking her down some streets she does vaguely recognise but mostly down streets that she doesn't. They once again end up on a boulevard of Georgian opulence, with the sat nav lady again pronouncing in her husky voice:

Your destination is on the left.

But it isn't her destination. It's the same destination they were at ten minutes beforehand. It can safely be assumed that Carole is both confused and angry, swearing audibly at the sat nav lady, then immediately feeling bad for swearing, because the kindly sat nav must have had some kind of breakdown: some form of software malfunction, no doubt temporary. Carole actually does feel sorry for her; somehow this electronic fault makes her sat nav less of a machine and more like a proper person with real faults and foibles, and momentarily unable to make love to Juan, sip a cocktail *and* hold a map. She wants to reach into the dashboard and pat her on the head although she doesn't know how to open the dashboard, or what the sat nav lady looks like or whether she has a head. Nor does she know who to take the sat nav lady to for counselling, if that's what required; is there some kind of psychiatric mechanic who specialises in such things? She rather thinks not, and that the sat nav would simply be ripped out and replaced with a healthy stranger, which would make her feel uncomfortable, like putting down a much-loved family pet.

She looks around her at the opulent houses and wonders who lives in them. Financiers, most probably, because making money from money is how the world seems to work, although Carole does consider it somewhat immoral. She leaves Ray out of that equation because he is in the business of lending money to smaller businesses and therefore helping companies get off the ground and create employment. He is, she has to concede, the responsible face of banking, or the least irresponsible face of banking. But then she notices that one of the grand houses has been converted into a swanky hotel, with a burnished aluminium name over discreet bonsai plants in pastel blue pots that flank the entrance.

The hotel is also on her left, just as the sat nav lady said, and she wonders why she has been taken to this destination (twice!) when she wanted to go somewhere else entirely. It's a mystery to her, a sat nav malfunction obviously, but Carole is also curious. So, she switches off the engine and goes to have a closer inspection, leaving her car parked unobtrusively on a double yellow line.

Up close, the hotel is even more opulent, with heavy drapes at the windows, and it exudes a sense of discreet exclusivity. The kind of place for romantic weekends, or illicit liaisons. She shudders to think how much a room here would cost but, having been brought here, pushes open the

73

front door. Inside is a carpet that, if it was a lawn, would need mowing. There is also a grand staircase in dark wood leading upwards into enigmatic shadow. It is the kind of hotel that Carole can only dream of staying in, of being carried up the grand staircase to a four-poster bed, violins playing in the background, and being told that she's the most beautiful women in the world: the kind of hotel that the sat nav lady is presumably well used to, or was, thinks Carole, remembering that her friend may now be ill and unable to fly to Barcelona.

She thinks about this while taking in the opulence around her; from the discreet check-in desk, complete with twig-thin and beautiful receptionist, to the silk wallpaper and subdued lighting. This is definitely not a hotel for passing businessmen; it is a place for romantic reverence, legitimate or illicit – and probably the latter. Wives, in her experience, quickly find themselves relegated to budget hotels or remain at home while their husbands spend lavishly on their expense accounts. She thinks sourly of Ray; this hotel is the kind of place he might stay on business, but never a place he would take Carole to.

The bar is also a shrine to romance, with heavy partially-closed dark red curtains, and the bar itself in polished dark wood, with small downlighters picking out particularly fine bottles of brandy or whisky. She briefly ponders again why she is pandering to a sat nav lady with a mental health issue when she sees the barman.

'My God, Joe!'

Her old flatmate with the inappropriate libido takes a moment to recognise her, which instantly flusters her. Has she changed that much? Is she now an old crone? Is it that she's wearing clean clothes? Or, remembering the open door to the bathroom, any clothes? He, on the other hand, doesn't seem to have changed at all. A bit of additional weight and a few flecks of grey hair, but still instantly recognisable.

'Carole! What on earth brings you here?'

'I just happened to be passing,' she lies, taking a seat at the bar, which is empty of other patrons, except for a couple in a distant corner holding hands with their heads together. The man looks old enough to be the girl's father, and Carole's suspicions about the hotel's illicit goings-on seem confirmed. Carole orders a small glass of wine, and is hardly surprised by the price. She could have bought three bottles at her local supermarket for the same amount.

'Well, it's good to see you,' says Joe. 'You look great.'

Carole is flattered, before remembering Joe's libido and that flattery is no doubt an important part of his job.

'I thought you were going to be a biologist?' she says.

'Actually, I am a biologist. Working at a research centre next to the Edinburgh Royal. Doing research on gene therapy.'

'Dolly the sheep, and all that?'

'No, nothing to do with Dolly the sheep.'

Carole gives a small laugh, to indicate that she was making a joke, which she wasn't. She doesn't really know what gene therapy is or what it does. 'Doing something useful,' she now says.

'Well, I hope so. Slow work, but rewarding. The fact is that research can take years and years.' He shrugs. 'We spend most of our time collaborating with other researchers.'

'Like I said, doing something useful.' She's distracted by the couple in the corner who are suddenly laughing at something, and she realises how similar she is to the young woman. Well, the young woman is much younger than Carole, but they both share the same figure, face and eyes. They could be mother and daughter or, thinks Carole optimistically, I could be her *slightly* older sister. She also looks more closely at her male friend and sees similarities with Ray. He's a bit older than the real Ray, but looks uncannily like a future version of himself. She wonders

75

again whether this is the kind of hotel that Ray frequents, and whether he goes to them alone, or whether looking at them online is as far as it goes.

'So why is a biologist working in a bar? Or are you secretly testing new therapies on unsuspecting customers?'

Joe shrugs. 'I was owed holiday and the barman who works dayshift here sprained his ankle. Tripped over his dog's lead, or that's his story. I'm just filling in for a few days.'

'That makes no sense whatsoever,' says Carole.

'My parents own the hotel. I'm just helping out.'

'Then that does make a bit of sense, although I didn't know you were descended from hotel royalty.'

'It's a boutique hotel,' he confides. 'Trouble is, there are many other boutique hotels in Edinburgh to choose from. Mostly closer to the city centre, closer to all the attractions and amenities, and therefore more popular than ours.'

'Oh, come on, Joe! This is perhaps the swankiest hotel I've ever been in.'

'With a barman working for free because the owners want to save money?'

To Carole, it doesn't seem possible that a place like this could be doing anything other than printing large sums of money. But, then again, apart from the other couple in the bar, she seems to be the only other patron.

She takes a sip from her glass. 'But do you actually know how to be a barman in a place like this? Suppose I asked you for a Bellini?'

'Two ounces of peach puree with four ounces of Prosecco.'

Carole notes that he hadn't hesitated. 'Singapore Sling?'

'Gin, cherry brandy and Benedictine. Add ice and Angostura bitters. Pour into a tall glass and add pineapple and lime juice.'

'You really do know your stuff,' she replies, having no idea how to make a Bellini or Singapore Sling and whether

Joe is right or wrong. She decides that, in a place like this, it probably does involve peaches and Prosecco, or cherry brandy and Benedictine, and would probably involve taking out a second mortgage to buy one.

Joe again shrugs. 'I used to work here in the summer holidays, back in uni days. Back then, there was more of a demand for cocktails. Fashion, I suppose. I therefore had to learn how to be a mixologist.'

'A mixologist?'

'It's a bit like being a biologist. A bit of this and a bit of that and, hey presto! A cocktail! You still look great,' he suddenly repeats, making Carole wonder if he remembers the episode in their shared bathroom.

'You haven't changed much,' she offers in response which, sadly, is the case. Certainly, she's changed and knows it. She looks again at the young woman in the corner, at her exuberant youthfulness, remembering herself as she must once have been. 'Married? Family?'

'Married. Three daughters. Living in the Old Town. You?'

'Ditto married. One daughter. East Lothian, in the sticks.'

'And still at the university, I suppose.'

It's not quite a question because Joe has assumed, *she* assumes, that she wouldn't have given up her career for motherhood. 'Actually, no,' she concedes.

Joe is looking surprised. 'But you were always so single-minded about it. I heard you got a doctorate and become a lecturer.'

Carole wonders how he knows this, but also feels inadequate, and doesn't immediately respond. 'I suppose motherhood got in the way,' she replies rather lamely.

'Then I revise my opinion,' he says. 'You may still look great but you've also changed.'

'We all change, Joe.'

'Christ, Carole, you were the only one of us who used to

77

actually study in the evenings!'

He makes it sound like an accusation, which Carole knows it probably wasn't, but she still feels a pulse of anger. Joe may not have been saying anything serious, but he's struck a nerve. 'You certainly didn't do a lot of studying in the evenings, I seem to remember.'

It's perfectly obvious what Carole is referring to, and Joe has the good grace to look a little sheepish. 'It's not something I'm proud of,' he says, 'but the truth is that they almost threw themselves at me. Honestly, Carole, that's what happened! If it's any consolation, I felt bad about it. At the time, I mean. It still makes my toes curl.'

Carole relents, mentally slapping her wrist. She'd been out of order, wanting simply to be hurtful because he had unintentionally been hurtful to her. 'What happened to them, do you know?' she asks in a quieter voice.

He shakes his head. 'No, sorry, didn't keep up with them.'

Neither had she, because both Kaitlin and Bernice still harboured lingering suspicions about her and Joe, and their friendships – if that's what they were – had been fractured.

'You're not married to Rob, are you?' he asks. 'You two were an item for years.'

Carole shakes her head. 'No, after graduation I went on to do my doctorate. He was offered a job in Wales … protecting and enhancing the past, apparently,' she says, remembering a difficult conversation with Rob on a beach in North Berwick.

No, they agreed, it would be a too-distant relationship, with plane or train tickets that neither of them could afford. A clean break was the sensible option although, maybe, their relationship had run its course; a patina of their passion had rubbed off and, like a glittery dress, the sequins had become faded. She was tearful for a while but then, to shelter from the rain, visited a pub and bumped into Ray and was instantly smitten once again. Maybe, she thinks, things happen for a

78

reason and that it sometimes takes years to work out what that reason was.

The couple in the corner have finished their drinks and the man is fiddling with a room key. It's clear to Carole what is now on the agenda. She also sees that the young woman *could* be her younger sister, and notices that the young lady is looking at her and perhaps drawing the conclusion that Carole could be her older sister or, God forbid, her mother. It's an unsettling moment, seeing herself as she was.

She finishes her drink and rather clumsily hugs Joe across the bar. 'Hope the proper barman gets better soon. Incidentally, your white wine is rubbish.'

'If you want, I could tell you all about its grape variety and the vineyard it came from,' he says.

'No thanks, Joe. All my wine comes from supermarkets, and probably only pretends to be made from grapes. That's all I need to know.'

She's almost at the door when she hears Joe's raised voice. 'Oh, and by the way, happy birthday!'

'But it's not my birthday.'

'But it soon will be.' He taps his head. 'Cocktails, biology and dates. The three things I'm good at!'

Back in her car she stares accusingly at the dashboard where the sat nav lady presumably lives, and wonders what psychotic episode she could have had. Carole makes a mental note to phone the garage the moment she gets back home. A deranged sat nav she can do without. But then again … her sat nav is just a bunch of bits and bytes, guided by satellites, and only able to make judgements to get her from A to B. Carole knows that. Yet the sat nav had unerringly taken her twice to meet Joe, and for him to simply remind her how much she had changed. Not for the better was his unspoken rebuke. She had seen it written all over his face, and Joe had never been good at hiding his thoughts. She decides, taking a deep breath, that today is making no sense whatsoever.

She's also been reminded of her impending birthday, and she wonders if Ray is scouring the shopping malls of New York to find the perfect gift. Or maybe he's already bought her a gift card from the shopping centre round the bypass, like he did last year. Or completely forgotten about her birthday, like he did the year before. She doesn't bother thinking about what Iona may, or may not, have bought her.

Seven

Then, for no reason, she remembers another birthday, years and years before, back when she was a student just about to graduate. It was a warm spring day and she and Rob were planning to have a quiet and romantic meal in the Italian restaurant near his flat, and near to what had also been her first flat. She was by then living elsewhere, but Rob was still in the same place. They still ate in the Italian restaurant on a regular basis; it was the only decent place in the area and Carole still liked being winked at by Luigi. Her parents were in Florence, gazing at Renaissance art, or so they said. Her mother adored art; her father less so. She supposed that her mother would be doing the rounds of galleries and museums, with her father safely deposited in a nearby bar or café.

It was one of the few days that she didn't have lectures or tutorials. Her work was all up-to-date and, as it was her birthday, she decided to walk into the city and sit in the gardens under Edinburgh Castle, or maybe just wander and see where she ended up. It was a wandering option that a great many other students had also taken, with a smattering of older people, some in suits, who should clearly have been in offices somewhere.

It was the perfect day for meandering and Carole, when she's in the mood, has always been good at meandering. She walked from the faculty past the Museum of Scotland, past the statue of Greyfriars Bobby, the faithful Skye terrier who stayed by his master's grave for fourteen years, and through the Grassmarket, with its profusion of pubs and cafés. Carole stopped to sit at a pavement café and slowly drink an iced coffee, watching the world go by. Then, after enough of the world had gone by, she walked down to Princes Street Gardens, in the shadow of Edinburgh Castle, and dozed off, being woken by an enormous bang, before realising that it was the one o'clock gun, the cannon fired from the castle battlements every day. It was a nice tradition for the city to have kept going, she often thought, despite most people now having watches, although perhaps not so good for anyone with a heart condition.

She sat up, stretching her arms above her head and yawning, and then saw Rob. He was about a hundred yards away, too far for immediate recognition but not too far to miss his garish blue and turquoise T-shirt. She'd bought it for him in a charity shop as a joke, and was then surprised and rather mortified when he started wearing it. Beside him, sitting on a coat, was Clarissa who, even at that distance, still looked like a Barbie prostitute doll, with a not-quite-there blue skirt and white clingy top that showed off her midriff. Rob seemed to be talking, moving his hands about for emphasis; then, strangely, Clarissa seemed to be replying, with Rob nodding like a metronome.

She watched them for a while, wondering whether she should go over, then decided against it. It was too nice a day for confrontations, and she didn't know what, if anything, she would be confronting. After all, they were all in same year and a casual conversation in the park didn't mean anything. Although it might, she also thought, narrowing her eyes and watching them closely. After a while, Rob stood up, waved rather airily at Clarissa and walked up to Princes Street. Clarissa continued to sit, staring straight ahead at the castle, perhaps wondering what it was.

Carole stood up, brushed grass from her jeans, and walked over.

Clarissa saw her approach and Carole thought she detected a hint of embarrassment behind her welcoming smile. 'Out by yourself?' asked Carole.

'Oh, you know how it is,' replied Clarissa.

'Not really, no.'

Clarissa pulled a book from under her coat. Carole tried to see whether it was an Enid Blyton for toddlers or something by Leo Tolstoy. Before she could get a good look, Clarissa had pushed it back under her coat. 'Too nice to be inside,' said Clarissa. 'I was just getting in a spot of reading.'

'Then I won't disturb you,' said Carole and walked off the way she had come.

That evening, she and Rob went to the Italian restaurant and ate pizza and drank white wine. She was on the point of mentioning Clarissa several times, but didn't want to ask anything because she didn't want to know the answer. She didn't want to be lied to, but she didn't want the truth either, whatever the truth was. She might have been witness to *something*, or to nothing at all. It was probably best to pretend that she had seen nothing, because that way she couldn't be hurt.

*

Still sitting in her car outside Joe's hotel, patting the dashboard rather soothingly, Carole now remembers another birthday, years and years before. She was carrying a slice of birthday cake wrapped in a paper napkin, and was taking it to her magic clearing in the woods. Her mother was almost as good at baking birthday cakes as she was at cooking Sunday lunch, and Carole had already eaten far too much of it. There had been a storm the night before so she was careful crossing the stream, carefully placing each foot on stepping stones. It was late in the afternoon, the sun low on the horizon, and the clearing was filled with shadows. Leaves were promising to sprout again on the oaks and, as always, they seemed to be saying something, but nothing she could hear. She wasn't sure why she'd come to the clearing, but it seemed nice to share her birthday with a place that had only recently given her a silver and sapphire brooch, even if it was broken and unwearable. She was just about to eat her slice of cake when she decided that she'd eaten enough cake, at least until she got home and could have some more.

'I brought you some cake,' she said to the trees and placed the cake, still in its napkin, at the centre of the clearing. The leaves rustled and whispered. 'I hope you like it,' she added, before slipping back through the trees, and hoping that her brother hadn't eaten too much of the rest of her birthday cake.

*

Rather than risk visiting Rob's old flat, as she'd been planning, Carole drives from Joe's family hotel back to East Lothian, without the sat nav's help and, only making a few wrong turns, arrives back at NAVARONE before Iona has made it back from school. She goes into the kitchen to make a cup of tea and there, as before, on the kitchen table, is the mussel shell.

This time she is unsurprised but nevertheless shocked. Small things seem to be happening that are out of her control, and Carole's life is mostly organised. She likes being in control, because she doesn't like nasty surprises that could, with a little forethought, have been anticipated. It's not that she can't be spontaneous, but it has to be organised spontaneity; like going to the supermarket and buying something that she wasn't planning on buying, or reading a book she wasn't intending to read. Carole likes it that way, for her mundane life to be planned out, hour by hour, so that she can avoid the unexpected. Carole only likes nice surprises, and they have been in rather short supply lately.

Iona arrives home a little later, in hockey kit, because it's a practice day, and looking every inch a personification of pain and exhaustion. She shuffles slowly, groaning out of her coat and dumps her school bag in the hall.

She finds her mother sitting at the kitchen table with a glass of brandy in front of her, and staring rather intently at an old shell on the table. This is new territory for Iona: her mother is usually polishing or dusting or, at least, *doing* something.

'How was your day, darling?' asks Carole absently.

'Terrible. I'm completely knackered.'

Iona is her team's goalkeeper, which to Carole doesn't seem to be a particularly exhausting position. Wisely, she doesn't offer this thought.

'It was also freezing,' adds Iona.

'It's winter, darling. Well, sort of winter. Not quite summer, anyway. It's supposed to be cold. Anyway, it'll soon be the Easter break, I expect. No more hockey for days and days.' Carole can't quite remember when or how long the Easter holidays are but, in spite of a rogue mussel shell, is trying to sound bright and cheerful.

Iona pours herself a glass of Coke from the fridge and sits opposite Carole at the kitchen table. Carole is still looking at the shell, and is frowning rather intently.

'What exactly is that?' asks Iona.

'A mussel shell.'

'I can see that. But what's it doing on the kitchen table?'

'I'd like to know the same thing,' says Carole, taking a swig from her glass. 'You didn't put it there, did you?'

Iona opens her mouth to say something, then closes it again.

'It's just something from my past,' offers Carole. 'I don't know why it's on the kitchen table. I suppose I must have put it there.'

'Your past?'

'Past, present and future,' says Carole suddenly, now

looking at her daughter. 'The past is what shapes our present, and our present shapes our future.' This is unusually philosophical for Carole, but it's been a strange day and she doesn't yet know what to make of it.

'Whatever,' says Iona. 'Is that supposed to be some sort of motherly advice, or what?'

'I'm not sure, to be honest.'

'Mum, are you drunk, or have you just gone madder?'

'Mad, maybe.'

'Whatever,' replies Iona and, finishing her Coke, stomps upstairs for a bath.

Carole now notices that the shell is inexplicably and spotlessly clean. Yet it had always been as Rob had given it to her, with the earth and mud of Skara Brae encrusted on it. Now, the grime of thousands of years has vanished. The shell's exterior is lustrous black and its inside is almost a mirror. Carole, still frowning, ponders this new revelation, or did she clean it earlier and forget about it? This, she concludes, is the only possible explanation, although she still can't explain the sat nav malfunction and meeting Joe after all these years. Her daughter is probably right: she is going mad.

Iona eventually reappears and looks suspiciously around the kitchen. Usually there are pots bubbling, or something sizzling on the hob, or something else in the oven. Instead, there is an absence of food preparation and her mother is still staring vacantly at the mussel shell.

'Well at least you've cleaned it,' says Iona, indicating the shell.

'I suppose I must have,' replies Carole. 'Except that I don't remember cleaning it.'

'I wouldn't worry,' replies Iona. 'It's probably the menopause. I learned all about it in biology. Go and see the GP, Mum, and get some hormone replacement stuff.'

But Carole is still too young for that stage of life, and

knows it every month, but doesn't reply to her daughter who knows everything about everything. Anyway, her body's cycles and rhythms are her private business.

'Are we actually going to eat this evening?' Iona now asks, no doubt desperately hungry from her hockey goalkeeping duties. Carole, distracted by the day's events, had completely forgotten about food. 'But nothing from the deep freeze, okay? I don't want to catch dead cat disease.'

Carole sighs, finds her handbag, and hands Iona a £20 note. 'Go down the street and get us some pizzas.'

'Gosh, Mum! Thanks!' says Iona. 'What kind do you want?'

'A round one,' replies Carole, whose knowledge of pizzas is hazy at best.

Iona, who had earlier exuded exhaustion, now bounds back down the hallway at high speed, leaving Carole to continue pondering the significance of psychotic sat navs and self-cleaning molluscs, whether they had any significance, and if there could be any connection between them.

Iona returns a little later carrying two square pizza boxes. Carole notes that one box is much smaller than the other, and therefore which box must contain her supper. She's right. They eat in silence in front of the TV because Carole can't be bothered with the kitchen table and watch an old spy film in which baddies try to take over the world. How precisely they intend to do this Carole doesn't know because she's still distracted by the day's events and isn't paying much attention.

She manages to eat only a few mouthfuls of her pizza, and puts her small box on the coffee table between them. When she looks at the table a few minutes later, she sees on it a very large empty pizza box and her smaller box on Iona's lap.

After supper, and once the baddies have been defeated, Carole takes both empty boxes into their small pantry off the kitchen and deposits them in the recycling container. Iona, yawning, announces that she's off to bed.

Carole returns to the kitchen and pours herself another glass of brandy, which is unlike her because she never drinks during the week. Then again, she's never had a psychotic sat nav to contend with or a wandering mussel shell. The neighbours' outside light is on, and Carole's garden is bathed in subtle patches of light and shade. She fancies she sees a small shape run across their lawn. A cat probably, or possibly a fox, although the indistinct shape looks too small to be a fox.

Carole's sensitive nose now detects a strong smell. It's the smell of the sea, of salt water and she can almost hear the screech of seagulls, the deck of a ship under her feet, and see Orkney fading into the distance. The smell is overwhelming, almost making her retch.

Go and visit him tomorrow, says a female voice from the corner of the kitchen.

'Who the hell?' says Carole, looking wildly round. 'Who said that?' She can hear Iona walking about upstairs, so it couldn't have been her.

Go and visit him tomorrow, says the voice again. It has the same, flat intonation as her sat nav lady.

Carole then notices a blue light spinning around the top of a black cylinder. 'Alexa, what did you just say?'

I'm sorry, I don't know that one.

'Alexa, you just told me to visit someone.' Carole's voice trembles and she feels suddenly cold. She's only ever used the Alexa to play music and to set herself reminders.

I'm sorry, I don't know that one.

'Alexa, who am I to visit?'

I'm sorry, I don't know that one.

Carole, utterly unnerved, switches on the main kitchen light and goes to examine her mad Alexa. Has it caught some electronic virus from her sat nav? Can electronic devices, like computers, pass on viruses? And can she return it to Amazon for a saner replacement? The blue light on the top of her Alexa has stopped spinning and Carole now notices something worse. Her Alexa is switched off at the socket.

Eight

Carole sleeps badly that night, trying to decide if things around her have gone mad, or if she is going mad. The only logical explanation is that the Alexa device must have somehow switched itself on and badly remembered a song that she'd asked it to play, except that she doesn't know any songs about visiting people, nor can she work out how a switched-off Alexa could have said anything. Or does it have a battery inside for use during a power cut? That also seems possible, if unlikely. However, even if it does have a battery, that doesn't rationally explain the moving mussel shell or her deranged sat nav. She tosses and turns, alternately worrying and trying to tell herself not to worry. I am not going mad, she repeats to herself, sometimes aloud, which simply convinces her that she probably is going mad. Eventually, she sleeps, worn out by worrying and by telling herself not to worry. Her one vivid dream is of being much older and being at a party. But it's not really a party because nobody seems to be having fun. She's back in a lecture theatre at her old faculty and her professor, who looks exactly the same as she remembers, is making a speech, telling everyone *what a fine member of staff Carole has been* and how she's *going to be sorely missed*. In the tiered seating of the lecture theatre are lots and lots of people, some of whom she recognises as the students she once taught. Ray is in the front row, alongside Iona. Both are smiling. Carole, in her dream, realises that she's retiring, and that her professor has a clock in his hands which he now hands over. It is ticking very loudly and the loudness of it wakes her up. It's still absolutely dark.

She looks at her bedside clock. Six o'clock, and at least an hour before she usually gets up. But she can still hear a clock ticking in her head, almost a headache, so she shuffles on her dressing gown and goes downstairs. To her surprise the mussel shell is no longer on the kitchen table and, when she goes to the living room, has somehow relocated itself back to the mantlepiece. Did she do that? It is also no longer pristine clean; the grime of ages has returned, which Carole is glad about because earth and mud again makes it authentic. Then she steps back from the mantlepiece, realising again that she may well be going insane. She had left it on the kitchen table; she's sure about that, and it was pristine clean. Should she speak to her doctor? Should she speak to Ray when he comes home in a couple of days? Even more bizarre, should she confide in Iona who is now the possessor of all knowledge?

She decides, at least for now, to confide in nobody, not until she can say with certainty how mad, or otherwise, she really is. She also knows precisely what Alexa's cryptic instruction from the night before was all about. She knows who she has to visit, but not yet why. She hasn't been with him for a long time, and she should have been to visit him before now. Her Alexa has both rebuked her and touched a nerve.

In due course Iona treads wearily down the stairs in her dressing gown and makes toast and marmalade without, of course, asking her mother if she could make some for her. It's their morning ritual, usually conducted in grunts or silences, and today is no different, except that Carole, who now has a new purpose to her day, seems to Iona to be particularly distant and distracted. She also notices that the mussel shell is no longer on the kitchen table which, to Iona, is a relief as she doesn't like the sight of dead things, except food.

After Iona goes back upstairs to change into her school

91

uniform, Carole puts the dirty plates and cups into the dishwasher and cleans crumbs from kitchen units and the table. She puts the marmalade back into its cupboard and the margarine in the fridge, wondering why Iona can't perform these simple tasks herself and whether she should say something to her. But she hasn't said anything for years, and can't be bothered starting now.

Iona reappears, looking less dishevelled, picks up her schoolbag, says a quick goodbye, and is gone. Carole crosses to the kitchen window and now sees that it's been snowing; not a lot, a mere dusting of white on their lawn. Springtime in Scotland! Flakes of snow are also blowing from trees, making the outside world look like a Christmas card. They hadn't had any snow at Christmas, which was the normal time to have snow, except that nothing seems normal any more. Yesterday hadn't been normal, and today was unlikely to be normal either.

Carole drinks another cup of coffee before having a shower and dressing in warm clothing. On this journey she has no need for the sat nav because it's only a short journey that she knows well. In any case, she no longer trusts the lady in her dashboard, who is either with her cigarettes and lover, or jetting off to Barcelona with Juan. Or wanting to take Carole to places that she doesn't want to go to, and meet old flatmates.

North Berwick used to be a small coastal town, now rapidly becoming a large coastal town, with many acres of new housing, although the town centre is still quaint and, in summer, is a magnet for day-trippers who walk its pristine beaches, play golf on its historic links, or simply meander down its High Street. Sea birds patrol the skies overhead and, just offshore, is the Bass Rock, home to gannets by the million. The smaller islands are the domain of puffins, with their clownish faces. Dolphins and whales sometimes come to visit, no doubt to marvel at all the new houses.

Carole parks and buys a bunch of flowers from Tulipa, the town's flower shop, probably grown in Dutch poly-tunnels and brought to Scotland by lorry. Carole doesn't know the shop owner, although she has met its delivery driver, who once came to her home with flowers from her mother. An older gentleman, she remembers, but still devilishly handsome and who once played rugby for Scotland, or so he claimed. Quite why he should have wanted her to know this, when all he had to do was hand her a bunch of flowers, she can't quite remember. Scotland doesn't really have flowers in winter; instead, the countryside folds in on itself, making landscapes seem brooding and desolate. Carole likes the Scottish countryside in winter; it looks and feels primaeval, and she likes the ancient past.

Then she drives out of town to a small house on a lane that was once her home, back when she was young and they were a complete family. It used to be a farmhouse, built in traditional Scottish style, with two main rooms downstairs and two bedrooms upstairs. She therefore had to share with Tim. They'd moved down from Edinburgh for the clean air and, well, because her mum wanted the peace and quiet of the country. Carole pulls onto the verge, still coated with a sprinkling of snow, and switches off the engine.

The house is much the same, although the garden is a little unkempt, which her father would never have tolerated. He was forever pruning or weeding or cutting things down. Her mother was responsible for planting things and making things grow. He was the destroyer; her mother, the nurturer. Carole also notices that the wooden window frames need a lick of paint. The house is in darkness, and there are no cars in the short driveway. Carole hasn't been here for years, and now wonders why not, because it's bringing back a flood of memories; of sliding down the bannisters, sitting by the open fire in the living room or family meals in the kitchen, with real conversations and laughter rather than grunts and silences.

Carole also remembers Tim sitting on her Dad's shoulders and being swung round and round, and Tim squealing with laughter. It was a time when anything was possible, and nothing bad could ever happen, because it simply wasn't allowed to happen.

Just down the road is the small river she used to play beside – in summer, just a wide stream with a narrow bridge across it. Carole walks down to the bridge. It was considered a blackspot, with unwary drivers not realising that the already narrow road narrowed even more as it crossed the river. One of Carole's abiding memories is of hearing loud crashing noises as cars bumped into one another on the bridge, sometimes then accompanied by equally loud shouting. Once there had been a fight, but both men were rather large and very unfit, and no damage was inflicted on either of them. But there were never any serious crashes; you simply couldn't drive fast on the narrow road. On each occasion her mother, unasked, would calmly make a pot of tea and take teapot, mugs, milk and sugar down to the scene of the accident. It always diffused tensions (even the brawling fat blokes) and, now, the memory of it makes Carole smile. A blackspot it may have been, but a very friendly blackspot.

Her other memory is her bicycle, speeding down nearby lanes on revolving feet, or the thrill of cycling into North Berwick, which was mostly downhill and therefore a racetrack. Sometimes, she remembers, the cold would leave her face puce-red and her eyes so sore with cold that all she could see was the dotted white line in the centre of the road.

There were also adventures, and daring games, and exploring further and further from their home, despite their mother always telling them to be careful. The only adventure she ever really lost on that bike was the puncture she couldn't mend, but that was what fathers were for. She also remembers the games that she and her brother would play, particularly the Death Game. This was played on an adjacent grass field down which was a muddy track. The rules were simple. The sibling not riding had to pretend to shoot the one who was, and the rider had to fall off their bike with all the pathos of a dying person. They each took turns although, being younger and less cautious, it was usually Tim who won.

Skidding was the other great. You rode as fast as you could towards a wall, jammed on your brakes and skidded to as close to the wall as you could. Again, it was usually Tim who won, although the wall often won as well. Their bikes bore the dents and scratches of their escapades, and they each proudly knew the source of each dent and scratch and the stories behind them.

Carole has now reached the bridge and sees that it's been replaced by a much wider one. The old bridge was stone and medieval; the new one is made from steel. It looks functional but soulless. This makes her both sad and happy; happy for all those insurance claims that now won't have to be made, but sad also as she remembers her mother stoically making tea.

On impulse, she walks down from the road to the small river. It seems more unkempt than she remembers it; there are small pieces of wood wedged up against rocks, and weeds and ferns clutter its banks. The water itself is a sludgy brown, and smells of decay. She remembers sitting on an outcrop of rock and eating bilberries, and she finds the rock outcrop and sits down on it. It's smaller than she remembers and she has no bilberries to eat. Back then, in summer, the small river gushed pure crystal water that she could drink, kneeling by the water's edge and making her hands into a cup. The water was always cold, even on the hottest day.

Then she picks her way up the slope, the woodland closing in on her as she climbs, the tree branches intertwined above her head. It's eerily silent, quieter than she remembers.

All she can hear is the receding sound of the stream and melting snow dripping from the branches. At the top of the hill she finds the small clearing. To her surprise, it hasn't changed. The oak trees still seem to have been planted in exact symmetry to create a perfect circle. Back when she first discovered it, then took her brother to see it, it seemed a place of magic; a place in which witches might gather or where a wizard would cast his spells: a hidden place in the middle of a woodland and designed never to be found.

It still seems a place of magic although she now assumes that the circle is an accident of nature. There are no paths leading to the circle, nothing to betray anybody's presence. And why build a circle in a wood anyway? Perhaps the last person to visit the circle was her, she thinks, walking slowly around it and touching each tree, as if for good luck. Then she pauses. The last time she'd been to the clearing she'd brought a slice of cake and instinctively she looks to the ground as if it might still be there. Then she touches each tree again, walking slowly across grass and ground elder; what with everything that's been going on, she needs all the luck she can get.

Carole suddenly shivers; there's a chill coming up from the stream and, looking up, the sky looks grey and thunderous. She hurries back down the slope to the river, then back up to the road, wondering again why she hasn't revisited her childhood home for so long, or her woodland circle. But, of course, she does know. It takes about a ten-point turn to get her car facing in the other direction and she drives slowly back towards the town, being careful on the corners where snow has gathered, and parks at the gate to the town cemetery.

Carole sits in her car for a few minutes and breathes deeply, then carries her bunch of flowers in both hands, and walks to Tim's grave. She finds it easily enough, having been several times before, but not recently. Does that mean that she's forgetting him? That his memory is of less importance now? In a Far Eastern religion that Carole can't quite remember, they believe that a person's soul only lives for so long as that person is still remembered on Earth. Does that mean that Einstein and John Lennon get to live forever, while everyone else only has a brief taste of the afterlife? But Carole has never been religious and swallows the thought. She looks at his gravestone. The marble stone is inscribed TIMOTHY DAY, with the dates of his arrival and departure. Underneath, ALWAYS LOVED. She remembers, before the funeral, her mother and father discussing what to put on the gravestone. *Always loved*, Carole had suggested, and her parents had both nodded in tearful approval.

She places her flowers next to Tim's grave, and picks up an old bouquet that had long since died. Her mum, she supposes, finding a nearby bin and depositing the dead flowers in it. Tim would be grateful for her gesture; he only liked sparkly new things. Dead flowers would have depressed him. She stands for some minutes, her breath fogging in front of her, remembering their shared childhood.

After his death, they moved back to Edinburgh and her mother found gainful employment in the retail trade, in arts and crafts shops that seemed to be springing up everywhere across the city at that time. North Berwick now held too many wrong memories for them, although Carole would have been happy to stay on, having made friends at school. She also wanted to be near Tim, where she could visit him, and probably would have done. Unlike now, she thinks, again feeling guilty.

Carole wonders why she was commanded by Alexa to come here, and is just about to say a *goodbye* to her brother when she notices a new headstone has been erected next to his. To her absolute horror it's inscribed CAROLE GUNN, but without any dates or fond words about how much she was loved. For a moment she can hardly breathe, her heart beating like a machine gun, and has to steady herself from falling over, bending over and putting her hands on her knees. She closes her eyes, feeling nauseous, but when she opens them again the gravestone has gone. In its place is the manicured grass that was there before, with its fine dusting of snow. Then she notices something else, on the spot where her gravestone had been. A mussel shell, pristine clean. She picks it up, her hands violently trembling, and puts it in her pocket.

Afterwards, she sits in her car with the engine running and the heating turned up to full blast. It takes some time for her heart to stop violently beating and her hands to stop shaking.

Why have I been brought to this place? she wants to ask, but doesn't know who to ask. What lesson am I being taught, or am I really becoming deranged? Carole has always enjoyed good mental health, but the line between sanity and madness now seems blurred, and she doesn't know on which side of the line she now stands. Then, unbidden, she starts to cry; for herself and Tim, and for not visiting him more often. She also wonders who brought the other flowers, the dead ones, although her mum still seems the obvious choice. A couple pass into the cemetery, also carrying flowers, and smile sadly at Carole, but she doesn't notice them.

After a long while, a strange sense of peace settles onto her. Although she doesn't yet know why, she now believes that was brought here for a reason. It's now up to her to find out what that reason is. A reminder of her own mortality, perhaps? As simple as that?

She starts the car and heads down the hill into town, past the rugby club and the hockey pitch which so exhausts Iona and turns into the small one-way High Street. But she's hardly turned onto it when the sat nav lady breaks the silence.

Your destination is on the left.

'What?'

Your destination is on the left.

'What fucking destination?'

Your destination is on the left.

'Holy fucking Christ!' she shrieks at the dashboard, loudly enough for an old woman on the pavement to purse her lips in disapproval.

Miraculously, on such a busy street, there is an empty parking space and Carole pulls into it, her hands once again shaking violently. But she also knows now to obey whatever command is given to her, even if it's only by a deranged bit of electronics that, she reminds herself, she hadn't switched on.

Nine

The place to which she's been brought is a restaurant specialising in high-end hamburgers and steak and, once she's regained some composure, she pushes open the door and steps in. It's not like Carole to visit restaurants on weekdays, or to visit them at all by herself, although she has been to this restaurant several times before, with Ray and Iona – the last time on Iona's birthday the year before. On this occasion she's more than slightly nervous, only managing to smile thinly at the young waiter who shows her to a table in a far corner. She supposes that single patrons make the place look like a refuge for the lonely and therefore, not being a good advertisement, are consigned to the most distant tables. As always, she orders a small glass of wine and, having only eaten a couple of mouthfuls of pizza the night before, also orders a steak sandwich. Strangely, despite experiencing an incipient panic attack, she's hungry.

The feeling of calm, almost of serenity, that settled on her outside the cemetery then returns again and, despite some nervousness, she also now feels a sense of anticipation. Although she knows that she might be going mad, it's madness with purpose. It's a madness that is taking her to places, real places or places within herself. She reaches into her pocket to make sure that the mussel shell is still there. It is, and she breathes a sigh of relief. She's become possessive about its whereabouts now that it seems to be more than a lucky charm given to her years ago by an ex-boyfriend.

It's still only twelve-thirty, and the restaurant isn't yet busy; a couple of matronly ladies are twittering gossip by the restaurant door and a mature man with a grey beard sits alone at a large table.

Carole consults her phone. She has only one message, from Ray, confirming that he'll be back on Friday evening. She has no emails, not even spam emails that she can pleasurably delete, when a voice booms across the room.

'Doctor Carole Gunn! My God!'

The man with the grey beard is levering himself from his chair and advancing towards her. He's smiling broadly and holding his arms out wide.

'Professor Dalton! Ditto, my God!' She resists the temptation to say that she'd dreamed about him the night before, thinking that might sound a little odd and inappropriate, remembering his reputation as a ladies' man.

He's now reached her table and she's come round to greet him, and they briefly and clumsily embrace. He's much taller than her and he has to stoop slightly. His beard tickles her forehead. 'What brings you here?' he asks loudly. The twittering ladies pause and look over, perhaps hoping that Carole might have an interesting answer.

'Early lunch,' she replies. The ladies start twittering again.

'Actually, to be precise about these things, I'm now Emeritus Professor Dalton. I couldn't go on being a burden to the university forever.'

He's still smiling, which makes the lines on his face deepen and, without being asked, now sits on the spare chair opposite Carole's. A waiter appears and he orders a large glass of red wine. He indicates her glass, but she puts a hand across it and shakes her head.

'You were never a burden,' says Carole, meaning it, remembering a more youthful professor at the front of her class, with his commanding voice and huge knowledge of ancient Egypt and Mesopotamia. Although not a specialist in the archaeology of Neolithic Scotland, he had been one

101

of her inspirations, but she doesn't quite know how to put this into words. He's older, much older than in her dream, but with the same presence; Professor Dalton was never someone you could ignore.

'So, you finally retired.'

'Two years ago. Time for the old order to give way to the new. That's what they told me, anyway,' he confides, leaning slightly over the table, and trying to lower his voice, not very successfully. All those lectures, Carole supposes, and making sure that the dullards at the back could hear every word. 'But they gave me a clock which, I suppose, was nice of them.'

Carole again remembers her dream from the night before and of being woken by the loud ticking of her own retirement clock. 'It's traditional, Professor,' she reminds him. 'Just remember to keep winding it up.

'No need, Carole. After a lifetime of devoted service, they gave me a clock with a battery inside. Mind you, probably just as well, what with my memory.' He smiles. 'Anyway, no more of the *professor* nonsense. Not now that I'm officially old and useless. I'm David. Not Dave, which I hate. Or Davey, which I hate even more. David, the name I was born with.'

'Then it's a real pleasure to see you again, David.' She smiles at him, feeling calmer and more in control.

'Moved to North Berwick after I was put out to grass. It's a rather nice place to retire to, being full of other old people. Some a lot older than me which, strangely, makes me feel quite young. Actually, I'm here to meet up with some old friends,' he explains. 'But I'm a bit early, or they're a bit late. One or the other. It's also good to see you.'

Carole notes that he's been speaking in the first person and that, presumably, he's still unattached. He always was, and his sexuality was a source of much gossip among Carole's first-year class, until a rumour went around that he'd been caught in the stationary cupboard with Miss Frobisher from Admissions. It was only ever a rumour, and neither the professor nor Miss Frobisher were ever going to confirm or deny it, and the source of the rumour was never identified. But Carole always believed it to be true, because of the mischievous twinkle that would come into his eye if he spied a pretty female student, although Miss Frobisher only ticked one of those three boxes.

'But still keeping busy?' she asks.

'As an emeritus professor I'm still wheeled out from time to time, which I'm grateful for, if only to give my mental faculties a little bit of lubrication. They could, of course, have simply dispensed with my services altogether. Quite why they didn't is a mystery to me. But it's in their gift to do whatever they like with me and, for some reason, they still value my input on certain things. By the way, my successor is Keith Bridges. Remember him?' he asks, one eyebrow raised.

She does indeed remember him, but as a rather intense lecturer with little sense of humour, and whose duties included picking up and dropping off students from their B&Bs on Orkney.

'Good gracious!' she says, then blushes, thinking perhaps that he'd been David's chosen successor. 'For some reason I never had him marked down as the professor type.'

'In my latter years at the university he became my sorcerer's apprentice. Not that I asked him to, of course. But he started making himself useful … doing things that he'd not been told to do … that kind of thing. I thought nothing of it, until I realised that retirement was on the horizon and the vultures would start circling. I suppose, therefore, that as the first vulture to circle, the powers-that-be saw him as the logical choice. How's your daughter?' he suddenly asks, looking at her intently.

'She's absolutely fine, thank you.' She takes a small sip of

103

her wine, her hand trembling slightly.

'Then I am truly delighted,' he replies, taking a large swig from his glass, which a waiter has just deposited in front of him. He still looks good, with his craggy face; exuding the kind of charm that Carole always liked: an infectious charm that made listening to his lectures so compelling. He'd inspired her, simply because his charm was also inspiring.

'But I still feel guilty,' Carole blurts out. 'I did intend to come back.' She becomes aware that her former professor is looking at her intently from across the table. 'Sorry,' she adds. 'Even thinking about it brings back bad memories.'

'Quite understandable,' he replies.

'I meant what I said,' Carole says, 'about feeling guilty.'

'Guilty for what?' Emeritus Professor David looks genuinely surprised. 'You had a sick daughter.'

'Even so.'

'You did good work with us,' says David. 'Several of your published papers are still required reading for our newer students. Not my field of expertise, of course, but your work on stone circles is still highly regarded.'

Carole smiles. Her research had also been published more widely in the trade press. Her picture had once appeared in *British Archaeology*, a photograph taken by Rob when she'd been in a bad mood, and which made her look rather intense and threatening, like a latent psychopath with a bad haircut. She still shudders at the memory of that photograph.

'Ancient history,' she reminds him.

'Maybe so, but some of your theories about Orkney did get people talking.'

'Hardly, David, but thanks for saying so.'

He leans back in his chair and takes another swig of wine. 'For example, I seem to recall your theory about the Brodgar and Stenness stone circles predating Stonehenge,' he now reminds her.

'Not my theory, David. By the time I came along, it was

established fact.'

'Okay, maybe not your theory, but you did put it in a wider context. It made people sit up and listen.'

At the time it was ground-breaking stuff; that some mystic early religion could have originated in the far northern islands of Scotland and travelled to the south of England, finding full voice in Stonehenge, the most dramatic stone circle of them all. All Carole did was to suggest that the Neolithic people were travellers and thinkers; able to communicate and convince; to have mystic ideas that they were able to take with them to mainland Scotland and, then, to the furthest reaches of the British Isles and to continental Europe. It was what she'd researched for her doctorate, and specifically the Orcadian stone circles of Brodgar and Stenness.

Carole's sandwich arrives and she eats it in small pieces with a knife and fork. She would normally perhaps have simply picked it up in two hands, but with her old professor sitting opposite that might have seemed a bit Neolithic.

'Well, thank you for saying so,' she replies simply.

He smiles. 'You were also quite good at finding stuff.'

'Just lucky, David.'

The twittering ladies all laugh, transforming the restaurant into a raucous bird colony. 'Shall I tell you a secret?' David leans over the table, still smiling, and still looking craggy, with his grey beard lending him a touch of Father Christmas. 'One of my duties is to chair the appointments board.'

Carole is mystified and takes another small mouthful of steak sandwich, delicately dabbing at her mouth with the paper serviette it came with.

'The thing is that we have a vacancy in the department. One of our lecturers has decided to decamp back to their native Australia. Quite why, I know not.' Carole simply looks at him, saying nothing. 'Keith Bridges also sits on

105

the panel, but he still regards me as his professor and goes along with everything I say, even if it's complete balderdash, which it often is. The rest of them are make-weights to give the impression that we're open and inclusive, which we're not. But it means that our meeting today could be rather fortuitous.'

'You're asking me to apply?' Carole is now utterly confused, remembering the person she once was, and knowing the person she now is.

'Well, why not? Of course, you'd have to look on our website and see what we've been working on. Get up to speed, as it were.' David has again raised an eyebrow. 'Nowadays, we post lots of our students' work online. Open-source, transparency, and lots of other buzzwords that I can't remember.'

'I already have,' she replies. 'At least, bits and pieces. I haven't completely walked away from it all.' It's something that she has only recently started to do, hunched over her laptop on the dining room table, with older ideas of who she is, or was, creeping in.

'Good gracious!' says David, genuinely surprised. 'So, not such a steep learning curve after all.'

'Well, as I said, only bits and pieces.'

'So, what did you think? Frankly, and I shouldn't really say this, but the current crop of students hasn't been our greatest.' He leans over the table. 'Repeat that and I would have to kill you, of course. Maybe they just need the right teacher,' he suggests.

Carole takes a deep breath. 'One of the bits and pieces I read was a paper you published last month on the positioning of stones around stone circles.'

'Your specialist subject, Carole.'

'A subject I still feel strongly about, David.'

'Of course, of course.'

'One of the points of my research was to prove that the

positioning of stones in a circle was important. I thought that was now accepted as fact.'

'Not by everybody, Carole. I seem to remember that you didn't have any conclusive evidence to back up your theory.'

'The student who wrote one of your bits and pieces would certainly agree with you.'

David raises his shoulders, almost imperceptibly. 'Research often involves disagreement, Carole. You know that and, after all, the Iron Age didn't leave us many clues about anything.'

'Ah, but that's where you're wrong. The Iron Age left us masses of clues. The trick is knowing where to look.' She takes another deep breath, forcing herself to slow down. For some reason, she feels irritated, more irritated than when she first read the idiot student's research paper. 'Or if not actually looking, then at least doing some *actual* research,' she says, and takes a sip of her wine. 'It was a sloppy piece of work, and I'm surprised that the university saw fit to publish it.'

'Sloppy?'

'Because your student, based presumably on no research whatsoever, said that the stones are just there to mark out a circle within which ceremonies could take place. But if you look at the night sky as it would have looked five thousand years ago, they align to a solstice or equinox.'

David is looking nonplussed. 'You actually did that research?' he finally asks, leaning back in his seat.

Carole nods. She doesn't quite know why she did the research, but stone circles were her specialty, David is right, and she still feels protective about them. She hadn't liked the idea of some spotty youth not taking them seriously.

'If you need proof, think of Maeshowe.'

'The burial mound? What about it?'

It's a place that Carole knows well, or did know well, having explored its inner recesses with a large torch; a grass mound that hides complex passages and chambers. For a long while, it was thought that Maeshowe was simply the largest and best-preserved burial mound on Orkney, and only a short distance from Brodgar, Skara Brae and Stenness, and joined to those sites by a Neolithic road.

'Not a burial mound, David, because very little in the way of human remains has ever been found there.'

'Apologies, Carole. I probably did know that at one time. Or maybe I didn't, I don't know. They were probably right to give me an electric clock. But Neolithic Orkney is your thing, not mine. Your point being?'

'Did you know that its central chamber is only lit up on the winter solstice?'

'No, I can't say that I did know that.'

'It suggests that Maeshowe was used as some sort of observatory and calendar. After all, it has an observation passage aimed at a nearby stone to indicate the summer solstice. Another watchstone indicates the equinoxes, and a further passage points to the north star.' She pauses for dramatic effect. 'Just like the pyramids of Saqqara, Dashur and Medûm, David, although that's your field not mine.'

He nods slowly, not taking offence, if any was intended. 'So, you're suggesting that, because Neolithic people understood a bit of astronomy, that the siting of stones on the circles would also have had significance?'

'Stands to reason. Stenness predates Maeshowe by hundreds of years. But that doesn't mean that the builders of Stenness weren't also astronomers, although a little bit more primitive.'

'Maybe so, young lady, but it's a bit of an assumption.'

Carole is flattered that he's called her *young lady* and smiles across the table. 'But, nevertheless, an educated assumption based on star alignments five thousand years ago.'

David suddenly gives a wheezing laugh, and Carole

momentarily wonders if he's amused or having a heart attack. 'In which case, Keith Bridges won't be happy. It was one of his students who wrote that research paper.' He taps a finger on the table. 'You really do still know your stuff, don't you?'

'I can't explain why, David, but stone circles have always fascinated me.'

'We were sorry to lose you.' He says this slowly, for emphasis.

'I was sorry to leave,' she replies, looking at the table.

David fishes in a back pocket and hands over a business card. 'Then why not send in your CV?' he suggests. 'Interviews are sometime soon, so I'm told.'

'Are you really being serious?'

'Look, Carole, you were a good researcher and a good lecturer, and there's no reason why you couldn't be again.' He leans forwards and lowers his voice, although the whole restaurant can probably still hear everything. The twittering ladies have their heads together, no doubt still exchanging juicy gossip. 'A chance also for field trips. Maybe test out your theory on solstices and equinoxes, which I would love you to do, Carole, if only to put one over *Professor* Bridges! Meagre salary, of course, but good prospects.'

But is this what she really wants? Carole has spent years hiding in the shadows, at first worried for her daughter, feeling guilty about her, and then drifting into being a housewife. For years, she has chosen easy options. So, does she really now want to return to the past? Or, worse, to attend an interview and be rejected?

'Can I think about it?' she asks, fingering his business card and then putting it into a pocket. Her thoughts are all over the place, leaping from the past to the present to, perhaps, pointing to a new future.

'Not really, no,' says David. 'Applications close at the end of this week.'

109

Just then, several other elderly gentlemen arrive, with one of them clapping David on the shoulder. 'Not chatting up the ladies, are we, David?' the new arrival asks and winks.

'A former and valued colleague,' says David, looking at Carole intently. Then he pushes back his seat and holds out a hand.

Carole finishes her glass of wine, pays her bill, and heads for the door. David and his friends already have several bottles of wine on their table, and it seems that lunch is likely to be a protracted and inebriated affair. She smiles at David on the way past and gives a small wave.

'Just send the bloody thing in!' she hears him boom as she opens the door.

Out on the pavement, her earlier calm serenity begins to evaporate and she again feels her hands start to tremble. The meeting with her old professor has confused her or, maybe, given her an opportunity too good to miss.

Back home, she realises that their domestic waste is due to be collected the next day, and she busies herself emptying the contents of their deep freeze and depositing everything in the wheelie bin at the bottom of their drive. Except for the dead cat, of course, which will remain there until Sunday, after which she'll disinfect the deep freeze, a small task that will at least keep Iona happy. She can't remember the last time she's cleaned the deep freeze, so the dead cat will perhaps have provided a last blessing.

But David and his potential offer are never far from her thoughts, so too the unnerving sight of her own gravestone with its unmarked dates and the mussel shell lying on the ground. But, oddly, it's as if she's become immunised against the madness around her, or the emotional and mental journey she's being taken on. She now knows, or thinks she knows, that she's being given some kind of lesson and that, while the learning of it might be painful, it's for her own good. But it's also a lesson in riddles; its meaning like trying

110

to hold onto the wind, or catch smoke.

Iona arrives home to find her mother at the kitchen table and tapping away on her laptop.

'How was your day, darling?' enquires Carole.

'Boring. As always,' replies Iona.

Carole bites her tongue. She wants to tell her daughter that education is good, that it offers opportunity and distant horizons. But she's had a lifetime of biting her tongue, of not telling Iona off, or not asking her to put the marmalade back in the cupboard. Emotional scars have left indelible marks on Carole's psyche, and she can't find the right words to rebuke her daughter, even if it would be in Iona's benefit.

Carole has once again forgotten to buy food and now can't be bothered going to the local supermarket. Once again, she hands over £20 and suggests more pizza, which Iona readily agrees to. Once again, they eat in front of the TV, this time watching a sci-fi movie which makes no sense to Carole although, to be fair, her mind is on other things. Like the night before, Iona helps her mother finish her pizza, and Carole puts the empty boxes in the recycling container.

With Iona safely in bed, Carole then puts the finishing touches to her CV, composes a rather formal email to David and, before she can change her mind, presses *send*. She then pours herself a brandy and sits at the kitchen table. The mussel shell is still in her pocket, and she now takes it out and lays it in front of her, thinking about her chance meeting with her old professor.

Why had she started to look at the faculty's website again? Until recently, she hadn't looked at it for years. Why had she made those astronomical calculations? For her benefit alone? To prove some spotty youth wrong? Or, somehow, was it some kind of preparation for a meeting that she hadn't yet had?

Then she once again smells the sea, almost hearing the screech of seabirds, senses a heaving deck beneath her feet, and sees that the switched-off Alexa is once more spinning its blue light.

Tomorrow you will go into Edinburgh. This will be your last meeting. Please listen for instructions.

'Alexa, who am I to meet?' Carole is more curious than panic-stricken.

I'm sorry I don't know that one.

'Alexa, please tell me!'

I'm sorry I don't know that one.

'No, of course you don't,' mutters Carole, taking her glass to the window. Tonight, the neighbours' outside light is off, and her garden is in darkness. Carole wonders what now might be in store for her.

Ten

Acute lymphoblastic leukaemia. That was the diagnosis, when Iona was a baby, and Carole was still a new mother. Iona didn't sleep, she ran fevers, bruised easily, looked anaemic, and simply wasn't developing the way she should. Various GPs offered various treatments, none of which worked, until she eventually saw the most intelligent GP in her practice who referred Iona to the Sick Kids' Hospital.

She remembers Iona undergoing tests, can still taste the hospital's disinfectant smell in her nostrils. She remembers sitting down with a young doctor, who looked too young to be a real doctor, who explained that Iona had a form of cancer in her white blood cells, the cells which help to fight infection. Acute lymphoblastic leukaemia, he explained, involves an overproduction of immature lymphoid cells that fill up the bone marrow and stop it making healthy blood cells. The young doctor seemed pleased to be using long words.

However, medical jargon Carole could do without. 'But will she get better?' she demanded to know.

'The good news is that most children with this illness do get better.' He looked momentarily pleased to be saying this, then looked serious again. 'The bad news is that treatment is long and, I'm afraid, rather arduous.'

'Arduous?'

'Difficult.'

'I know what arduous means, doctor! I just want to know what will be involved.'

'Treatment could take as long as two years, Mrs Gunn.

Regrettably, there's no quick cure. I'm afraid you'll have to be patient.'

'Two years? Treatment?' echoed Carole, somehow feeling guilty about her daughter's illness, as if it was her fault, remembering Tim and wondering if her mother also, in some way, blamed herself.

'The principal treatments are chemotherapy and steroids,' explained the boy-doctor. 'But she may also require radiotherapy and a stem cell transplant.'

'Two years,' she said, not quite making it a question. She'd half been expecting a bottle of pills and for Iona to be as right as rain in a few days. But the other half of her had long known that Iona's illness was more than something inconsequential.

'Maybe less,' he offered, smiling hopefully. 'We'll have to see how she responds to treatment.'

'But she will get better, won't she?' There was an edge of desperation to her voice.

'I'm sure she will, Mrs Gunn.' The boy-doctor gave her a reassuring smile despite, presumably, only having qualified the week before. His head seemed a little too big for his neck so that, when he nodded, it looked as if it might fall off. His shirt collar was a little too big for his neck, as if his mother had bought it for him in the expectation that he would grow into it. To complete the picture, his tie was covered in a jolly Mickey Mouse design. Carole thought it wholly inappropriate, then realised that he was a children's doctor and that, maybe, it was completely appropriate.

He was right, the treatment was long and arduous, and Carole's period of compassionate leave came and went, although the department was more than understanding. Take as long as you need, she was told. Your daughter must come first although, as Carole well knew, her job couldn't be kept open forever.

It was explained to her and Ray that the aim of the first

stage of treatment was to achieve remission, which would then allow Iona to produce normal blood cells. By then, Carole was a world expert on all aspects of childhood cancers, and able to converse with the boy-doctor using long medical words which he even seemed a little unsure about. It was her way of coping; of understanding what was being done to her daughter, and why, and not merely accepting that things had to be done. Perhaps it was the scientist in her wanting to understand everything about the medical procedures and her daughter's physical responses; but it was also her mother's instinct to know everything that there was to know, just in case it might be useful. Ray preferred not to know; to trust in the doctors and nurses looking after Iona. He wasn't medically qualified and nor was he a scientist. He put his faith in the medical team. Carole had lost faith because her brother had died, and she didn't want history to repeat itself.

But was she really a scientist, she would wonder? Despite the moniker of *doctor* before her name, she was only qualified to find stuff and dig things up. Her quasi-science was about the past, not the present: it was arcane and dusty, wading through mud in a rain-filled trench, examining ground radar readouts and telling people where to dig. It was sometimes about finding treasure, but usually not, and never about doing anything useful like saving someone's life. In those early weeks, she came to hate her title of doctor: her skills were useless against an illness that could kill her child. What use finding an axe-head when she didn't really know what a white blood cell did? Maybe that's why she so assiduously learned every aspect of Iona's illness; to make good her title of doctor and give it new purpose; to take her own useless title of doctor and, using her quasi-skills, make her a better mother. Usually, most evenings, she cried from tiredness, anger or frustration.

The first phase of treatment took weeks and weeks, with

neither Carole nor Ray sleeping much, with Iona sometimes in her crib beside their bed and crying for most of every night, or sometimes at the hospital with Carole sleeping, or trying to sleep, on a small bed beside her. It was a time of exhaustion, of little or no sleep and too much worry; a time without dinner parties or holidays; a time when most of life was put on pause. Some of her friends tried to coax her out of herself, plying her with cake or wine, telling her that, if she couldn't change anything, she had to learn to accept. But accept what? A shitty diagnosis? Shitty treatment? An uncertain prognosis? Instead, she would shake her head at her friends: there would be another time for wine or cake, or holidays in the sun. To have even pretended to enjoy herself, with her daughter so ill, would have felt like a betrayal, and Carole has never betrayed anyone.

One morning, Carole saw that there were lines on Ray's face that she didn't think were there the day before. It was also the time when Carole began to frown because arranging her face in any other expression didn't seem worth the effort.

In the morning, Ray would put on his suit as if it was a heavy suit of armour, and Carole sometimes felt angry that he could so easily leave her to worry alone at home, or worry alone at Iona's bedside. But Ray's work had to be done; bills had to be paid. In a way, she also felt sorry for him: having to go to work and behave as if everything was all right; making small talk with clients and smiling in the right places. Worry was her penance; work was his.

Carole remembers sobbing with relief when the first stage of treatment was successfully concluded, tightly holding onto Ray's hand. Or maybe it was his hand tightly clasped to hers. He had come to the hospital with her, as he tried to do as often as he could, and always to hear the result of the latest test. But it didn't end there because there needed to be a period of consolidation, another bland medical term, because not all the nasty cells would have been eradicated.

Cue more chemotherapy which made both Iona and her mother listless and cranky. There were also injections into her spinal cord and bouts of radiotherapy. Carole marvelled at her daughter's growing stoicism; she was crying less, as if Iona was slowly becoming used to pain; as if needles, vomit-inducing medication and constant suffering were what life was all about.

Back then, they were living in Edinburgh, in a Georgian flat that had seen better days. They didn't have much furniture when they bought it and hadn't yet got around to buying any. They had intended to redecorate, but hadn't got around to that either. It was therefore a flat with a lot of space, but not much in it to make it a home. In any case, they reasoned, neither of them had the energy to wield paintbrushes or search for furniture and, anyway, they'd been planning to move somewhere more rural; to escape the city's pollution and traffic noise. Or maybe just to escape a flat that had only accumulated bad memories, like her childhood home outside North Berwick. The Georgian flat was therefore a temporary refuge, disguised as a good investment. Its only advantage was that it was in the city and only a short drive to the hospital.

Carole took to visiting different churches during this period of Iona's treatment, although she wasn't – and isn't – religious, hoping maybe for Divine intervention or simply reassurance. She visited the High Kirk of Scotland, with its crown spire, and other less formidable places. She'd sit on pews in Catholic and Protestant churches, her nostrils alternately filled with incense or fading hope. Priests and ministers would ask if she was all right, and she would smile and say yes. She even visited Rosslyn Chapel, of Holy Grail legend, but tourists kept interrupting her quiet contemplation and she soon left.

She supposed that it was something to do with Tim, this sense of impending loss. That her family, somehow, had been marked down for unhappiness, maybe because of a past sin that was destined to be carried down the generations. It was a crazy thought, and she knew it, and she often wondered how her own mother had coped, when Carole obviously couldn't. Of course, she could have asked her mother, but never did and her mother, perhaps wisely, didn't offer any advice. She was like a primed bomb, and could explode at any moment, although her temper was usually reserved for her husband.

'You have to be strong for Iona,' was Ray's advice, which was as clichéd as it was unwelcome. She'd just come back from the hospital, having spent a day by Iona's bed. She was tired of squeaking trolleys, cheerful nurses and tepid tea.

'And what the fuck good will that do?' she retorted, screaming the words at him like an accusation.

Oh yes, they argued mightily at that time. It was never about big things, like what they felt about one another, or Iona's treatment, but always about little things; an unwashed pan in the sink was enough to set her off, or a dropped sock, or a smudge of butter on a kitchen surface. It was as if the small things had become the big things, and the big things had been squeezed out.

The boy-doctor was pleased with Iona's progress, but she then needed maintenance therapy to prevent relapse. This involved tablets, more tablets and regular injections of chemo drugs. The days seemed never-ending; long nights and false dawns. By then, Carole knew all about false dawns: she'd seen enough of them, the sun beginning to rise over the rooftops and then, somehow, deciding that it wasn't time for morning after all.

One morning, after yet another false dawn, Carole got up and simply told Ray that she was going out. She didn't say where, and Ray didn't ask in case that might trigger another fusillade. Dressed in her warmest clothes she drove to Edinburgh airport and caught a flight to Kirkwall, capital of the Orkney archipelago, and then took a taxi to the Stenness stone circle where she'd once discovered an axe-head, with orders to the taxi driver to pick her up in an hour.

She'd been back to Orkney several times since finding her axe-head, sometimes also working at the Brodgar circle, or at earth burial tombs, or the enigmatic Maeshowe, but always revisiting Stenness, the most ancient circle of them all; each time it felt like coming home: a different kind of home, a place of sanctuary, bounded by rolling water and a tugging wind. It's no longer a complete circle, so she walked round the remaining stones, touching each one, wondering as always how something so ancient could still be standing. Would they still be here in another five thousand years? She rather thought they would be.

There was also an undimmed power in the broken and incomplete stone circle that she could always almost feel; millennia ago, an ancient culture would have seen divinity in the full Moon and Sun, and replicated them on Earth, and it's that faith that Carole felt: a belief that what they were building would stand as an eternal reminder that people once lived and worshipped there. For Carole, it was only by standing within a stone circle that their symbolism became clear; their representation of wholeness and the life cycle and, maybe the universe. She thought about Iona, and the building blocks that make us, our DNA – mostly interlocked circles that give us shape and substance, health and illness, happiness and despair. We are made from circles, she thought; circles without beginning or end, because a circle has no beginning or end. Like the wedding ring on her finger, because love has no beginning or end.

But why was she there, when she should be at her daughter's bedside? Was she there for Iona or herself? Maybe for both of us, she decided, standing now in the centre of what had been the circle, imagining the rituals and feasts that would once have taken place, a community honouring its dead, and charting the turning Earth from the position of the Moon and stars. The wind was funnelling off the sea, white-flecked waves rolling in. She listened to the wind, and the almost-words that it seemed to be speaking to her. She remembered that a lifetime ago the circle had once spoken to her, or seemed to have spoken, and she closed her eyes and tried to concentrate on the wind, and its unspoken words. Instead, she felt peaceful and grateful, walking again around the circle, her circle, touching each stone almost with affection.

She walked to the spot where she'd found her axe-head, but it was grown over, the marks of their excavation long since lost. But it was then that Carole felt a new kind of equilibrium; that children were only ours on loan, never given to us, and that someday you had to let them go; that nothing, especially life, lasts forever. It was an enigmatic feeling: a sense of hope mixed with fatalism: a realisation that this ancient place would also have seen happiness and unhappiness, hope and despair, and that, perhaps, she wasn't alone. As always, the stones were comforting; a reminder that history was merely a sweep of time, marked by sunrises and sunsets and ticking clocks, and that none of us is here for very long.

The next day, the boy-doctor was all smiles. 'Your daughter seems much better today,' he said simply. 'You'll be glad to know that I think she's on the road to full recovery.'

Iona had regained some colour. Yes, her face was still ashen, but little spots of red had crept onto her cheeks. She also smiled when she saw Carole and they held hands while Iona went back to sleep.

*

In total, it did take two years before Iona was declared cured, by which time the boy-doctor had grown a stubbly beard and looked like a proper doctor. They had almost become friends, although Carole mostly thought of him as a schoolboy pretending to be a doctor. By then, she could have draped his stethoscope around her neck and practiced as a children's oncologist, and the boy-doctor knew it. She felt somehow that, by learning everything there was to know about the treatment of acute lymphoblastic leukaemia, she had gained a second doctorate, or made her first one seem more worthwhile.

The night Iona finally came home, free of doctors and tablets and injections, Carole sobbed uncontrollably over the kitchen table while Ray massaged her back and said soothing things in her ear.

'I'm sorry,' she said to him. 'All the stupid things I've said.'

'It doesn't matter,' he replied, kissing the top of her head, and reminding her why she had married him. He had always been more understanding than her; more able to forgive, or simply to recognise than some things, and some words, don't need forgiveness.

'I'm still sorry,' she repeated.

But things didn't work out the way she had planned. She had always thought that she'd go back to work; it was what she had studied for, trained for. But, even with Iona back to full health, Carole still needed to be near her daughter, making sure that she stayed well, and bothering her GP practice over the smallest of ailments. Then when Iona started nursery, Carole needed to be only a phone call and a short drive away. She needed to be at home when Iona came home from school, always looking for signs of illness, and never quite shaking off the sense that she had been responsible in the first place, and hardly noticing when the months became years.

Eleven

Friday morning follows its usual pattern of grunts and silences, breadcrumbs and jars not put away. It's a ritual that's been in place for so long that Carole would now find it hard to converse with her daughter over breakfast. She could ask about school, of course, but that would simply be met with a grunt; she could ask about homework, but Iona would merely roll her eyes. To Iona, Ray is the provider and Carole is responsible for everything else, including breadcrumbs and marmalade. But the fact is also that Carole has spent too long wrapping her daughter in cotton wool to risk confrontation; she's still attentive to every cough or fever, every morning and afternoon and, although it's an obsession that's quietened over the years, the memory of Iona in hospital, with drips in her arm, and nurses fussing around her, is never far from Carole's mind.

But the last few days seem to have brought a new perspective; that things can change, that the past has no direct connection to the future without the intervention of the present. Carole has yet to think through what it all means, but it does mean something, she is sure of that. She's also decided that, for now, she's on the sane side of the mental health line and that, whatever has been happening, is the work of something else. She doesn't speculate on what that *something else* could be because mussel shells and electronic devices don't on the face of it have much in common.

She is, of course, still deeply unsettled, veering from nervous anticipation to deep anxiety; but she feels that whatever is happening is taking place for a reason; one of her deepest anxieties is that she will reach the end of today without understanding what the rest of the week has all been about. Her *last meeting*, Alexa had said. Her last chance therefore to put everything into a new or different perspective. But who is she to meet? She switches on her Alexa.

'Alexa, who am I to meet?'

I'm sorry, I don't know that one.

'Alexa, am I mad?'

I'm sorry, I don't know that one.

'Alexa, am I sane?'

I'm sorry, I don't know that one.

Iona dutifully leaves Carole to clean up everything, picks up her schoolbag, and heads out the door. Carole sits alone at the kitchen table for a while longer, drinking two more cups of coffee, and thinking about the day ahead. Then she dresses sensibly in a warm red dress, shuffles on her warmest winter coat, and follows Iona into the outside world.

She backs her car out of the driveway and onto the road, its bonnet pointing towards Edinburgh. But for a while she just sits there, the handbrake on, prevaricating. Carole, normally decisive, is feeling unusually indecisive. What if she were to ignore her Alexa, and simply go back to bed? Or do some dusting? Or go to the supermarket? Would the strange things stop happening? Would she be free to make decisions without the intervention of mussel shells and clever, but insane, software? But, deep down, Carole knows better. She has followed every instruction so far, and following them one more time to some kind of conclusion seems the best option.

She also reminds herself that Ray will be back later and, at the thought of him, her face softens. Although he's only been away for a few days, either in New York or a spa hotel in the Cotswolds, she's missed him. She always does when he's away. It's as if she sometimes doesn't notice him when he's at home, and is only aware of a gap in her life when he's not there. But she's also glad that he's been away; the oddities that have piled in this week were not for sharing, and Carole doesn't like *not* sharing everything with Ray. She sits in her car, thinking about her husband, smiling.

You don't seem to be going anywhere.

Her car is switched off, although that doesn't seem to bother the sat nav lady, who sounds merely curious.

'I'm thinking.'

You have to be there for one o'clock.

'Where?'

You don't therefore have to leave now. You're too early.

The sat nav is speaking in her usual husky voice, and has neatly evaded Carole's question. She no longer imagines her sat nav as a real person, in a real bed, with her hunky Spanish lover beside her, a cigarette daintily held between two fingers. Carole now simply regards the sat nav lady as a conduit, but a conduit to what or where she doesn't know.

'I'm going to visit my mother,' says Carole.

That's nice.

'How would you know?'

There's a small silence. *Do you wish to be guided?*

'Thank you, but no.'

It's a route she knows well enough, and she doesn't want company. In any case, by answering back to the sat nav, she may have inadvertently been rude. Instead, she wants space to think or, even better, to clear her mind of all thoughts.

It's a slow journey into the city because rush-hour hasn't quite ended. But Carole is in no hurry, dawdling on the dual-carriageway into Edinburgh, and slowly negotiating her way to the salubrious suburb of Morningside and parking her car down a side street. It's near where her parents still live, the same house in which she spent the latter part of her childhood, and her mother only has a ten-minute walk to and from her shop.

Her mother's shop is called BESPOKE ARTS and it has become something of a destination for lovers of quality arts and crafts. It therefore stocks only items that people don't actually need, although it is very successful because the residents of Morningside like buying things they don't need. Carole never knows whether or not to call it a *shop*, as that suggests somewhere functional; her mother's shop would better be described as a gallery or emporium, a place only fit for refined people with exclusive tastes and large wallets. Carole, who isn't particularly refined, always feels slightly uncomfortable in it.

Carole pushes open the door. Her mother, tall and bony with pink and blonde hair expensively coiffured, is behind the counter, wearing half-moon spectacles and peering at a piece of paper. She's worn well, Carole's mother, who is dressed in designer jeans and a white shirt, over which she has draped a grey cardigan. Her mum looks up and peers over her spectacles, expecting a customer and smiles broadly.

'Caro, what a surprise! It's not often that you grace us with your presence.'

'I was passing, that's all,' lies Carole. 'Thought I'd call in and see how things were doing.'

Mary, her mother, is the only person who calls her Caro. Carole likes the diminutive and wishes that more of her friends and family would use it. She's tried to suggest it to people, but usually after a few drinks at parties, and nobody therefore remembers. Carole, stubbornly, has remained Carole.

Mary gestures around her, at the artworks on the walls and the glass cabinets in which sit all manner of crafts, from colourful scarves and cashmeres, to delicate fairies on almost-invisible threads and complex pieces of blown glass. It's a shop full of unexpected treasures, and Carole has always liked visiting it, when she's had the time, despite feeling a little out of place. Carole only really buys things that have a function, and has never bought a sculpture or decorative vase in her life. Her home is therefore quite sparsely decorated, without ephemeral knick-knacks or unnecessary clutter. She likes it that way, and it makes dusting easier.

Also, despite not doing a lot, Carole finds that her time is always at a premium, what with cooking, cleaning, ironing, and putting marmalade jars and butter back where they belong. She never really has the time, even if she had the inclination, to visit shops selling unnecessary things.

'Well it's good to see you,' says Mary, taking off her spectacles and coming out from behind the counter. Mother and daughter kiss on both cheeks, her mother holding tight to Carole's shoulders. 'Come and see some of my new acquisitions,' she whispers rather reverentially, as if they were in a library or museum.

Although Mary likes to think of her shop as selling *acquisitions*, this isn't quite true. What Mary has an eye for is quality and what will appeal to her discerning clientele, who no longer just come from the immediate area. Mary's shop now has a wider reputation, and a website, and sells to a national and international audience. Mary therefore exhibits stock from artists and artisans whom she has personally chosen, and takes a hefty commission on every item sold. It's a business model that involves little cost beyond rent and rates and, of course, dumpy Molly, Mary's assistant, who now appears from the back of the shop and rather formally shakes Carole's hand. Mary has other part-time assistants as well, allowing her the time to visit art exhibitions and up-market artisan fairs and so *acquire* new stock or suppliers.

'Here's someone new,' says Mary, standing in front of a wall of seascapes in striking and unlikely colours, painted in thick oils with bold strokes. 'These are my Hemingways.'

'Not the author, presumably.'

126

'Don't be silly, darling. George Hemingway. Lives somewhere in …' Mary struggles to remember. '… well, I suppose, he must live somewhere. Aren't they fun?'

Carole doesn't think that they are much fun, with each painting making the sea look fearsome and dangerous. It's how the Orkney sea can look sometimes, with strong winds sweeping in from the north or west.

Mary has marched off to another part of the shop, and Carole dutifully follows. 'And these are my Adele Wallace cashmeres. There aren't many individual craftspeople making cashmere these days. She's one of the last, bless her.'

Carole takes a blue jersey off the shelf, looks at the price tag and winces. You could buy a small car for the amount that Adele Wallace, and her mother, are charging. 'Her cashmeres are considered something of a status item,' Mary confides, leaving Carole to her own devices as the bell over the door tinkles and an elderly lady hobbles in. Mary seems to know the old lady, greeting her effusively, calling her by her name and, Carole thinks, enticing the customer to actually buy something.

Carole saunters around the shop while her mother effortlessly chats up the newcomer, enquiring politely after her grandchildren, her arthritis and what she might be looking for, and whether it's for herself or a gift, and leading her towards a cabinet in which sit bronze sculptures of naked women, naked couples and galloping horses. The old lady seems more captivated by the horses than the naked people, and soon leaves with a BESPOKE ARTS carrier bag in one hand.

'It's what I knew she would buy,' says Mary, once the door has closed. 'I'm pretty good at guessing peoples' tastes.'

'Well, you've been at it long enough,' Carole reminds her.

Mary is looking at her with a crease on her forehead. 'If I may say so, darling, you don't look at all well.'

'Not sleeping, that's all.'

127

'Caro, I only saw you a few days ago. You were fine then.'

'I'm just tired, Mum, that's all.'

Mary's forehead is still creased. 'It's not anything to do with that bloody cat, is it?'

Carole shakes her head. 'No of course not. But you will be there on Sunday?'

Mary sighs dramatically. 'We come to you most Sundays, remember? Anyway, it's your birthday! Of course, we'll be there! But grudgingly for the funeral, if that's what you want to call it, and certainly not from any lingering affection for the damn thing.'

Carole knows better than to reply to this. Her mother, practical and unsentimental, doesn't understand how Granny had been one of their family, and probably hadn't meant to pee on her dress. Instead, she asks, 'How's Dad?'

'Exactly the same as he was on Sunday and, come to think of it, the same as he was the Sunday before.' Her mother is looking at Carole intently.

'Pottering in the greenhouse, I suppose.' This isn't really a question. Carole's dad, released from servitude as an accountant, does very little except potter in the greenhouse. In summer, her parents' garden is a riot of colour, unlike Carole's which is mostly grass that needs cutting and weeds that need weeding. The gardening gene has not been passed from father to daughter, and Ray hates weeding or mowing the lawn and rarely does either. Carole likes to think of her garden as being deliberately wild, a haven for honey bees and other insects, which gives her a measure of satisfaction, but which doesn't convince anyone else.

'Pottering with intent, now that the days are getting longer. Are you sure you're okay?' Molly is now behind the counter, trying to look busy. She's looking at the same piece of paper that her mother had been looking at, using the same pair of half-moon spectacles. 'Come on,' says Mary, having given Carole more than enough time to answer her question, which Carole hasn't. 'Time for a cigarette.'

She takes Carole by the arm and leaves the shop in Molly's hands. Outside, on the pavement, Mary lights up.

'Mum, you should really quit,' advises Carole.

'Which you keep telling me to do every damn time I see you. But, as I keep telling you, it's one of my great pleasures, and not something to be cast aside lightly. And, frankly, at my age I need all the pleasure I can get.' Mary winks at her daughter, while pluming smoke into a cloudless blue sky. It's also an observation that Mary has made several times before.

'Mum, can I ask you something?'

'Ask away, Caro. It's what mothers are for.'

Carole now doesn't know what to say or what to ask. 'Have you ever had strange things happen to you?' It's the best she can manage, and feels immediately stupid.

Mary gives her a sideways look. 'Strange things? What kind of strange things?'

'I can't really explain. For example, suddenly meeting people you haven't seen for years, that kind of thing.' It doesn't really explain anything about what Carole has been through, but the unvarnished truth would probably involve swift admission to a psychiatric unit.

'It's called coincidence,' advises her mother. 'Have you suddenly been meeting people?'

'Not really, no.' Carole doesn't mention her old professor, as that would open up a completely different line of questioning.

'Is that why you're looking tired?'

Carole shrugs, while her mother stubs out her half-smoked cigarette on a nearby bin and deposits the remains inside.

'I'll make some tea,' says Mary. 'That'll make you feel better.'

Back in the shop, Carole takes another wander around her

mother's cabinets and pictures, marvelling at the prices and, despite herself, rather liking many of the things she sees, while not being remotely tempted to buy any of them. But she can understand the shop's allure: its absolute adherence to one-off individuality, and the sheer craftsmanship of everything on display. It is therefore a shop that has found a niche and a loyal following, and maybe the reason it has featured in several Sunday supplements, her mother standing behind the till and grinning broadly, or peering closely at a picture with the artist also peering intently at it.

There's a cabinet full of ceramic vases, each slightly different and painted in vivid blues and greens; in another, complex jewellery, with bracelets woven from strands of silver, and pendants with intricate Celtic crosses; in another, large but delicate glasses engraved with country scenes – a horse drinking at a trough, two pigs with their trotters intertwined and lying close to one another, and a sitting cat looking straight out from the glass, and reminding her of Granny.

Her mother hands her a mug of tea. 'I put sugar in yours. To give you some energy. If you're tired, you need energy.'

'I visited Tim yesterday,' says Carole abruptly. 'Felt a bit guilty that I hadn't been for a long while.' Carole takes a deep breath, feeling it ragged in her throat. Her mother's tea is strong and aromatic; some kind of exotic blend, and very sweet. Her mother was always experimenting with strange teas. 'I took flowers, and threw away some dead ones that were there.'

'They would have been mine,' says Mary. 'I try to see him every few weeks. As often as I can,' she adds.

'Maybe we could go together next time.'

Her mother firmly shakes her head. 'I like to go alone, Caro. To be by myself. God, sorry, that sounds terribly rude!' Mary suddenly laughs, then falls silent for some moments. 'Children aren't possessions,' she then says. 'You look after them for a while and then you bid them farewell. You, I said goodbye to years ago. With Tim, I never had that chance, so he's still mine.'

'I understand, Mum,' says Carole, remembering Iona and her mad trip to Orkney, and having that exact same thought. Maybe she has inherited some things from her mother, and momentarily wonders if this is a good thing. She then says more brightly: 'I also visited our old house. Did you know that they've replaced the old bridge with a new one?'

But before her mother can answer, the little bell over the door is tinkling and her mother is off again to charm another customer. This customer her mother doesn't know, but she greets him like an old friend, fussing over him and asking whether he's buying something for himself or, perhaps, as a gift and, if so, a *special* gift for a *special* someone?

While Mary determines her customer's tastes and intentions and the level of his disposable income, Carole takes her mug of tea on a final lap of inspection, this time taking in a distant part of the shop that is mostly hung with oil paintings. There's a dead fish on a slab, which Carole finds rather gross; and another of a dead fish in a basket; and another of a salmon hanging on a fishing line. But, despite his output consisting of dead fish, she can also appreciate the artist's talent; each fish scale seems luminous, each strand of the wicker basket precise and interwoven. She could almost be looking at dead fish photographs. All have been painted by someone called Roy McGregor. She's about to turn away when her eye is caught by a much smaller picture, hung further down the wall. It's a simple picture of an empty mussel shell lying, it would appear, on a wooden slab, much like Carole's kitchen table, but without its dents and scratches. It's an image that makes her heart stop for a moment, although it's nothing more than a dead sea creature picture among other dead sea creature pictures.

'Ah, I see you've found my McGregors.' Mary's voice

is almost reverential, her voice back to its library whisper. 'He's among my best-sellers. Huge talent, don't you think?'

'How much is this?' asks Carole, pointing at the mussel shell picture.

Her mother names a price and Carole once more winces. But she also knows that it's a picture she must have. It looks exactly like her own – real – mussel shell but, then again, all mussel shells must look much the same.

'Of course, I give discounts to valued customers,' says her mother. Carole hasn't, as far as she can remember, ever bought anything from her mother's shop, but doesn't remind her of this.

'Then it's a deal,' says Carole.

'However, in advance of your birthday, let me give it to you.'

'Mum, it costs a fortune!'

'Well, I haven't been able to think of anything to give you, so this sorts your birthday present out.' Her mother leans in close to Carole's ear. 'In any case, it didn't cost me a fortune, did it?'

'Then, thank you.'

Her mother shrugs. 'Think nothing of it, Caro. But, yes, I did know the bridge had been replaced. Years ago. You really didn't know?'

'I just haven't been back to our old house for a while, that's all.' Carole smiles. 'You were quite the Good Samaritan back then, Mum. Making tea, taking out biscuits.'

'I've always believed in doing the right thing, Caro. Tea and biscuits weren't much of an effort.'

Carole lifts the mussel picture from the wall. 'I'll treasure it,' she says, not entirely sure if she will treasure it, or where to hang it, or what Ray will say.

Once she's said her goodbyes to Mary and Molly, Carole walks slowly back to her car and places her new acquisition, inside its fancy carrier bag, on the back seat. Then she sits in her car and thinks about lots of things and about nothing in particular. It's like her thoughts are a jigsaw jumble that's been tipped out, and she can't find the mental stamina to pick up just one piece and think one coherent thought.

Instead, it's the sat nav lady who interrupts her chain of confused non-thought. She still hasn't started her car.

In two hundred yards, turn left.

Twelve

Carole does turn left in two hundred yards, and then takes the second exit off a roundabout. She is being taken back into the city, away from the riches of Morningside and the discerning clientele of BESPOKE ARTS. Her mind is still a jumble of thoughts, and she drives on autopilot, carefully guided by the sat nav lady who seems unusually solicitous, speaking more slowly than normal and repeating even the most mundane of instructions. Carole is, however, surprised to find herself closing in on her first flat, the flat that Joe so successfully broke up.

Your destination is on the left.

Amazingly, or perhaps not, there is a parking space right outside the pub that brought back so many memories the last time she was in it. When was that, she wonders? Yesterday? Two days ago? But, whenever it was, it seems an eternity ago, back when electronic devices behaved themselves and mussel shells stayed on the mantlepiece and didn't clean themselves. She steps out of her car, her anxiety level at full blast, and looks up at wall-to-wall blue sky. It's cold, and her breath plumes from her mouth, much like her mother's cigarette smoke.

But she now sees that there is one small and solitary cloud right above her, and she's immediately reminded of a field trip to the north of Scotland. It must have been in her second year at university and they were to carry out excavations around the Stones of Stenness, perhaps the oldest stone circle in the British Isles. There were six students, three girls and three boys, although Rob had chosen to give this Orkney field trip a miss – perhaps remembering the disastrous last time that they had been on the islands.

But it was on that trip that Carole's abiding fascination with standing stones was born; not out of any romantic sense of the distant past, but out a genuine admiration for the ancient people who constructed them, gave them purpose, and then took that purpose to other parts of the British Isles.

The surviving four stones, out of an original twelve, sit on the bank of a stream that joins the end of the Loch of Stenness with the Loch of Harray. It is a majestic but bleak place, the sea wind-flecked with white; a flat landscape devoid of trees, and which can't have changed much since it held ritual significance. The horizons seemed distant, and the sky enormous; to Carole, it was like standing at the edge of the world, as it must have seemed to the ancient people who first gave it mystic purpose. Its name comes from the Old Norse for stone headland. Unlike the Brodgar circle, the Stenness stones are huge, some six metres tall, and stand within an enclosing ditch and earth bank. It would have been over one hundred and thirty feet in diameter. It's the scale and age of the Stenness stones that captivated Carole. They are the same age as the first and second Egyptian dynasties, the brick temples of Sumeria, and at least two centuries before the Golden Age of China.

For Carole, on that week of unexpected and perfect sunshine, it was also the most magical of times; carefully working away in her trench from early morning and then falling into bed exhausted at the end of each day. The unsmiling lecturer leading the dig told them all in no uncertain terms before they set off from Edinburgh that there was to be no hanky-panky at their respective B&Bs, looking at Carole as he said this and making her blush. But it was okay: there was nobody on the trip who Carole would have considered having hanky-panky with, even if Rob never found out. The three boys were dull; the other two girls not much better.

There was one particular stone that Carole was particularly fascinated by, although it no longer existed. Known as the 'Odin Stone' it had a circular hole pierced through it. It was reputed to have magical powers and loving couples since early times would hold hands through it and pledge their love. It would have stood slightly apart from the rest of the circle, probably making it seem more aloof or important than the other stones. But why was it set apart from the others, and why the circular hole? The story goes that a farmer, an incomer, destroyed the stone in 1814, outraging local sentiment. Orcadians, then as now, retain an affinity for the stones; they're part of the landscape and part of their shared history. The incomer was chased off the island.

A mile away is the Brodgar circle, which would once have comprised sixty stones, although less than thirty are still standing. It was built after Stenness, and designed to be the greatest circle of them all. At Brodgar, there would have been great feasts – the amount of cattle bones excavated prove that. It was a place of celebration and revelry; a place in which to affirm life, as well as honour the dead. But, unlike some of the other students who would much have preferred to be digging at Brodgar, Carole liked the less majestic Stenness circle. She liked them for their age, predating Brodgar by half a millennium; but she also liked it that Stenness would have been a place of quieter contemplation, a more personal place to reconnect with the dead: a more sober place where the ideas and mysticism of the island would originally have been honed and fine-tuned, finding later affirmation in Brodgar and, later still, at Stonehenge.

It was the last day of their dig and Carole's back was mutinying. None of them had found anything of value, and this last day seemed pointless. Everyone was looking forward to a last-night visit to the pub, and a hungover drive back to

Edinburgh the next morning. They were digging a little way from the circle although, like before, aerial photography suggested that there might have been a pathway leading away from the circle, and who knew what they might find?

Carole straightened from her trench and stretched her back, rubbing the bottom of her spine with both hands. Above was clear sky with just one solitary cloud directly over her head. She decided that a quick walk would ease the ache in her back and she walked the short distance to the place where the Odin Stone had once stood. She reached out a hand, mentally putting her hand through the hole although, with no Rob on the other side, there was nobody to hold it. She wondered what he would be doing now in Edinburgh; maybe just slumped in front of the TV not doing very much. Or maybe slumped in front of someone else's TV; she was never sure what he got up to when she wasn't around, but never asked. She didn't want to know.

In any case, Rob didn't need to come on field trips. Not only did they usually take place in the holidays, they weren't compulsory. Some students never went on them, although Carole would usually volunteer for any trip to the north of Scotland or, even better, the islands. It was in her nature she supposed; to exercise her passion for the past by trying to find fragments of it.

She walked back to her trench, looking at her watch. Only a few more minutes and their week in Orkney would be over, with nothing to show for it. But this was what archaeology was all about; sometimes you got lucky, usually you didn't. The important thing, she knew by then, was to keep looking because, without looking, you'll never find anything.

It was then, looking into her trench, that she thought she saw the faintest of protrusions poking from the earth. She would have missed it but for the angle of the sun, now lower in the sky and casting shadows. It was in a part of the trench that she had already meticulously searched with

137

her small trowel and brush and, fascinated, she went back into the trench to excavate further. Twenty minutes later and she had unearthed a small but perfectly-formed axe-head; probably gold, too small and too impractical for ordinary use but, maybe, something ceremonial. Its wooden shaft had long since rotted away.

Carole looked at it from all angles, holding it almost reverentially. 'I did find you, didn't I?' she whispered.

Then she carefully marked where she had found it and took it across to the empty tent in which their finds were to be photographed and catalogued on trestle tables. The trestle tables were mostly empty. Their lecturer was sitting in a canvas chair with his feet up on the main trestle table, which was covered in maps and ground radar read-outs. Wordlessly, Carole handed over her axe-head.

That night, Carole's find transformed everyone's mood. They had actually found something that the Museum of Scotland might want to exhibit. Consequently, everyone had even more to drink than they had planned and the trip back to Edinburgh the next morning was interrupted several times by two of the boys having to get out of the minibus to be sick. The third had already been sick on the ferry back to the mainland.

Carole still visits her gold axe-head in the Museum of Scotland – it's now on permanent display – and it's a constant reminder to her to never stop looking, no matter what happens in life. She likes it when other visitors to the museum look at it closely, and then stand back to admire it. She likes that, in a small way, she has added to what's known about ancient Orkney. Maybe that's been the reason for her recent melancholy; that she has folded in on herself, not looking beyond herself and her family, forgetting the anticipation of finding something, and the thrill of actually unearthing an object of historic value.

She remembers vividly her discovery, how her lecturer's

feet descended from the table when she handed him her treasure, his smile. She remembers him washing it carefully in warm water, peeling off earth with his fingers. She remembers that his hands were shaking. Then, standing at the mouth of the tent, he'd held the axe-head up, so that it caught the dying sun. She now wonders if her love of ancient history is somehow connected with the events of this week; that, inexplicably, a bit of the past has sought her out to repay the debt of its discovery. The axe-head wasn't the last of her finds, but has always been her most special. Her first great discovery, and a vindication that the past can always be unearthed. Over the years, there were also coins and pottery, the blade of a medieval knife, and an ornate piece of jewellery, probably 12th century, and also in the Museum of Scotland. There were more discoveries, some of intrinsic or historic value, and some of no value at all, except to Carole. To her, every bit of the past has a value – to her, if to nobody else. She had, or has, an instinct for finding things, or maybe things had, or have, an instinct for finding her.

For Carole, past and present have now become melded together, interwoven into a pattern she can't discern, or teaching her something that she doesn't yet understand.

*

Outside the pub where the sat nav has deposited her, Carole locks her car and again looks up. The solitary cloud has disappeared. Instead, like a child's scribble, there is the wispy trail of an aeroplane.

Inside the pub, and the large mirror is still behind the bar, with its twinkly and incongruous Christmas lights. The red wallpaper is still ghastly and the pub's resident drunk is still sitting at the bar on the same barstool nursing a pint of beer and large glass of whisky. She wonders if, like Luigi in the Italian restaurant, he ever goes home. She looks at

139

him closely, her heart beating a drum-roll, because his hair is once again brown, and years have been stripped from his face. Only the pint of beer and glass of whisky are the same.

She also now realises that she's soaking wet and that the pub's bright interior is fading to semi-darkness, like at the start of a film when the house lights go down. She turns to look at the pub's large windows and now sees that the outside world has turned to darkness and that rain is pouring down, cascading loudly over the pub's windows in small rivers.

'Ghastly weather,' says the barman, who she immediately recognises from years before, and who also doesn't seem to have aged. 'How are you doing today?'

'Wet,' says Carole, who can think of nothing else to say, and sits heavily on a barstool before she falls over. Her breathing is shallow and fast, matching the staccato rhythm of her heart, and even saying *wet* is an effort.

The barman, who clearly knows her as well, plonks a gin and tonic down in front of her without being asked. Instinctively, she reaches for her handbag, only to discover that she doesn't have a handbag. Instead, she's wearing a small backpack. So, she reaches into that and finds a purse that she threw away years ago. She is, however, relieved to find that it does contain money, paper money, but banknotes that have probably been out of circulation for years. She used to drink gin and tonic back then, when she could afford to, in her latter days as an undergraduate, thinking it made her sophisticated.

She now makes a closer inspection of what she's wearing: instead of a warm red dress, she's wearing rather tatty jeans; instead of a warm coat, a light blue anorak; instead of her cardigan, an equally tatty jersey that perfectly matches her jeans. It was her undergraduate uniform; the sensible clothes she could wear day after day, blending in with all the other impoverished students – or the rich students pretending to be impoverished. She also seems to have longer hair, because it's flopping over her face, and she tucks it back over her ears, as she remembers doing years before. Then she feels sick, and puts a hand over her mouth in case she is sick, and closes her eyes. She forces herself to take deep and regular breaths and, slowly, the nausea passes and she opens her eyes. The barman is looking at her with a look of concern on his face.

'You okay?' he asks.

She nods. 'Just a hot flush,' she replies, knowing that no man, in the history of mankind, knows what a hot flush is, but does know that women are prone to them, even on cold, wet days. The barman looks satisfied and heads to the other side of the bar to serve another customer.

She shuffles out of her anorak and lets it drop to the floor, her heart slowing and her breathing becoming more regular. Out of all the madnesses that she's been subjected to, this is the maddest of the lot. But, she thinks, she's clearly here for a reason, although, looking around, she can't think what that reason could be. There is only a scattering of other drinkers – the rain probably discouraging most people – but, scanning faces, she recognises nobody. Except, of course, the drunk at the end of the bar, who she does remember, and she looks at him for a moment wondering if he is the reason she's been transported back in time or, more likely, hallucinating about travelling back in time. In the real world, the one just beyond the pub doors, she's probably still sitting in her car, and dreaming all this. She considers going back outside, and rejoining the real world, but her legs feel wobbly and, for the time being, she's probably safer on her barstool. But despite extreme anxiety, she wants to stay. The madnesses haven't yet tried to kill her; they seem benign and, taking another deep breath, she decides to remain where she is and see what happens.

After several more deep breaths she begins to feel more in control, although her hands are still shaking. But she no longer feels as panic-stricken as she did in the graveyard, with her own gravestone next to Tim's. The happenings of the last few days also seem now to be oddly reassuring; nobody and nothing means her any harm, she is sure of that.

She also notices, then feels, something else. The wrinkles on the back of her hands have vanished and she's experiencing a surge of energy. It's the energy of youth, the energy she remembers, but which has drained out of her over the years. She has been transported backwards, in body if not in mind. She is to meet someone, and she can't guess who. She looks at her hands again, feeling their dexterity, and noticing that her wedding ring, which has never left its appropriate finger, is now missing.

She searches through her backpack. In it is a notebook with some squiggled words. It takes her some moments to decipher them, and realise that she must have written herself a shopping list. *Pasta*, says one squiggle; *tomatoes*, says another. A squiggle at the bottom of the list remains just that: a squiggle. Carole's handwriting was, and is, appalling. After each lecture, she would have to write out her notes properly because, in a few hours, they would have become gibberish. She's often tried to learn how to write properly, even buying a fancy fountain pen that she thought might help, although none of her strategies worked and the fountain pen leaked down the front of her best cream blouse. She'd filled it with red ink, so that for the rest of the day she'd looked like the victim of a stabbing. Carole looks at her shopping list and tries to think what she might have been doing that day, all those years ago. Cooking for herself? For her flatmates? But they never really cooked for one another, and had separate shelves in the fridge.

But the old shopping list has taken her mind off her present predicament, and she is able to look around the pub again with greater equanimity. A week ago, the idea of time-travel would have been palpably absurd: an impossibility in which only the deranged could believe. Now, Carole tells herself again that she's *not* deranged and that time-travel is perfectly normal if you have the right sat nav, Alexa or mussel shell, and, with her hands trembling a little less, pours a little tonic into her gin which she drinks back, then pours in more tonic. Carole weighs up the only two options, apart from madness, that might explain where she now was: time-travel or hallucination. Neither seem remotely plausible, although one them was probably the real explanation.

She's about to again tip the glass to her lips when the pub's door opens, letting in a howl of wind that ruffles Carole's hair and dislodges it from behind her ears. The burst of wind is followed by a young man in a blue overcoat, collar turned up against the rain. He's about her age, is carrying a briefcase, and looks thoroughly wet and miserable.

Carole's glass of gin and tonic falls to the floor and shatters. She barely notices.

It's Ray.

Thirteen

In Carole's world, except for this week, things usually have simple or obvious explanations. The world operates to known laws of space and time; physicists and mathematicians have made sure of that. The universe and our world run like clockwork. Light from the Sun takes eight minutes and twenty seconds to reach Earth. Our world rotates once in about twenty-four hours in relation to the Sun, and once every twenty-three hours, fifty-six minutes and four seconds if you measure it to other distant stars. The Earth rotation is slowing, so that a day was shorter in the past. It's slowing because of the tidal effects of the Moon. Carole knows all this stuff, because she has recently been working on the alignment of stones. Yet, despite the Earth slowing down a tiny bit, time moves at a fairly precise pace, measured in seconds, minutes and hours. Except for today, time has always moved forwards; sand in the egg-timer dripping downwards, the hands on her watch moving clockwise. She checks, and finds that she's wearing a cheap and shoddy watch that she lost, accidentally or on purpose years ago, and that it seems to have stopped. She gives her wrist a shake and looks again. The hands on her watch seem frozen.

In Carole's world, the right answer to a problem is usually the most obvious or logical one. Only when you've run through the more obvious explanations, can you consider the unlikely ones. If there's a nasty mess on the kitchen floor, it was probably the cat vomiting up a furball. It might also be something that Iona has trodden in. Moving down the scale, it might conceivably be something that she has trodden in, although Carole is fastidious about brushing her shoes. But it probably won't be a wasps' nest or a baby crocodile. But, here, in this pub there are no explanations, however obvious or unlikely. She is facing an impossibility: on her scale of probable to conceivably possible, the impossible is standing in front of her. Carole is now in the company of someone who becomes her lover and husband, the father to her only child; except that she knows it and, presumably, he doesn't because he's looking a little disapprovingly at her, and the shattered glass on the floor, and assuming perhaps that she's a little drunk and, literally, can't hold her liquor. He might also be wondering why this mad woman is staring panic-stricken at him. She quickly tries to rearrange her features and looks away.

The barman is now on her side of the bar with a mop, brush and pan.

'God, I'm sorry!' says Carole, a little too loudly, but intended to let Ray know that she isn't drunk, or mad. Ray doesn't look convinced, plonking his briefcase on the floor and not looking in her direction.

'Don't worry,' says the barman. 'Happens all the time in here.' He nods down the bar to the resident drunk, who is staring intently at the opposite wall, and doesn't seem to have noticed the sound of breaking glass. 'Him, usually,' confides the barman, sweeping glass shards into his pan and mopping the floor dry. 'There, no damage done. Except to your drink, obviously.'

'And my reputation!' says Carole, again a little loudly and tries to laugh. It emerges as a kind of hiccup.

'I wouldn't worry about that either,' says the barman. 'You dropped a glass last week as well.'

Carole doesn't remember doing this and blushes. The resident drunk has looked round and has raised his pint glass to her, making her part of some fraternity of inebriated people who can't hold onto glasses.

145

Ray, a little uncertainly, has parked himself on the barstool next to her, largely because all the other barstools – not that there are many – are being used by other people. He picks up his briefcase and opens it, and Carole sees that it's full of big serious-looking files. It's an old briefcase, slightly battered and one that Carole remembers, before he traded up to a better briefcase after his first real promotion. Carole looks coyly from the briefcase she remembers to her future husband, who is absently sifting through files but not actually doing anything with them. God, we were both so young! she thinks.

'Gin and tonic, please' says Ray to the barman, and casts a glance in Carole's direction, 'and maybe another one for her as well.' She concludes that he doesn't think she's mad or drunk, and tries to remember how their original conversation started, all those years ago, but it's been wiped from memory.

All she can immediately hold onto is that she's in the company of someone whose faults and foibles and, yes, redeeming features, she knows so intimately. Was this how it all started? She has to remind herself that he knows nothing about her.

'Very kind of you,' replies Carole, a little breathless, remembering just in time not to call him by his name. She tries to smile, forcing her mouth muscles to produce what she hopes isn't a psychopathic grimace. Her heart is again hammering, and her breath is coming in short gasps. 'I don't usually drop things.'

'Apparently, you do. Last week.' He indicates the barman, who is now behind the bar, and reaches a hand across the gap between them. 'I'm Ray,' he tells her, as if she needed to know.

'Carole,' she replies, which he presumably does need to know. 'With an "e," she adds, because she's always been punctilious about it.

He looks her up and down, from her tatty jumper to her tatty jeans, but is too polite to jump to any conclusions. 'And what is it you do?' he asks instead, presumably to find a pigeon-hole to slot her into. 'When you're not dropping things,' he adds.

'Actually, I don't usually drop things,' she replies. 'Well, maybe just today and last week, apparently. Anyway, I'm a student.'

'Ah, a student,' he says, as if she couldn't have been anything else. 'Studying what?'

'Archaeology.'

Ray nods and takes a mouthful of his drink. 'Do you know, I don't think I've ever met an archaeologist before.'

'I wish I had a penny for every time someone has said that to me,' says Carole, suddenly feeling brighter and less anxious. He's bought her a drink and is still talking to her and, for reasons she can't fathom, she needs this conversation to go on, even though she knows that he goes to the gym twice a week, has a small birthmark on his bottom, hates his name, and can't dance.

'Really?'

'No, not really. But there aren't many of us archaeologists. So, not much chance of bumping into one.' While she can't remember their first conversation in this pub all those years ago, something tells her that he did say that to her. *I don't think I've ever met an archaeologist before*, rings a faint bell. 'However, being a student and therefore penniless,' she informs him, 'I get to meet lots of bankers. Actually, just one. My bank manager, but lots and lots of times.'

Ray is looking confused. 'How did you know I worked in a bank?'

Carole almost bites her tongue. 'I suppose it must be the suit.' It's not a very good answer, but Ray seems happy with it. She mentally curses her stupidity. He's now taken off his coat and, underneath, is wearing a charcoal-grey suit and

147

red tie, unbuttoned at the neck. 'A very *nice* suit, I may add, so I wasn't being rude, or anything. Actually, it was just a lucky guess.' She takes a deep breath, willing herself to stop babbling and think rationally. You know everything about him; he knows nothing about you, she keeps telling herself.

'I suppose that archaeologists get to make lots of guesses.'

She doesn't know how to answer this and, instead, pours tonic into her gin. She's relieved to see that her hands have stopped shaking and that, despite still suffering from high anxiety, is beginning to slightly relax into her role. She supposes it's how actors must feel as they walk onto a stage; nervously standing in the wings, then becoming someone else and speaking their lines. The trouble is, of course, that Carole's only role is to be herself, despite playing someone many years younger and without a script. But, once again, she senses that nothing bad will happen. She hasn't been brought to this place to be humiliated; all she has to do is improvise. She takes a gulp of her drink, feeling it course down her throat and into her bloodstream. 'We try to keep guesswork out of it, Ray. It's sort of a branch of science, so we're always looking for evidence.'

'Only sort of?'

'Well, maybe not a proper science. But enough of one to try to find evidence for things.'

He nods slowly at her inarticulate answer. 'Evidence to back up your guesses?'

'Something like that.'

Down the bar, the resident drunk suddenly coughs, finds a handkerchief in a pocket, and sneezes into it. The handkerchief, she notes, is spotless and perfectly creased. Has he ironed it himself? Does he have a wife or partner to iron it for him? Somehow, the small fact of his handkerchief momentarily depresses her; it has given him a new dimension; turned him from a caricature into a real person: someone with a life outside the pub. She wants to go over and tell him that he'll always be here if he doesn't get a grip on himself, but resists the temptation: what would she say and why would he believe her, particularly as she's now someone who also has a habit of dropping glasses?

'So, a student,' Ray says, and Carole doesn't know whether this is a question.

'Well, almost a post-grad student.'

'So, almost maybe going to continue being a student?'

'That's the idea, although the university may have other ideas,' she replies, knowing full well that she does get the doctorate she wanted and then, much later, another doctorate in oncology that she didn't want.

'And what will your doctorate be on?' he asks. 'Assuming, I suppose, that it's on anything. Sorry, I'm not good on the mechanics of academia.' He scratches his head. 'Come to think of it, I don't know many clever people.'

Carole is pleased that he seems to consider her as someone clever, and feels a sudden warmth inside, although that could be the mouthful of gin that she's just swallowed. 'Standing stones,' she replies. It doesn't sound very interesting and Ray simply looks bewildered, so Carole launches into one of her lengthier explanations of what they are, who built them, and what they were likely used for, although nobody really knows. 'So, they're still a bit of a mystery,' she finishes, hoping that she hasn't entirely bored him, 'because we know next to nothing about Neolithic religious beliefs.'

'Or if they had any?' says Ray, making it a question, which suggests that he might actually be interested in what Carole had been telling him. Then again, she has to concede, maybe he was just being polite.

'The stone circles were places of ceremony so, yes, they must have had some kind of religious belief.' She shrugs. 'We can assume that they venerated their dead, because other Stone Age peoples seem to also have done the same. But I doubt we'll ever really know for certain.'

149

'Maybe that should be your life's work,' he says. 'To solve the riddle of Stone Age religion. But maybe you'll find that they were landing sites for flying saucers.' He gestures to the barman and indicates their empty glasses. Carole immediately reaches for her purse, but Ray waves a hand. 'I'm enjoying being educated,' he says. 'In exchange for ancient knowledge, I will provide gin and tonic.'

'That doesn't seem like a fair exchange,' Carole replies. 'Anyway, I'm sorry if I've been boring you.'

'Not at all. Ten minutes ago, I didn't really know what a standing stone was. Now I do, and I can tell all my friends about them. Could they have been landing sites for UFOs?'

'Now you're being rude!' she rebukes him, but carefully with a smile. She doesn't want to frighten him off by saying the wrong thing. 'I knew I was boring you! Everyone gets bored when I start talking about standing stones. It's a gift,' she adds. 'I can be very, *very* boring.'

'Not a bit of it,' he replies, raising his glass, 'and I wasn't being rude.'

'But if I do find they had something to do with alien green blobs, I'll be sure to let you know.' She gestures round the pub and its ghastly wallpaper. The drunk at the end of the bar has his head cradled on one hand, elbow planted on the bar, and looks to be nearly asleep. His handkerchief is back in a pocket. 'Anyway, what brings you here?' she asks, getting back to boring trivia when all she really wants to do is put her arms around him, to kiss him all over, and tell him that she loves him. Her emotional journey with Ray has run a rather longer course, and she has to keep reminding herself that this is the first time he's met her. She's also aware that she's drunk rather a lot of gin and that good sense could soon slip, perhaps irrevocably. She dares not risk losing him, when she hasn't even properly found him. Why is she being gifted this first meeting again?

'Dropping off my car to be mended. Some idiot smashed

one of my rear lights. Then it started to rain, and then I saw this place. A refuge, I thought, until the rain passes.' They both look at the pub's plate-glass windows. Rain is still cascading down. It's the same reason, all those years ago, that Carole had for also sheltering in the pub. 'If it ever passes,' he adds.

'Which it might by September. We're in Scotland, don't forget.' She goes to touch her wedding ring, a habit of hers, to absently turn it round and round, and then realises that it's not on her finger, and briefly wonders if it ever will be again. 'What made you go into banking?' she asks, although she's known the answer for years.

'It seemed like a safe career option,' he says rather lamely, 'but I'm also greedy and rapacious.' Carole knows this to be untrue; among Ray's redeeming features is his generosity of spirit. She wisely decides not to say so. Instead, she asks: 'Are you? Greedy and rapacious, I mean.'

'Not really,' Ray concedes. 'Actually, I lend to small businesses. Theoretically, I help them get off the ground and become bigger businesses.' He shrugs. 'What I do, I hope, has a kind of positive social purpose. Creating jobs, that kind of thing. There. I'll get off my high horse now.'

Carole can remember virtually every one of their courtship excursions (what an old-fashioned word! she thinks) – trips to the cinema and theatre, meals in romantic restaurants or, at weekends, simply strolling in a park somewhere in the city. She can remember walking in the gardens under Edinburgh Castle, its ancient battlements looming over them, the same garden in which she'd confronted Clarissa, which once triggered a sense of an ending.

With Ray, it was as if they both knew that this relationship was special, and therefore to be taken slowly. She can also remember their first proper kiss, Ray walking her back to her flat. In those days she was still with her archaeology flatmates, both girls, not far from the university, and on a busy road that would keep her awake at night. But, although she has twinges of memory about this first meeting, she still has no real recollection of what was said. Maybe this is a re-enactment of that past meeting, or maybe an entirely new version. Either way, Ray is still talking to her and seems to be enjoying her company, despite her tatty jeans. She has resisted the urge to go to the loo and look at her face; she doesn't want to be reminded of what she once looked like, back when she didn't frown and still did have longer hair.

The gin is now doing what it does best, and Carole no longer feels anxious, although she forces herself to remain guarded. Her feet are still on a tightrope of past and present, and she dare not reveal something that she isn't supposed to know. Her heart is beating more normally again and her breathing is no longer coming in ragged gulps. She finds that she's smiling at Ray, perhaps a little too intimately for a first meeting, and he looks away for a moment.

'I guess the other reason I went into banking is that I'm not very creative,' he says, looking back at her. 'That ruled out a whole bunch of career options.'

'Ridiculous, everyone is creative.'

'Not me.'

'Then think back to primary school,' says Carole. 'Didn't you do lots of painting? Didn't you have crayons and colour in lots of little masterpieces?'

'I suppose so, although I doubt they were masterpieces.'

'Well, there you are then. Everyone is born creative.'

'And then life beats it out of you,' he says.

'Exactly!' she agrees, taking another swallow of gin and tonic. 'Education becomes about learning things so you can pass exams. Creativity gets forgotten about, or gets buried under boring stuff. You just need to dig it up again.'

'That's more your field than mine,' he reminds her.

Suddenly she can't think of anything to say. It's as if she can feel her feet slipping on the rope beneath her; she doesn't know what to say, because she already knows everything. 'Do you enjoy being a banker?' she asks rather lamely.

'Most of it, at least sometimes. But not the paperwork.' He indicates the briefcase in front of him, still open, and still filled with big files.

'Who does?' agrees Carole.

They talk on, mostly about inconsequential things, finding some common ground in places they've been. She steers clear of films they might have seen because she can't remember what films were around back then. Likewise, TV and books. Likewise, restaurants, because they're forever changing identities. One minute, a Chinese; the next, something vegan and unappealing. Then again, veganism been invented back when she first met Ray. Carole therefore sticks to safe subjects, always acutely aware of asking things that she already knows the answer to, and of trying to avoid telling Ray anything that she shouldn't yet know. It's a balancing act; of knowing, but not revealing: a trapeze act of past and present, with her feet always precarious on the rope beneath her.

But she's again drawn to Ray, as she must have been all those years ago. He has brown-blonde hair and an easy smile. Wide lips and a lithe body; tall but not too tall. He also seems confident but not commanding, seemingly genuinely interested in her and what her studies entail. If standing stones bored him, he didn't show it. He's always been a good listener, she decides, another redeeming feature and one of the reasons she chose him in the first place.

They finish their gin and tonics and, before Carole knows it, another one has been laid in front of her. 'I hope you're not trying to get me pissed,' she says, but with a smile.

'Now why would I do that?' he asks, one eyebrow raised.

She laughs, perhaps properly for the first time that evening. Did all this happen the first time around? Did they *really* say the same things to one another? Did she really laugh? But she simply can't remember, despite remembering everything that came afterwards. This one evening, their first evening together, and it's a complete blank.

'I don't even know your surname,' she says, wondering why on earth she's asked that.

'Gunn,' he replies.

She feigns thought, eyebrows furrowed. 'That means you're called Ray Gunn.'

'On my business cards, I'm *Raymond* Gunn. That way, not so many people make the connection.'

Carole is pretending to think. 'You're named after something in *Star Trek*?' She's fairly sure that the Starship Enterprise was around back then.

'My parents had a strange sense of humour,' he says, looking rather embarrassed. 'In revenge, I have, of course, killed both of them and buried their bodies in a forest. But, for strict accuracy, in *Star Trek* they used phasers not ray guns. As in *phasers to stun*.' Ray does a passable imitation of Captain Kirk.

'I rather like it,' she replies. 'It's … different, in an odd sort of way.'

'Different, yes, but something that's been the bane of my life. Can you imagine a childhood spent with a name like that?'

'A bit tedious, I would imagine.'

'Tedious doesn't get close. And yours?' he asks.

'Day. As in night and day. Very boring.'

Her train of thought is interrupted by a phone ringing.

'Hadn't you better answer that?' says Ray.

Carole hadn't immediately recognised her old ring tone, hardly surprising after so many years, and rummaging in her backpack, locates her phone and then stares at it blankly. It takes her a few moments to realise that it is, or was, one of those flip-phones that has to be opened. She manages this and puts it to her ear.

It's time to leave now.

The sat nav lady seems certain about this, although Carole has remembered one crucial detail of her first encounter with Ray and, rather rudely, reaches into his briefcase and extracts a small ring-bound folder. She also locates a biro tucked into a small leather loop on the briefcase lid. She opens the folder, makes to scribble her phone number, and then realises that she doesn't know her phone number.

'Do you really have to go?' he asks.

'Don't want to, but have to,' she says. 'It's my birthday next week, and my *bloody* mother is planning a birthday party.' It's the first thing she can think of, and immediately it sounds like the lie it is.

'That's mothers for you.'

She has her phone in one hand and Ray's biro in the other, and she now looks rather blankly from one to the other. 'I don't know what my number is,' she says.

'Then let me help.' Ray takes her phone from her, opens it, taps on its keyboard, then writes a number, presumably hers, on the folder. 'You should really try to remember it,' he suggests.

'I do have it written down somewhere,' replies Carole rather absently, knowing that she probably does, or did, but can't remember where. 'Anyway,' she adds, nodding to the folder, 'that's just in case you ever want to be bored by more archaeology stories.' He's examining his scribbled handwriting to make sure, she hopes, that he can read it. 'Anyway, thanks for the drinks.'

'Think nothing of it.'

She shuffles on her anorak and backpack. The rain outside seems to have eased to a drizzle, and she zips up the anorak and pulls its hood over her head, feeling that something is either about to end or something about to begin.

He raises his glass and smiles, the same smile that Carole both remembers and knows so well. 'Happy birthday,' he says.

Fourteen

If walking into the pub had been like the start of a film with the house lights fading to darkness, then walking out of the pub is like the end of the film with the house lights coming on again. Carole again finds herself in bright spring sunshine, her breath again ragged. Anxiety has gushed in, and she forces herself to take deep breaths. Above is blue sky. She looks at her watch, which is the watch that Ray gave her on a previous birthday, and which she's always worn since. Just after one o'clock. She has enjoyed a long conversation with her future husband, drunk several gin and tonics – and all within the space of a minute. She looks again at her watch. Its second hand is reassuringly moving in the right direction. Time is once again doing what it's supposed to do.

She's back in her warm coat and red woollen dress. The wrinkles are back on her hands and her wedding ring is back on its finger. Good things and bad things in equal measure. Absently, she twirls her wedding band with the fingers of her other hand. The familiar habit calms her. She also feels older again; the bounce and vitality of youth has gone from her step. She makes to brush hair behind her ears, but her hair is again sensible and short. For a moment, she considers walking back into the pub, to reconnect with Ray, to carry on where they'd left off, to be young again. But to what purpose? To drink another gin and tonic? To tell him that he's a father, or will become a father? To ask him about hotels in the Cotswolds? But she also doubts that Ray would be there anyway; she is back in her own timeline, completely sober, and the link to the past would have been broken. The clocks have started ticking again. The second hand on her watch is still moving clockwise.

She sits in her car for a while, with her mind once again a jumble of thoughts, anxieties and memories. Nor is she sure what's just happened; a precise enactment of what happened years ago? Or something completely different? All she can remember about that first meeting with Ray is that they didn't exchange phone numbers. This time, he has her phone number. Does that one difference between now and then have any significance? She suspects that it must, otherwise why transport her back in time to meet someone she's already married to?

Now that she's in her car, in the clothes she put on that morning, with her wedding ring back on its finger, what's she's just experienced seems both surreal and ridiculous, and she wonders if it *has* actually happened. Okay to bump into Joe or her old professor: those were chance meetings in the here and now. But *Ray*? Has the last few minutes or hours been a dream: some kind of hallucination? She's not sure, because the idea of time-travel is absurd, but *something* has happened. Hallucination seems a more likely explanation, as it was when she saw her own gravestone next to Tim's, and if hallucination *is* the explanation, then she most certainly has gone mad.

It's a tempting label to stick onto everything that's happened to her, because the list of absurdities has grown too long for simple sanity, from sentient electronic devices to chance encounters that couldn't be just coincidence, not forgetting a mussel shell that no longer likes to live exclusively on her mantlepiece. Like before, her mind is full of fragments, rearranging themselves, but never forming a pattern. I am mad, she thinks, because that is the only likely explanation. But I am also sane, she also thinks, because she has eliminated all likely explanations to arrive at the logical explanation that time-travel is, of course, perfectly possible, and that electronic devices and seashells can, of course, be sentient and intelligent.

She starts the car, but doesn't switch on the sat nav, although that doesn't seem to matter to the sat nav lady who, Carole now knows, regards *on* and *off* to be merely optional. There's also a text from Ray saying that he should be back by seven. She looks fondly at his text: simple and short, merely telling her something that she should know. But he's put an XX at the end of it, and that does seem to mean something. He doesn't usually put kisses at the end of his texts, although he rarely has any need to send her any. She replies to his text, without words. Just XXX, with an extra X to outdo him.

This simple task complete, Carole is now ridiculously happy, brain chemicals whizzing all over the place, an emotion she hasn't felt for a while, and she wants to hold onto this unexpected feeling, pickle it, make it a part of who she is now, rather than just who she was. Years back, she was always happy; now her life has sometimes simply felt like existence. Maybe that's what this week has all been about; giving her back an equilibrium that had been lost somewhere, down behind the sofa cushions, perhaps where Iona keeps the key to all wisdom. I am mad, but I am also sane, she thinks. If that makes me happy, so be it.

But, unbidden, she remembers something else. A memory of Orkney when she was still with Rob, and Ray hadn't yet appeared on the scene. It was the field trip to the Stenness stones when she'd found her axe-head.

She stops the car, the sudden weight of memory making it impossible to drive.

*

It was their second last night on the islands, and their landlady had cooked something wholesome but utterly revolting: something that involved meat from an animal species that Carole couldn't identify, with mashed potatoes that were semi-liquid, and frozen vegetables that had been microwaved to oblivion. Even by their landlady's abysmal standards, this set a new low, and Carole and the other two girls stared dumbly at their plates with fading appetite. It was also irritating because the three boys, staying in a nearby B&B were always telling the girls how good the food was in their place. (They only found out later that the boys had been lying; their food had been equally disgusting.)

It was therefore a meal that Carole only ate only because, after a day scrabbling around in mud and earth, she was hungry. But it sat heavily on her stomach, as did the apple pie that followed, that had similarly been cooked beyond redemption. They all watched TV for a while until Carole, her stomach still in uproar, went up to her room and swallowed indigestion tablets.

Try as she might, she couldn't sleep. She lay in her narrow bed, missing Rob, turning one way and then the other, and then lay on her back staring at the ceiling. Opening her curtains, she saw that it was a cloudless night with a panorama of stars from horizon to horizon. It was one of those clear night skies that she had only experienced in the far north of Scotland; an impossibly-huge sweep of stars, with Carole standing at the edge of the world So, she got dressed in her warmest clothes and crept down the stairs. She used her small torch to guide her along the upper hallway and down the stairs. From behind her landlady's door came the sound of contented snoring. At least someone enjoys their own cooking, thought Carole, soundlessly opening the front door and stepping out into the night, and another world.

Being so far north, in winter there are no proper days on Orkney; in summer, no proper nights. But, always, there is a quality to the light that you can almost taste; to Carole, it has always tasted of history and magic; a time of dragons and giants and, if you were lucky, a time to watch mermaids swimming in the shallows. The islands, barely scratched by their human inhabitants, are still a magical place.

She'd only gone outside to sit for a while on the wooden bench that sat outside her B&B. It was pushed up against the white-washed wall outside the kitchen and faced the sea. She sat still, marvelling at the sweep of stars, watched as a shooting star carved a brief path above her head, and breathed deeply, tasting the succulence of the night, listening to the call of some distant seabird. Then she stood up, filled with unexpected energy, and walked the few yards to the small road that passed her B&B. Here she stopped, debating whether to turn left or right; then, turning her face to the sea, climbed the small wall on the other side of the road.

The Stenness stones were only a thirty-minute walk away and she'd made that walk several times during the week. In this remotest of places, she liked the solitude: the wide-open spaces and the ancient and unforgiving landscape. Usually, she made the journey in the morning, after a breakfast of toast and marmalade. (The bacon and sausages, which she could have had, either looked dangerously undercooked or cremated. Their landlady didn't seem to have mastered a happy medium in anything.) Under a canopy of stars and washed by moonlight, it was an easy walk to make in Orkney's twilight night, although Carole also used her torch from time to time to pick her way around outcrops of rock.

She was on a rough pathway that took her over a low hill and down to the stones on the other side. It was a route that, presumably, had been carved by generations of cattlemen or other farmers. She liked to be walking on this centuries-old path, adding her footsteps to those who had come before her. It was cold, but invigorating, and a gusty wind was blowing in from the sea.

She reached the top of the hill and started on the downward slope, walking into the natural amphitheatre in which the stones have sat, solid and immovable for five millennia and more. In the semi-darkness they looked both welcoming and forbidding; a place of worship, but a place in which she didn't belong at dead of night. She walked to the centre of the site and looked around, sensing the history about her, almost hearing the voices of the long-dead people who once come here to worship or honour their dead or, like her, to simply feel the presence of the stones. For Carole it was always more than simply wanting to understand the ancient world; without written records, much of the Neolithic period will always remain unsolved. Rather, it was to understand what those ancients must have felt, standing within the symmetry of stones, protected from the world outside by the perfect alignment of slabs of rock. One tradition is that the circle was formed when an unwary horde of giants, dancing the night away, were caught unawares by the rising sun and turned to stone. It was a story which Carole could almost believe; that while magic may have drained away from the real world, it still existed in desolate and untouched places.

Carole half-closed her eyes, imagining the other stones, the ones now lost to the site, growing around her; the very act of creating them must have offered power: a perfect circle designed to amplify each chant or incantation and, with absolute precision, transmit that energy to the Sun, Moon and stars.

Then she walked to where Odin's stone would once have stood, separate and aloof, with its circular hole for young couples to declare their love for one another. Carole stood on the spot, mentally running her hands across the cold face of the stone, momentarily feeling like an intruder in a place where she didn't belong and then, imagining, pushed her hand through the hole.

A sudden gust of wind blew against her and she had to steady herself. The wind was in her ear and seemed to be whispering something. She listened but the words were indistinct; merely a sea breeze catching in her hair. She looked out to the sea, at grey-flecked waves; almost a mirror-image of the stars above.

Then, feeling less bloated from her landlady's evening meal, and energised by her walk to the stones, Carole walked back slowly, back up the hill and down the other side. She used her torch more often on this return trip; she had never walked back to her B&B, always too tired at the end of each long day in her trench to do anything other than climb into the back of the university minibus.

Her B&B was still in darkness when she arrived back and she crept up the stairs and into bed. This time she went immediately to sleep, dreaming of the stones and of stars. But she also dreamed of putting her hand through the circular hole in the Odin Stone, and of feeling a sudden gust of wind against her ear. But in her dream, she could hear the wind speaking to her in a clear and commanding masculine voice:

Search for me. Find me. Treasure me.

It's an unexpected memory, plucked from nowhere, reminding her again of the thrill of discovery. But it's an ambiguous memory, seemingly unconnected with her impossible meeting with Ray or with anything else that's happened. Once more, Carole can discern no pattern in anything she thinks, or in the things that are happening to her. Her last visit to Orkney was a lifetime ago, although she does wonder why she's never been back. It just seems like something else that she's turned her back on.

Fifteen

She drives home via the garden centre to choose something to plant on Granny's grave. She's decided on catmint, but the garden centre doesn't have any. This doesn't surprise her. If Carole goes to the supermarket, whatever she wants is the one item it won't have. If she's shopping for clothes, nothing she wants will be in her size. Then she goes to the supermarket which, remarkably, does have everything that she needs, buying groceries for that evening with Iona and Ray, and more provisions for the weekend. She also remembers to buy a leg of lamb for Sunday lunch, the day of Granny's funeral and, she reminds herself, her birthday. Her parents will also be coming to stay the night, as they sometimes do on special occasions. They rarely see Ray's parents who now live in a retirement home near Inverness; too far for regular contact, although Ray phones every week, and tries to visit once a month. They'll probably drive up, the three of them, sometime soon, with Iona sitting wordlessly in the back with her earphones on and playing computer games. Carole supposes that she's lucky to have parents on her doorstep, parents who are still relatively young and active, although the weekly Sunday lunch can sometimes feel like an imposition: an obligation to cook expansive meals when she'd rather be doing something else. But doing what exactly? Despite having no time to do anything, time also hangs heavy on Carole. She can go a whole day being busy and, in the evening, only remember that she did a bit of dusting and hoovering. But, she concedes, there's not a lot else in her life and the smallest of tasks can exponentially expand to fill the time available.

But maybe there will be more time now, she thinks, having composed her CV and emailed it to her old professor. Now that it was with him, and no doubt circulated to God knows who else, Carole's great fear is of rejection, which might still happen, having yet to make it to a shortlist, let alone an interview. She has, after all, been away from the faculty for fourteen years. A lifetime, really, although she has kept up with some of the research, good and bad.

But she's still happy, deciding that the visit to the pub and meeting Ray has been a good thing. Or maybe just a strange, but nice, dream brought about by malfunctioning electronics. She wonders again if she's gone mad: what would Ray or Iona say if she told them what's been happening to her? Most probably, a quiet recommendation to go and lie down while Ray phoned for the doctor. In their shoes, it's what she would do. In a way, it's what she'd done with Iona all those years ago, harassing doctor after doctor at their GP practice, until they all must have concluded she was delusional. Until, she reminds herself, one of them got so sick of her that he referred Iona to a specialist in Edinburgh.

She's jolted back to that time; of drips and injections, of tears and tantrums (not all of them Iona's) and of the crushing uncertainty of it all. It had overwhelmed her, turned her world upside down, made her reassess her place within their family, and the new priorities that Iona's illness had thrown up. And then, once Iona had recovered, there was always that lingering sense of doubt; that she, Carole, was now Iona's protector, emotionally unable to leave her side until the young Iona went to nursery and then primary school. But Carole was always there, a phone call away, always there if needed, and always there at the end of every school day, making sure that Iona's cheeks were still rosy, and worrying every time Iona sneezed or blew her nose. But isn't that what all mothers are supposed to do? she thinks;

a lioness protecting her cub, until the cub is old enough to leave home. She remembers her mother saying that you have to say goodbye to your children, but never had that chance with Tim, so that he was still hers. Had she said that only today? But Carole can understand it; Iona is now at an age when she's already spreading her wings. Sometimes Carole can almost hear them beat; the fledgling not quite able to fly, nearly but not quite. Soon enough it will be time for Carole to give Iona away, as her mother did with her, and all the way back down the generations, to a time when ancient peoples built stone circles, or when dancing giants were caught unawares by the rising sun.

It's a powerful thought; that Carole's role as a mother has been simply to make sure that her daughter can take that final step from the nest and fly. To also make sure that she has the skills and aptitude to fly somewhere sensible, and not flutter and fall. But is that enough now for Carole? To have simply defined herself as mother and protector; defining herself not by who she is, but by her relationship with her family, and particularly her daughter. She supposes not; not now that she has seen the past and present in a new perspective. A small part of her has changed; a stitch in her tapestry unpicked: a small shift of perspective. It's also making her think in new ways; not about who she was, or is, but also who she could become, or should have become already. The fledgling may not quite have flown the nest, but Iona is close to the edge, wings flapping, with adolescent eyes looking to the horizon. Maybe it's time, Carole thinks, that I did the same.

On some of the field expeditions that Carole went on, all they would find were pieces of pottery and, sometimes, lots of pieces that could be put back together like a jigsaw. It was a painstaking process, occasionally ending up with a complete beaker or pot, but more usually finding that pieces were missing. Carole always marvelled at the intricacy of the patterns on each pot: delicately carved with a fingernail or piece of bone or wood. Once she came upon a fingerprint, and it made her cry; the link between here and then suddenly overwhelming. But who were those designs made for, she used to wonder? For the maker, whose design it was, or the customer who may have asked for something specific? Was making a pot a solitary activity, or something more communal, binding families or communities together in a common activity?

Does Iona have my fingerprints all over her? Carole thinks, and supposes that she must have. A mother can't leave no trace of herself, and Iona's new-found key of wisdom has, in no small part, been given to her by her mother. It's a comforting thought, what with her mind being full of a jumble of other thoughts.

She remembers sitting in the faculty, with the table in front of her covered in pieces of pottery, trying to fit them together. A jigsaw, certainly, but without a picture to tell her what the finished beaker or pot should look like. In a sense, Carole thinks, that's what's happening to me now. But will she end up as something incomplete, a new version of herself but with pieces still missing? No, she decides, because she now has enough pieces to make sense of herself. She has been temporarily gifted Iona's key to all knowledge, and it's all now up to her.

Back home, groceries bought and catmint ordered, Carole finds Iona at the kitchen table and tapping away on her phone.

'You're home early,' she remarks to her daughter.

'It's Friday, Mum. School finishes at lunchtime on a Friday.'

Carole feels a little foolish to have forgotten this small fact. 'Of course, of course. How was school?'

'Boring,' her daughter replies, now looking at Carole's heavy shopping bags and no doubt concluding that carry-out pizza won't be on the menu tonight.

'Your dad's on his way back. Should be home this evening.'

'I know,' says Iona. 'He texted me.'

This always slightly unnerves Carole. Although Iona is also his daughter, and therefore deserves texts, Carole can't help but wonder what else Ray tells Iona; things, maybe, that he doesn't tell her. But it's a ridiculous thought, and she knows it, and pushes it away, just as Iona pushes back her chair and escapes upstairs to her room.

Carole unpacks her shopping, and lays the mussel shell picture from her mother on the kitchen table, and stands back to admire it. Away from BESPOKE ARTS, it looks small and insignificant and Carole wonders where she can possibly hang it. It's also not the kind of art that Ray likes, not that he really likes any art. If anything, he prefers sweeping landscapes, or pictures of birds in flight; he doesn't much like miniature simplicity, and certainly won't like Carole's latest acquisition. It would have to be hung in their spare bedroom, she decides, a place to which Ray has little need to venture, and so, perhaps, will never see.

Pleased with this decision, she starts to chop onions and big pieces of chicken into smaller pieces. She's going to cook curry, with samosas, onion bhajis and naan bread (bought from the deli counter: Carole knows her culinary limitations) which both Ray and Iona enjoy, although she's never been one for curry and will mostly eat rice and a samosa.

But it's been a strange and emotionally tiring day and she finds it difficult to concentrate, nearly cutting her fingers on several occasions. Chopping onions and chicken is something that Iona could have done, if Carole had ever given her the chance, but – as the designated cook in the house – it's a task for Carole alone, despite fatigue and the unnerving feeling that she's missed something from the day's events.

167

It's not a feeling that she can pin down and, distracted, she barely notices that Iona has come back into the kitchen and is pouring herself a glass of Coke from the fridge.

'Mum, what is it with you and mussel shells?' Iona is looking at the small picture on the kitchen table.

Carole turns from the chopping board. 'Do you like it?'

Iona doesn't reply which signifies that she doesn't like it.

'Your granny gave it to me as a birthday present.'

'Why?'

'Maybe because it's my birthday on Sunday?' Carole suggests.

Iona is slurping from her glass, looking intently at the picture. 'How do you know this guy?'

'What guy?'

'The painter.'

'The artist? I don't know him.'

'So how come he's painted *your* mussel shell?'

Carole puts down her knife and comes to stand by her daughter and, together, they look at the picture.

'It's just a mussel shell, darling. All mussel shells look the same.'

Iona isn't convinced. 'But if you don't know the guy who painted it, how come he got into our house?'

'What do you mean?'

Iona reaches down and moves the picture a little to the left and turns it slightly. 'Because he painted it on our table, that's what.'

Carole peers more closely and, sure enough, the mussel picture *was* painted on their kitchen table, or a representation of it. Top left, there's a faint red stain: the aftermath of a red wine accident, not fully cleaned up. Bottom right, there's a scoring in the wood, where a sharp knife was accidentally dropped on Iona's birthday last year. Carole looks from the picture to their table and back again, feeling slightly nauseous.

'Coincidence,' says Carole brightly.

'Hardly coincidence, Mum.'

'Look, darling, I don't know the painter, I've never met the painter, and he's never been in our house, okay?' Carole has said this rather loudly, not meaning to, and Iona looks at her sharply.

'Whatever.' Iona shrugs and retreats back up the stairs to her room. Carole hears Iona's bedroom door closing.

Carole sits heavily at the table and stares at her mussel shell picture. Was it like this in her mother's shop? Or has the picture changed since she got it home? But Carole is also acutely aware that, until now, the madnesses going on around her have only been seen and felt by her. Now that Iona has seen the picture, and its mirror-image depiction of their kitchen table, the contagion seems to have spread.

*

Ray arrives back a little before seven, looking tired. His eyes are red and the bags under his eyes seem more pronounced. He drops his suitcase and briefcase in the hall, and goes to give Carole a kiss on the cheek, and is surprised when Carole puts her arms around him and pulls him close. She doesn't want to let him go, to have her sat nav lady say that it's time to go.

'I've missed you,' she says, nuzzling into him. 'I've had a hellish week.'

Ray pulls back from her, unused to such bold displays of affection. 'Is it the dripping tap?'

Carole shakes her head. 'No, that seems to have fixed itself. Divine intervention, perhaps.'

'Then what's the matter?' he asks.

Carole sighs, holding him tight. 'Nothing important,' she says. 'Nothing important.'

'In which case,' says Ray, pulling himself clear, 'it's

probably time that we both had a drink. God, I hate flying! A crying baby in front of me and another crying baby behind me. Do you think I could ask British Airways for a refund?' He pours out two generous glasses of white wine and hands one to Carole.

'Actually,' he says, 'you do look a bit peaky.'

'Peaky? What's that supposed to mean?'

Ray puffs out his cheeks. 'A bit frazzled, that's all. Actually, you were looking a bit peaky before I left. Now you're looking a bit peakier.'

Carole resists the urge to put her arms around him again, wondering where her sudden affection has come from. She looks at him more closely, remembering the younger Ray she met only a few hours before. He still looks much the same; the same lips and smile, and the same eyes, although slightly dulled with fatigue. He's smiling now, although looking a little unsure: overt displays of marital affection from Carole are rare and, he's probably thinking that it means she's done something awful and is only slowly building up to tell him. It wouldn't be the first time.

But the added years do suit him, she decides; he has a few grey hairs and a few more lines on his face. He's older, that's all, and the passage of years simply lends him gravitas and an air of responsibility, although Ray has always been the most responsible of people. Okay, a few unwanted pounds around the middle but, she reminds herself, who isn't guilty of that small misdemeanour?

'Peakier isn't a word,' she says, 'and you look knackered. Anyway, how was the Big Apple?'

'Lots of meetings, lots of people to meet. Actually, it was mostly a waste of time.'

Carole knows that lots of sitting around and meeting people isn't in his nature. 'So why did the bank send you?' she asks.

'Because we have policies to agree, that sort of thing.

Quite why it couldn't have been done by email or over the phone, I don't know.'

'And did your secretary like New York?' she asks, eyebrows raised.

'Carole, I don't have a secretary. You know that.'

'But you weren't alone, I assume?' Carole is only half-joking, thinking back to spa hotels.

'No, bankers are like the police. We always go in pairs. If you must know, I was with Simon McGuire. If you remember, you met him at that ghastly office party last year.'

Carole does have a vague memory of meeting Simon McGuire. It was indeed a ghastly affair, held in a swish Edinburgh hotel, and intended to team bond Ray's loans department with everyone's families. It had mostly involved standing around and making small talk with people who Carole knew she'd never see again, and who she didn't want to see again, and who probably didn't want to see her again.

'Small chap, red hair, red beard.'

'The very same,' says Ray, extracting the wine bottle from the fridge and refilling their glasses, 'although he's shaved off the beard. He now only has a rather fetching red moustache, or so he likes to believe.'

They're interrupted by Iona who has appeared at the kitchen door. She's wearing giant earphones and, by the sudden look of surprise on her face, clearly didn't know her father was home.

Ray gives Iona a big squeeze and lifts her off her feet, with Iona squealing like a small child. Ray has that effect on her; while Iona is all grown-up in Carole's presence, she can immediately revert to childhood with Ray.

'I have gifts!' he announces, fetching his suitcase from the hallway. For Iona, an *I Love New York* T-shirt and a computer game that she's been dropping hints about for weeks; for Carole, a small bottle of perfume that Ray says was made from unicorn tears, or something equally rare and expensive. 'If you don't like it, just give it to your mother,' he advises.

'Or me!' Iona pipes up, who has begun experimenting with makeup when she thinks that Carole won't notice. Carole is again reminded of her fledgling standing at the edge of the nest, testing out her wings, and anticipating that first step from the safety of home and family. A tentative first step but one, no doubt, she would do with immaculate makeup. It's a thought that makes Carole momentarily sad, but also a little happy because Iona has been allowed to grow up, in no small part due to Carole's fierce doggedness. She clearly remembers all those visits to the GP surgery. She remembers shouting at one particularly self-satisfied GP that mothers have an instinct for illness, only to be told that GPs actually have the training to spot it. After the real diagnosis, and on another trip to the surgery, that particular GP had the good grace to look embarrassed, although not to actually apologise. For Carole, it had been a small victory.

'Anyway, I haven't seen you wearing that for a while,' says Ray, after Iona has retreated back upstairs, no doubt to start playing her new computer game.

'This? It's just an old jumper.'

He taps his chest. 'The brooch, Carole.'

She looks down. Her silver and sapphire Luckenbooth that has always lived, or used to live, in the childhood treasures box that she keeps at the back of her wardrobe is now pinned to her jersey. The sapphire and the silver brooch have joined themselves together, and the brooch seems cleaned and polished.

'I don't think you've worn it since the first time we met.' For some reason, he's looking a little disappointed.

'I haven't?' she echoes, not quite sure what else to say. She hopes that she isn't looking too astonished, or panic-stricken, although the floor under her seems to be swaying as if she was on a boat. She has *never* worn the brooch, because

172

she's never been able to. When she dug it up, in her clearing in the woods, the clasp was broken; so too the mount into which the sapphire slotted. It had always remained two separate treasures which, much later, she'd thought about restoring several times, but had always decided it would be inappropriate. It was someone else's Luckenbooth, given in love for good luck. It had never been hers to wear, except that she now was wearing it, and was once more finding it hard to breathe.

'That evening in the pub?' he continues. 'I came in, you dropped your drink and I assumed you were a derelict student.'

'So?' she manages to squeak.

'Then I saw your brooch, which seemed far too nice for a derelict to be wearing, so I then assumed you might only be a semi-derelict student and introduced myself.'

Carole sits on a kitchen chair, taking deep breaths. 'Then you bought me a drink,' she manages. She tries to think back all those years, to their first meeting. But she couldn't have been wearing it because it's always, always, been in bits.

'Stupid of me, I know, given everything that happened afterwards.' He smiles, but a little sadly she thinks. 'Still, nice to see that you're wearing it again.'

Ray goes off to change and unpack, leaving Carole and the distant past both sitting at the kitchen table. She runs a finger over her brooch, tracing its outline, remembering how she'd found it, and the mad professor in Edinburgh who had explained what it was.

Oh God, she says inwardly. Not you as well.

Sixteen

In the kitchen, with husband and daughter upstairs, it takes Carole a large brandy to regain her composure. It seems that more and more things are taking on a life of their own, and she looks suspiciously at the cooker before daring to turn it on, in case the cooker might take that as a conversational invitation, or turn into something else. Her Alexa is still firmly switched off and unplugged.

But, having drunk the brandy, and once she's decided that the cooker is safely inanimate, and does turn it on, Carole then cooks supper.

The chicken curry satisfies everyone, crunching their way through poppadums and samosas, with only a few drops of blood from a cut finger, as well as a second bottle of wine.

Iona only once demands to know if any of their meal has come from the deep freeze, and is reassured by Carole saying that she bought everything today. She omits to mention that the chicken breasts did come from the deep freeze, a day previously, but from two shelves above Granny than therefore, she presumes, too far distant for the transmission of dead cat disease, or whatever Iona is worried about. Ray hasn't much to say about New York because he didn't get out much, being stuck in meetings and presentations. Iona doesn't have much to say either, having been at school all week. Carole, who has had the most spectacular week of anybody's life, also says very little.

It's not until the end of the meal when Carole is clearing up plates and Ray is soaking pans in the sink that Iona asks,

'Mum, have you shown Dad your gross picture?'

Ray turns off the tap. 'Have you?' he asks Carole.

'I was waiting for an appropriate moment,' she replies, touching her brooch for good luck or just to confirm that the latest insanity is still pinned to her jersey. 'Anyway, it's not gross. My mother gave it to me,' she adds.

'Dad, it's hideous and spooky. Mum, where is it?'

Iona retrieves the picture from the cupboard under the stairs, an out-of-the way place filled with household items such as cleaning fluids and the hoover, and therefore somewhere that Ray wouldn't normally venture. She's still planning to hang it up in the spare bedroom the next morning, but without telling anybody. Carole sighs, outmanoeuvred by her daughter, and by events she seems powerless to control.

Iona plonks the picture down on the kitchen table and stands back. She gestures to it rather triumphantly. 'There! Utterly gross!'

'It's a mussel shell,' says Ray after a few moments. 'Maybe not the most appealing of pictures, but—'

'Look at the table, Dad!'

There is a small silence. 'Your mother gave this to you?'

'In case anybody is interested, it's my birthday on Sunday. Yes, Ray, my mother gave it to me.'

Iona sighs loudly. 'Look at this bit, Dad. This is where you dropped a knife, remember?' She points to a scar on the table in the picture, then at the same scar on their kitchen table. Iona moves her finger. 'This is a wine slop from when Mum was drunk.'

'I was nothing of the kind!' protests Carole. 'Well, maybe a little bit,' she relents, remembering a raucous dinner party, but not remembering who they'd invited.

'It's the same table!' says Iona loudly. 'We're being stalked by a painter!'

'I hardly think so, darling,' says Carole, and tries to laugh.

175

'Then how do you explain it?' asks Iona.

'Coincidence and claptrap,' says Carole, more firmly than she feels. 'Lots of tables have stains and marks on them.'

'Your mother didn't paint it, did she?' asks Ray, who is still looking at the mussel painting but, Carole is relieved to see, also seems amused.

'No, of course not.'

'Your father?'

'Now you're being ridiculous! My father's never painted anything in his life. Well, their downstairs hall, which doesn't really count … *and* they had to get someone in to repaint it properly.'

Ray picks up the painting and takes it to the window. He looks at it from a variety of angles, even upside down, giving a fairly good impression of an art expert about to give his verdict on a potential Rembrandt. 'It's not a very nice picture,' he says at length.

'Mum has a thing about mussel shells.'

'Does she?' asks Ray. 'Do you?' he asks Carole.

'No, I do not have a *thing* about mussel shells,' she replies. 'I merely keep one on the living room mantlepiece for good luck.'

There is a small silence. 'As one does,' says Iona.

'Listen,' says Carole, 'I agree that the picture does, sort of, depict a mussel shell on what, sort of, *could* be our table. But it isn't our table because *nobody* has been in our house to paint it, okay?'

There is another small silence. 'You keep a mussel shell on the mantlepiece?' asks Ray. 'How long has that been there?'

'Since we first moved here.'

'Good gracious! Why?'

'I found it on the first dig I went on.'

'All that time,' says Ray, 'and I never noticed.'

Iona again sighs loudly. 'Well I think it's utterly gross!

176

It's also freaking me out a little bit.'

'Only a little bit?' asks Carole. She catches Ray's eye. He's trying not to laugh.

'Please, Mum, give it to a charity shop! Maybe just burn it.'

'My mother gave it to me,' Carole reminds her. 'She'll be offended if we don't hang it somewhere.'

'Then hang it somewhere out of sight. In the garage, maybe. Even better, in someone else's garage.'

'I was thinking just here might be nice,' says Carole, indicating a spot right beside the kitchen table, 'so that we can look at it all the time.' Ray is still trying not to laugh.

'Whatever,' says Iona and stomps off to her room to listen to music or play her new game; something about ridding the world of vampires or zombies. Carole sometimes wonders why computer games are so violent: does it encourage violence in those who play them, or act as a beneficial release valve? She doesn't know.

'It does look a bit like our table,' says Ray when they're alone.

'Don't you start!'

'Anyway, I'm going to bed. Long flight, jet lag and crying babies.' He kisses her on the cheek.

Carole sits alone at the kitchen table for a while, alternately looking at the mussel shell picture and fingering the silver brooch. She wonders again who might have bought the brooch, and who he had given it to. Luckenbooths were always bought by men, usually given as a betrothal or wedding gift. Sometimes they were worn by nursing mothers to help their milk flow; it was also sometimes called a witch-brooch because it saved children from the evil eye. She remembers the mad professor telling her all this, and also saying how strange it must feel to have dug up someone else's love after such a long time. It's the reason why she's never had it restored. It was never hers to wear, but was

177

always part of the reason she studied archaeology.

'Alexa, do you like my new picture?' she asks.

Silence.

'Alexa, do you like my brooch?

More silence. Her Alexa, still switched off at the mains, perhaps now understood that it required electricity to function.

Then she too goes to bed, and climbs in beside Ray and puts an arm over his back, snuggling in close. He's had a shower and smells warm and clean and soapy. Then, unexpectedly, he turns to face her and they kiss, his arms now around her. They make love slowly and languidly.

Afterwards, Ray says, 'It's been a while since we did that.'

'Too long,' she replies. 'Then again, I've been a bit peaky, remember?'

'Peaky and peakier.'

'I still refuse to believe that peakier is a real word.'

She hasn't told him about her chance meeting with her old professor and that, maybe, her role as housewife may be coming to an end. After so many years, she doesn't know what he'll feel about that. She supposes he'll be happy for her, because Ray has always been supportive. But it's not something that she wants to discuss, not now, what with other things going on.

They sleep in each other's arms, which they also haven't done for a long time, and Carole dreams about her day, and of meeting the younger Ray. She can't remember wearing the silver brooch back then, and couldn't have done because it had always been broken. Then she sits bolt upright, her breath coming in short gasps.

She's remembered something, and that the meeting with Ray today must have happened. When she first met him, all those years ago, they hadn't exchanged phone numbers. She *knows* this, because she'd kicked herself about it afterwards.

It's the one clear memory she has of that first encounter. She'd wanted to give him her number, but felt that he should be the one to make the first move. If he'd wanted to see her again, so she thought, he would have asked for her number. This time, having been told to leave the pub by her sat nav lady, she *had* made sure that he had her phone number.

But more than that. She had *chosen* to give him her phone number. After all these years of marriage, she had chosen again to choose him.

She had somehow gone back in time and rewritten her past and, by rewriting her past, written her present. She clearly remembers each trip she and Ray later took to cinemas, theatres and restaurants. She can remember laughing at the same things and holding hands. She can remember going to restaurants, and what she ate. She can remember introducing him to Luigi, and Luigi looking disappointed, as if winking at her over his pepper grinder had been more than just casual flirtation. She can remember introducing him to her parents. She can remember their first kiss, and nervously meeting his parents. Although she can't remember Ray's initial phone call, he must have phoned because he's right beside her now, and Iona is in the next bedroom saving the world from the undead.

She had *chosen* to give him her phone number because, she realises almost with surprise, she loves her husband and always has done and, maybe subconsciously in the pub earlier, had wanted their life together to actually happen.

Seventeen

Saturday morning, and Carole is a woman possessed. She's filled with a fierce optimism and bubbles and fizzes with energy. Her anxieties have disappeared; in their place is a sense of being remoulded, like a clay pot, but a clay pot with all its pieces that she, Carole, is painstakingly fitting together. It's not a feeling that she can put into words, and nor does she want to; what this week has taught her is merely to accept the unexpected, because everything will eventually make sense.

Then, putting all this new-found energy to good use, she makes Ray a bacon roll, and takes it to him on a tray with a cup of (real) coffee and glass of orange juice. Ray smiles at her, rubbing sleep from his eyes, and kisses her lightly on the cheek.

'You really must have missed me,' he says, looking at the tray.

'Just don't take breakfast in bed for granted. Anyway, I'm off to Edinburgh,' she informs him.

'Edinburgh?'

'It's a city, Ray, just west of here. It's where we lived for a while. Come to think of it, it's also where you work, when you're not in New York.'

'I was really asking *why* you're going to Edinburgh. Not, of course, that I will be remotely interested in your answer.'

She kisses him on top of his head. She avoids his mouth; there's a smudge of tomato sauce on his upper lip. 'I'm on a mission.'

'Ah, a mission. Could I ask what kind of a mission?'

'A secret mission,' she replies.

'Then good luck.'

From the moment she woke up, she's had a compelling urge to drive into Edinburgh. It's an urge so forceful that it's like the sat nav has been speaking to her, although it's not until she's on the main road into Edinburgh that she knows where she's headed.

Treasure me. The two words that had popped into her head when she woke up.

It's a route that she's taken many times before, so she doesn't use the sat nav. In any case, the sat nav lady could take her anywhere, and she has no desire to meet anybody else from her past. But she also misses the companionship of the sat nav lady, and wonders if they might get back on proper speaking terms again. They were friends, she thinks, or maybe just acquaintances, despite the sat nav lady not actually being real. She misses being told to turn left; she misses being told what exit to take off a roundabout: she misses being told what to do, rather than having to think of left or right turns for herself.

On the city bypass there's an overhead gantry with a sign covered in lots of little lightbulbs. Usually the little lights are to warn her of roadworks, which her sat nav may also have warned her about. Sometimes the sign says CHECK YOUR FUEL. For what, Carole would think? Alien lifeforms? The meaning of life? Or it sometimes says DON'T TAKE DRUGS AND DRIVE. Does paracetamol count? she would think. She approaches the illuminated sign with some trepidation, thinking that it might be in league with her sat nav lady. But her sat nav lady has been quiet all the way into Edinburgh, and has perhaps gone back to sleep after a night of passion, one arm draped across her lover and a half-full ashtray beside her bed. The sign, unusually for something so bossy, is blank. Carole accelerates past.

The sign both depresses and irritates her. While the

roadworks information can, she concedes, be useful, its other exhortations are generally nannying and patronising. WINTER WEATHER EXPECTED. DRIVE WITH CAUTION. Well, who wouldn't? CHECK YOUR TYRES. Again, for what? To check that the car still has four of them? Carole doesn't like to be told what to do or think, except by her sat nav, and metes out advice only in small portions, usually only to Iona, who doesn't usually pay much attention.

She only now advises her mother not to smoke, which her mother also chooses to ignore. The first time that Carole told her that smoking was dangerous, her mother agreed and told her a story about driving to Glasgow years before, and lighting a cigarette with a match, which she then dropped onto her lap, nearly setting herself on fire and almost crashing. *I therefore know how dangerous smoking can be*, her mother had concluded, completely missing Carole's point, probably intentionally.

In the city itself, there are traffic jams everywhere, with half of Edinburgh on the move, doing things that Carole can only guess at, although she is in no hurry. The pavements are also full of people, many laden with shopping bags, although perhaps not filled with gifts for Carole's birthday. Amazingly, she finds a parking space just outside the National Museum of Scotland, puts money in the meter, and goes inside. She only briefly considers why she's come here, when she has a funeral to prepare for, let alone a dead cat to defrost. But the urge to come into the city was too persuasive; an overwhelming sense that it was something that she had to do.

It's an impressive entrance, a giant atrium over several floors, dominated by a T-Rex skeleton; a scary welcome for young visitors, and a reminder that history can be counted in the hundreds of millions of years. In other parts of the museum are galleries devoted to the Egyptians, and artefacts from Asia. There are old aeroplanes and whales hanging from ceilings, and all telling an interwoven story of the history of the world and Scotland's place in that story. There are also galleries exploring Earth's place in the universe, and the geological forces that are constantly shaping and reshaping our planet. Carole has spent many days there, lost in the history it tells, and the human stories it weaves into the telling of it because, she thinks, that's what history really is: the stories we make for ourselves, and the stories we leave behind for future generations to discover.

But Carole isn't there to visit those galleries, although she has done many times. She's here to visit the Early People gallery, centred on the artefacts that have so far been discovered across Scotland, and telling the incomplete story of Scotland's early history and the Neolithic Stone Age. In this gallery are intricately carved carnyx and gold torcs, stones carved with sophisticated artistry and symbolism and, of course, her gold axe-head. It's in a glass cabinet, along with intact beakers and pots and pieces of jewellery. But her axe-head is still front and centre of the cabinet, with a brief description on a piece of white card. *Neolithic gold ceremonial axe-head, probably 5,000 years old, and discovered at the Stones of Stenness on Orkney. The gold was probably mined in the north of Scotland. Its fine decoration demonstrates the remarkable craftsmanship of these early people.* In smaller letters, the inscribed card also tells visitors when it was discovered, and that the discovery was made by a team from the University of Edinburgh's archaeology department. Carole is always amused by this; the rest of the team had discovered nothing of value all week.

Carole is pleased that it's still the star of the show, and that newer discoveries in other nearby cabinets have yet to match or excel her own piece of treasure.

Search for me. Find me. Treasure me.

Carole touches the heavy glass of the axe-head's cabinet, as if trying to form a bond with it, when she's startled by a loud voice behind her.

'Carole! Good gracious! Thought it was you!'

It's her old professor, dressed in tweeds and incongruously wearing a Panama hat. 'David, what a surprise!' says Carole, although nothing surprises her anymore.

'I thought I saw you come in and guessed that, if it was you, I'd find you here.' He doffs his hat, which makes Carole smile.

'David, nobody wears a Panama at this time of year.'

He leans towards her. 'That's *exactly* why I'm wearing it. Now that I'm an *emeritus* professor, I'm cultivating an air of eccentricity. In summer, I'll wear something equally inappropriate like a diving helmet or baseball cap.'

'It's good to see you again,' says Carole.

'Coincidental and fortuitous.'

'Certainly coincidental,' agrees Carole. 'What brings you here?'

'To deliver some notes,' he informs her. 'Some Byzantine stuff has just come in and the museum wanted my thoughts, such as they are. Rather second-rate pieces, I had to tell them, which hasn't pleased the curator. Nice fellow, when he's not being given bad news. Do you come here often?' he asks with a wink, and removes his Panama hat. 'Come to admire your treasure, have you?'

Carole is glad that he's called her axe-head *treasure*, because that's what it is, and always has been to her. She's also flattered that he called it *her* treasure, as if giving her possession of it.

'Only sometimes,' she replies. 'Mainly to see if anything else has taken its place.'

'Don't be silly, Carole. Your axe-head is the finest example of its kind yet discovered.' He seems to mean this and, again, Carole is flattered. 'You are, however, looking pensive.'

'Pensive?'

'As if there's something on your mind. Pensive pretty much sums it up.'

Carole bites her lip then gestures to the axe-head. 'It's just that I've been thinking, David.' She then can't think of anything to say.

'Thinking is good,' he prompts.

'What most people don't understand is how complex a process was involved in making this,' she blurts out, wondering what she's doing in the museum, staring at an axe-head she's stared at many times before. She also wonders why she now seems to be lecturing him. David might have been the department's Middle East specialist, but he knows a thing or two about the Scottish Neolithic period. After all, it's the part of Scottish history that outclasses the rest of the UK. Orkney first, Stonehenge much later. It's therefore a subject that David had to know something about, if not teach. She ploughs on. 'It required crucibles and clay moulds, lots of different tools, and the skill to make liquid metal.' She looks fondly at her axe-head wondering, as always, whose hands first held it.

'Is that why you're looking pensive?'

She shakes her head. 'Anyway, David, you said that our meeting was fortuitous. Could I ask why?'

'Because I have a question to ask,' he replies.

'Then ask away.'

'How much do you want this job, Carole? I mean, really want it.'

She takes a deep breath. 'I now want it more than anything,' she replies, surprised by the firmness in her tone. Yes, a week ago she would have been uncertain; too rooted in her role as mother and housewife, and feeling that her old job was just that: something old that couldn't be recaptured.

'That's what I wanted to hear' – he leans in closer again and Carole can feel his breath against her cheek – 'because I've put you on the shortlist.'

'Good gracious!' Things are moving faster than Carole had expected.

'You will of course receive notification in the post,' says David, reverting to formality. 'Interviews still in a few weeks, so I'm told, although that doesn't mean a great deal. What I'm told will happen, and what actually does happen are often two different things. Sometimes they forget that I actually chair the appointments board. Interviews could be anytime, quite frankly.'

'I'm flattered,' says Carole, whose heart is beating a little faster.

'Don't be. Remember, I get to choose the shortlist. The other candidates are therefore only there to make up numbers. Utterly useless, the lot of them.'

'I'm sure they're not, David.'

'Well, maybe a couple of them are sort of okay, but no more than that. It's just that I would hate to have you on the shortlist if you really weren't too sure about the job. It would make me look a bit silly, frankly.'

'Yes, David, I would like the job.'

'It would be a wrench, I expect, having to get up early every morning.' He's again winking, one eyebrow raised.

'I get up early every morning.'

'Carole, the department needs someone like you, and you're the only person who is remotely like you, if you get my drift. What I'm trying to find out is whether I'm making a mistake.'

'Trust me, David. I do want the job.'

'Then let me give you a bit of advice. At the interview, try not to dribble or talk gibberish.'

'I'll certainly try.' She thinks for a few moments. 'Is that what I used to do?'

'Not that I can remember, no. I just can't think of any other good bits of advice, that's all.' He leans in very close, and almost whispers in her ear. 'Then the job is as good as yours, although I shouldn't say so, of course.'

Carole smiles again, her heart beating even faster, feeling once more that the axis of her life has slipped; that while her life might still be bound in her past, her past is inexorably linked to the present, and what she does now will influence what happens in her future.

They're interrupted by a party of Asian tourists draped in cameras and speaking in Chinese, or Korean, or Japanese, or something else entirely. They look into various cabinets but don't seem very interested. Carole has to concede that the Early People gallery isn't very interesting, except to the initiated. There are no aeroplanes hanging from the ceiling, or audio-visual displays of dinosaurs lolloping across open plains. The tourist party moves off taking surreptitious photographs as they go, strictly against museum rules.

'You're looking pensive again.'

'Then let me tell you a theory,' she replies.

'All ears, as always.' He touches one of his for emphasis.

Carole gestures to the glass cabinet. 'It's always been assumed that the axe-head was accidentally lost, right?'

'I did agree with that supposition at the time,' he says. 'Keith Bridges ... sorry, *Professor* Bridges was adamant that there was nothing else to find.'

'But think of all the skills that it took to make it. All those crucibles and moulds. Now take a closer look, David. Look at its decoration. Look at the craftsmanship. This isn't something that someone accidentally loses. Or intentionally loses, for that matter. It would have been, back then, an object of great value.'

'It still is,' he reminds her.

'Being gold, an object of great value *and* status. Maybe even a symbol of authority. So, what happens when this very important person realises that he's dropped it?'

David doesn't say anything, but his lips are pursed. 'I suspect that you're about to tell me.'

187

She goes on. 'The first thing that would happen is that this very important someone would go and look for it, stands to reason. After all, possibly, the axe might be his source of authority. Without it, maybe he's just another nobody. He therefore and absolutely has to find it. And then, if he can't find it, the whole community would be roped in as a search party. The axe would have been found.'

'You have an alternative theory, I assume?'

'It's just something that's been bothering me for a long time, that's all. Actually, mainly in the last few days,' admits Carole. The madnesses have also made her think again like the archaeologist she once was. 'I just don't believe that his axe could have been lost accidentally.' She takes a deep breath. 'I think there might be something more, underneath where this was found.' She gestures to her axe-head.

'Something more?' David is intrigued, both eyebrows raised.

'Maybe a burial chamber.'

David now looks sceptical. 'But surely the site was mapped out before you started digging?'

'Of course, of course.' It had become standard archaeological practice to use radar at all their sites, helping the team establish where to look. 'But the ground at Stenness is all large rock formations and stones. Easy enough for even the ancient people who lived there to excavate underneath, create a chamber of some sort, and cover it over with rock and stone.'

'But the geophysics, Carole …'

Carole gestures again to her axe-head, realising how much she still thinks of it as *hers* and not the university team's nor, now that it's in the national museum, as the nation's. 'But what would it have showed up, David? Just rock and more rock. In any case, ground radar didn't pick up on the axe-head, did it?'

David nods slowly. 'What you're saying is that, over the

millennia, the axe-head became detached from the rest of what might still be down there?'

'Exactly! We know that the area has been prone to major geological shifts. So, why not a burial chamber? Of course, it might be something more than that.'

'Something more?'

'Maybe the community felt threatened. Armed migrants from the mainland, perhaps. We know that the period saw great shifts in population. Maybe the community buried all its valuables for safekeeping, but for some reason never unburied them. Maybe that's when the inhabitants of Skara Brae also upped and left.'

'It sounds fanciful,' he says.

'Does it?

'Well, maybe not fanciful, but a bit like putting two and two together and getting—'

'Four,' says Carole, and there's a tone of certainty in her voice which makes David pause and nod. 'After all, think of Howard Carter.' This is a bit of an underhand jibe, and David knows it; Howard Carter, the discoverer of Tutankhamun's tomb who had so very nearly given up on his quest, with everyone saying that everything of the pharaohs had been discovered and he was wasting his time.

'I take it that you think we should go back there and have a better look.'

'It's just a thought, David.'

He rubs his chin, looking neither convinced nor unconvinced. 'I did say that our meeting today was fortuitous,' he says eventually.

'I could, of course, be completely wrong,' she replies, looking again at *her* axe-head.

'At least it's something to regale the interview panel with. That and your theories on the alignment of Orkney's standing stones. Equinox and solstice, and all that.' He looks at his watch and jumps to attention. 'My goodness! Is that the time! Sorry, Carole, things to do, people to meet, that sort of thing.'

'Then it was good to see you again, David.'

He replaces his ridiculous Panama hat, doffs it, turns to leave, then stops. He looks at her, eyebrows raised again. 'Just no dribbling, okay?'

'Or talking gibberish,' she adds.

'That too,' he agrees.

'Meeting you feels like a very strange birthday present.'

'Is it your birthday?'

'Tomorrow.'

'In which case, happy birthday,' he says, and is off, his loping stride taking him with surprising speed from the gallery.

She looks again at the axe-head, at its craftsmanship. On its blade is a perfect hole, a decorative and precise circle; the perfect embellishment for a ceremonial gold axe to be held in a stone circle. Then, as now, it probably represented the infinite, eternity, timelessness and the cyclical movement of the universe; it would have symbolized the perpetual movement of everything, the circle of the zodiac, the great rhythms of the stars. Every point on the circumference of a circle is the same distance from its centre.

Carole touches the glass cabinet one last time and says a private goodbye.

Eighteen

Leaving the museum, Carole has other tasks to perform, but she decides instead to procrastinate. She's done rather a lot of that over recent years, so a little more won't matter. She stands outside the museum for some minutes, watching the lines of tourists snake in, and wonders how many of them will visit the Early People gallery, and how many of them will pause to look at her axe-head. Not many, she readily admits, because small implements can't compete with dinosaurs or aeroplanes hanging from the ceiling. She then walks past the National Library to the Royal Mile, Edinburgh's original High Street that joins the Castle with the Palace of Holyroodhouse. Despite history oozing from every stone, it's mostly a street that now only sells things of interest to visitors, of which there are a great many filling the street. You can still buy a suit, so long as it's in tartan; or food, so long as it's shortbread or haggis in a tin; or bottles of alcohol, so long as it's whisky. Some tourists are strolling hand in hand, others in family groups. There is also a party of Asian tourists and Carole recognises them from the museum. She wonders if any of them took a photograph of her axe-head, and whether it'll be shown to family or friends, and whether any of them will marvel at its craftsmanship, or be remotely interested.

For no very good reason, or for one very good reason, Carole has come to St Giles Cathedral, the mother church of world Presbyterianism, although you wouldn't immediately think so. Unlike other cathedrals, with their delicate spires and soaring windows, St Giles has a solidity to it. It doesn't

191

aspire to mimic God's majesty, or to reach towards the skies. It doesn't offer architectural metaphors for the faithful; St Giles is rooted to the earth: a reminder that we're human, and shouldn't be silly and have grand aspirations.

Carole sometimes came to the cathedral when Iona was ill, sitting quietly with her thoughts, always choosing the quietest spot she could, and she remembers that bleak time, and briefly considers going inside the church, but decides against. A minister once came up to her and asked if she was okay. He'd seen her before, he explained. To her embarrassment, she'd been crying. No, she was fine, she told him, but never went back again. Next to St Giles are the country's High Courts, God and mammon side by side. But once the area would have been filled with stalls and workshops selling jewellery and trinkets. They were the city's first proper shops, where silversmiths plied their trade. The stalls were called Luckenbooths and it was here, nowhere else, that Carole's brooch would have been bought. The young man who bought it would have experienced a different Edinburgh, a jumble of small stalls, and among the babble and filth, he would have searched out and found *his* Luckenbooth. *Their* Luckenbooth. Not just a random choice, but a perfect choice. A brooch to be searched for and found, and then treasured. Maybe the young man was rich and could easily have afforded the brooch. But Carole doesn't think so, because she thinks she knows who bought it, and who it was given to because, around their old home outside North Berwick there were no grand houses; only their modest house and small cottages nearby. He would have been a farm labourer, Carole has decided: someone living nearby. Maybe she also worked close by: a milk-maid or weaver. The clearing in the woods would have been their secret place, as it had been her secret place. The brooch is still pinned to her jersey, and she fingers its outline: two hearts joined together: an eternal reminder that, like a circle, love has no beginning or end.

Then she retraces her steps, drives to North Berwick and, once again, visits Tim's grave. The flowers she laid only days before are still there, looking just a little jaded; she decides to leave them where they are. She looks nervously to the empty plot next to Tim's, but it's just grass. She doesn't know what to say to him, or whether he would hear her, so she says nothing and, head bowed, just stands for a few minutes.

She remembers the last time they were out together, riding into North Berwick from their small house. It was a strange day because it was usually Tim who made it into the town long before her. That day, she was the winner by some distance, with Tim looking a little ashen. They had only returned home from Orkney the day before, with Tim complaining about his sore head, with Mary feeding him a regular diet of painkillers, but looking a little worried. A mother's instinct, thinks Carole, remembering endless visits to their GP practice before someone took her seriously, or got tired of being shouted at by a neurotic mother.

She remembers how they had parked up their bicycles which, oddly, were never stolen, and then bought ice creams. It was a warm day, but with scudding clouds casting chasing shadows across the small High Street, and they walked the length of the street licking them slowly, making them last. The High Street was filled with people, many of them foreign-looking: the town is a magnet for tourists, being home to a world-class golf course, the Scottish Seabird Centre and pristine beaches. It's also home to a great many charity shops, making North Berwick a destination for bargain-hunters on the look-out for unidentified Renoirs or Rembrandts and, maybe, a pair of cheap trousers.

Sometimes they would paddle in shallow water; sometimes, but only on very hot days, actually swim. Once they jumped from the harbour wall, a dubious thrill that Carole never wanted to repeat. But that day wasn't hot enough even for a paddle, and Tim's forehead was creased with pain.

'I wish it would go away,' he'd said.

'It will,' Carole promised.

'Promise?'

'Cross my heart,' said Carole, 'and hope to die,' and made a cross sign on her chest.

It was enough, and Tim looked up at his big sister and smiled. He was still at an age when big sisters could be mostly trusted. It was probably the last time that he did smile because, when they got back home, Tim was in tears with the pain and Mary, her mother's instinct at full blast, called an ambulance, and went with him in the back to the Sick Kids Hospital, the same hospital to which, years later, Carole would take Iona. Carole saw him the next day, hooked up to drips, with his hair shaved off and livid stitching across his scalp. It was the last time she saw him.

Now, she looks down at Tim's grave. 'I'm sorry,' she says out loud. 'I didn't keep my promise, did I?'

Having said a goodbye to Tim, she drives down to the town's High Street and buys an ice cream from the same shop where she and her brother had bought theirs. That's one of the nice things about North Berwick, she thinks: nothing much changes. Okay, there may be more cafés and charity shops than she remembers from her childhood, but the important things haven't changed, like ice cream shops.

She takes her ice cream down to the east beach, with its spectacular view of the Bass Rock and its zillions of gannets. It looms white and massive a mile offshore and, in summer, is fringed by a multitude of birds circling and diving into the water. She licks her ice cream, but isn't enjoying it. It's far too cold for ice cream, but she keeps licking until it's all gone because it's what Tim, even with his headache, had done.

She then walks to the end of the beach and clambers over rocks until she reaches a large flat piece of stone. At her feet, small waves are breaking against the rocks. Above her, golfers are putting out on one of the town's golf courses. Higher still, seabirds turn and tumble on the thermals. Towards town are a few dog walkers but, otherwise, Carole is alone with her thoughts which have turned from Tim to Rob. How strange, she thinks, that the two loves of my life have both had abbreviated first names of three letters, and both beginning with an R. She holds no candle for Rob now, of course, but part of coming to this beach, this rock, is to remember how it ended.

Although they'd been going out pretty much through their undergraduate years, with only a few forays into forbidden territory (mostly Rob, and Carole always forgave him his trespasses), it was a relationship that never seemed to be going anywhere. She remembers the first heady morning when they first slept together, and how she felt that Rob might be the one to make her truly happy. It was a feeling that she'd clung onto, and in their first year together – and probably longer – she held onto it with a positive certainty: this person, with his lop-sided smile, and happy-go-lucky attitude might be the one person in the whole world she would ever be truly happy with.

But, time passing, it then seemed that they were on different trajectories. He couldn't wait to graduate and earn a living; she couldn't wait to graduate and, hopefully, be accepted as a post-graduate. He was the practical one, seeing university as a stepping-stone; she saw academia as a calling and, perhaps, a refuge. He loved the idea of travel, of jumping onto aeroplanes; she hated flying, and loved the idea of staying where she was.

It came to a head at graduation. Carole was on tenterhooks because an administrative glitch meant that she didn't know whether she'd been accepted for a doctorate; Rob, too, was on tenterhooks but for reasons that Carole couldn't fathom. She kept wanting to ask, but something stopped her. Maybe a distant look in his eyes; a distracted sense that she didn't actually want to know. She realised that this person that she had shared everything with had become almost a stranger. She had shared everything with him, she realised, while he was keeping things back from her.

On a particularly hot day, they caught the train to North Berwick and bought ice creams and walked the east beach. It's a rocky beach, unlike the west beach which is just perfect sand, fringed with large houses, so is always quieter. People don't often swim from the east beach, with its hidden outcrops of rock just below the surface of the water; it's therefore given over to people with dogs, or to occasional people without dogs. Rob and Carole walked slowly over the sand to the beach's far end, clambered over rocks, and sat on a large flat slab.

'I've been offered a job,' he finally said, not looking at her.

Carole nodded, not surprised. 'Where?'

'South Wales. Working in local government.'

'And do you actually *know* anybody in south Wales?'

'No, but what's that got to do with anything?'

'Nothing, I suppose.'

Carole wondered how he could have found himself a job, presumably only after an interview, without her knowing. Then she remembered that he'd disappeared off for a few days to Aberdeen, without taking her with him. By then, Carole had met his parents many times; she was almost family. He'd made an excuse to go home alone – a stag party or something. She'd taken the hint and stayed in Edinburgh. Instead, without telling her, he must have travelled down to Wales. He'd therefore lied to her, and not for the first time, remembering his sins with other women.

'Doing what exactly?' she'd asked.

'Working with house builders and developers, people like that. Making sure that anything archaeological that they find is at least looked at.'

'And is that really what you want to do?' she asked. Rob had never said what it was he *did* want to do, beyond finding a job and earning a living. She realised that, despite spending most nights together, there were significant gaps in her knowledge about Rob. She was open about her hopes and dreams: she told him everything. He, it now seemed, was a firmly closed book when it came to long-term plans.

'Well, it's a start,' he replied.

'Then what about us?' she asked, the most important question of them all.

'I guess we stay friends.'

'Friends? Is that all?'

'Look, Carole, you'll be in Edinburgh and I'll be at the other end of the country. Trains and planes cost money.'

'So that's it?' Oddly, she wasn't too upset, not yet, and simply needed clarity.

'I guess so,' he replied, still not looking at her. 'But you have to admit that things haven't been hunky-dory between us lately.'

He was right of course; those wildly differing trajectories with their different kinds of ambition had put distance between them. The passion they'd once felt for one another had trickled away, but so slowly that Carole had hardly noticed.

'Could I ask one question?' she said. 'Did you ever sleep with Clarissa?'

'Whatever made you ask that?' The words were aimed at the sea.

'I saw you both in Princes Street Gardens. On my birthday, no less. You looked to be more than friends.'

'Is it important?'

'Not particularly, no. But did you?'

197

'It didn't mean anything,' replied Rob, resorting to well-trodden cliché.

She didn't say anything, not for a while, and didn't want to do anything stupid like cry. 'Then do me a favour, Rob,' she eventually said. 'Please leave because, right now, I'd rather be alone. I'll catch a later train.'

He stood up, almost eagerly, she thought, then hesitated. 'Will I see you later?' he asked.

Carole was abruptly angry. 'What you mean is, will I be available for sex later. No, I won't see you later.'

He accepted this with the smallest of nods, raised a hand, and was off across the rocks back to the sanctuary of the sand and out of earshot. After years together, that was the end of it; no fond words or shared memories. But it was a final parting that she'd been expecting. Rob was the traveller, if only to south Wales; she was the stayer. He had made her happy for a long while; but then the magic had faded.

She'd hoped and hoped that things could be made better, but then realised that maybe they couldn't be. She never saw him again.

*

Carole remembers all this vividly, but without regret. Rob and her would never have worked. They were too different, with different paths to follow. They'd kept in touch for a while, mostly by text, but then that too faded to silence. The last she heard, he was still in local government, living somewhere near Swansea. She hoped he was happy.

She's still sitting on the same slab of rock where it all came to an end with Rob, and she reaches into her coat and takes out her mussel shell, the one he'd given her all those years ago. She looks at it, remembering their ignominious departure from Orkney, with the islands disappearing behind them, the screech of seabirds, and the taste of salt.

She smiles at the memory, turning the shell over and over in her hand, encrusted with grime and dried mud; it's the colour of Orkney and, putting it to her nose, she can almost smell its antiquity.

Once, digging near the Brodgar stones, she'd found a pile of mussel shells, each with a small hole in them. It had once been a necklace, a common adornment at that time, but whether worn by men or women nobody knows. But what Carole does know is that seashells had importance for early religions: the scallop for Christianity, the conch for Buddhism and Hinduism, and the cowrie for indigenous Native Americans. The list goes on. Perhaps, for the Neolithic people of northern Scotland, with their intimate relationship with the sea, the mussel shell might also have had significance. For a few moments, Carole imagines the man who owned her axe, standing inside the Stenness circle, with strings and strings of mussel shell necklaces around his neck.

Then she throws the shell into the water. 'It's time you went back home,' she says aloud.

The shell floats for a few moments, but then becomes engulfed by incoming waves, and slowly sinks.

Carole walks back to her car, task complete.

Nineteen

Back home, and Ray is in the kitchen and Iona is in her room. Carole plonks shopping bags on the table.

'Successful mission?' asks Ray.

'Very.'

'So, a successful and *secret* mission?' he persists.

'Yes.'

'Which probably means you've been to the museum to look at your axe-head.'

Carole pauses from putting things in cupboards. 'How could you possibly know that?'

'Witchcraft,' he replies with a smile. 'Actually, it's where you usually go when you tell me you're on a mission.'

Carole hadn't realised that everything she did was so obvious. 'Do I always say that?'

'Every time,' he replies.

'Good God!' she breathes, feeling a little stupid. 'It's just that I like to see if it's been replaced by something else. Collections do get moved around from time to time. I know it sounds possessive and silly, but I did find the bloody thing, and it's why I don't tell you.' Carole smiles. 'Anyway, if I never tell you I've been to the museum, how come you always know where I've been?'

'Because you eventually do tell me. You're also not very good at keeping secrets.' Until this week, Carole has never had any secrets from Ray. 'You're just not a very secretive person,' he says, and she wonders how much of the last week she might eventually tell him. Probably nothing. Secrets are all very well, she thinks, because secrets are things that are *actually* real or which have *actually* happened. Her secrets are about things that weren't real and which couldn't possibly have happened. In a way, she thinks, that doesn't really make them secrets, which immediately makes her feel better.

Carole takes a deep breath. 'I've kept my secret lover a secret.'

'You don't have a secret lover. That's something I would definitely know.' He taps his nose.

'His name's Juan and he's from Barcelona. He's much younger than you, and runs marathons just for fun.'

'No, he isn't, and no he doesn't.'

Carole has a vivid mental picture of what Juan looks like, clothed and naked, and how he would speak and then realises that she's thinking about her sat nav lady's boyfriend, and feels guilty for mentally borrowing him. 'Well, maybe he doesn't quite exist. I also visited my brother's grave,' she says, to be a little bit honest about something, although she omits to mention that she also visited it earlier in the week.

Ray has the good grace to look at little abashed. 'I'm sorry,' he says. 'That I didn't know.'

'I don't know why, but I suddenly felt guilty. Stupid, I know, but I realised I hadn't visited him for years. A bit silly, what with him being so close. Anyway, I thought it would be nice to take him some flowers. Mum still goes regularly,' she adds, momentarily wondering what her mother thinks about when she visits Tim's grave.

Ray doesn't know what to say to this, although suddenly he's smiling again. 'Actually, I've got you an early birthday present. To cheer you up.'

'Do I need cheering up?'

'You were looking peaky, remember? Although not so peaky today.'

Ray has never given her surprise birthday presents before, and Carole doesn't know whether to be happily expectant or,

201

simply, suspicious.

'Wait there,' he says, and disappears outside, returning a minute later with a wicker basket; it's their picnic basket, given to them as a wedding present, which Carole doesn't think they've ever used, not having been on any picnics.

He carefully puts the basket down and Carole, rather nervously, undoes the clasp and looks inside. Looking up at her, and looking equally nervous, is a very small and entirely black cat.

'Out with the old, in with the new,' says Ray. 'Anyway, that's what I thought. I got him from the same shelter we got Granny. Except, not being a geriatric cat, I didn't get a discount.'

The kitten gives the smallest of small squeaks as Carole, grinning stupidly, picks it up and holds it in the palm of one hand. 'That, Ray, is the best present you could have given me.' She kisses Ray on one cheek, now carefully holding the cat in both hands. Granny might have been a bit cantankerous, and wary of any affectionate gestures, but she had been a presence in their home; sometimes not a very welcome presence when she was being sick, which was often, but a part of their family. Carole had grown used to Granny sitting on her knee in the evenings in front of the TV, or checking which bit of the floor she was lying on so that she didn't accidentally step on her. She had been around for years and, she realised, had left a cat-shaped gap in her life.

'I've got lots of kitten clobber,' he says. 'A litter tray until he can go outside, cat litter, kitten food, the works.'

'We'll have to think of a name,' she says.

But Ray is one step ahead of her. 'Why not name him after your brother?' he suggests quietly. 'Maybe just to stop you feeling guilty.'

She thinks about this, holding the kitten in front of her, and hears a louder squeal from the doorway. Iona is also grinning inanely, and rushes over to pet the kitten, rather roughly, and much to its alarm.

'Careful, careful!' admonishes Carole and puts the kitten down on the carpet, where it turns around several times and then heads for the safety of an armchair, limping slightly, and crawls underneath.

'It's tiny,' squeals Iona.

Carole squats down beside the armchair. 'By the power invested in me by the Gunn family, I now christen you Timothy. Tim for short,' she adds.

'Tiny Tim!' says Iona, now lying flat out by the armchair and trying to tease the kitten out.

'It has a bad leg,' Ray informs them. 'Happened at birth, apparently. Dislocated hip, or something. But it should get better fairly quickly. If it doesn't, we can always have him put down.'

'Don't you dare think that!' says Carole, slapping him playfully on the arm, then holds Ray's hand, feeling ridiculously happy, while Iona now tempts the kitten from its bolt hole with a cat treat stick that Ray has also bought. Tim crawls out and eats the treat, and also seems happy. Iona watches the kitten eat the treat and looks equally happy.

'He's purring,' says Iona.

Carole squeezes Ray's hand. 'So am I,' she says.

*

That night, Ray and Carole again make love again and sleep in each other's arms. Carole dreams of a clearing in the woods and of talking to the trees which nod and whisper, and of the far north of Scotland, with its wide-open expanses, tugging winds that can almost form words, and Orkney's magical and ancient rings of stones, and of what could, maybe, lie beneath.

Twenty

She's still in Ray's arms when she's jolted from sleep by a scream. Ray, probably still tired from doing very little in New York, turns over, snuggles deeper into his pillow and sleeps on, oblivious. She envies his ability to ignore the real world, particularly in what seems to be a crisis. To her knowledge, Iona has never screamed before. Carole tugs on her dressing gown, bounds downstairs and finds Iona, horror-stricken, standing by the kitchen door.

'God! Whatever's the matter?' she asks, instinctively putting a comforting arm around her daughter. Iona wriggles free and points with a trembling finger.

'Look!'

At first Carole doesn't know what Iona is pointing at, until her gaze falls to the floor which is mostly covered by a wet sheen.

'It just looks like a bit of water,' says Carole reasonably. 'Nothing whatsoever to worry about.'

'It's not just water, Mum! Christ! It's the bloody cat!'

'He's a bit small to have done all that,' she replies.

'Not the new cat! The old cat. The *dead* cat, Mum!'

Carole remembers looking out all the utensils she would need for the big deep freeze clean, then switching the deep freeze off, and propping the door open with a floor brush. She'd been quite pleased with her late-night activity.

'It's just water,' Carole repeats. 'I'll get it cleaned up, don't worry.'

'It's not just water! It's water mixed with dead cat juice! God, Mum, how could you have been so stupid!'

Carole doesn't know what dead cat juice is, and doesn't want to speculate. But sometimes it's only in retrospect, she thinks, that stupidity can be measured. 'I had no idea that Granny would defrost so quickly,' she says to Iona who is now backing off towards the stairs. Carole wonders why Iona is up so early. Normally, at the weekend, it's Carole who is first up. Normally, come to think of it, it's Carole who is up first every morning. Normally, therefore, this small disaster would have been dealt with before either Iona or Ray made an appearance. 'Don't worry,' she repeats. 'I'll get it sorted.'

'You said that the cat was wrapped in a plastic bag.'

'She is wrapped in a plastic bag. Ironically, a Tesco Bag for Life.'

'Mum, please don't do jokes.'

'I wasn't making a joke,' says Carole defensively. 'However, it would appear that the bag must have a rip in it.'

Iona continues to back out of the room, having not succeeded in getting whatever it was she wanted from the kitchen, and treads heavily up the stairs, making each step sound like a rebuke to her mother. 'By the way,' she shouts from the top of the stairs, 'happy birthday!' Her tone doesn't carry much sincerity.

Sighing, Carole quietly gets dressed so as to not wake Ray, fetches a mop and bucket and sets to work. First, she sponges up the liquid and then disinfects every inch of the floor, making the kitchen smell Alpine fresh for the first time in years. Granny's cardboard box, she discovers, when she gets the ripped Tesco bag off, is now soggy and still leaking water and cat juice. Being practical, and a little unkind, she puts Granny's shoebox into the sink with some dirty dishes from the night before, where it can't do any more harm.

Half an hour later and the deep freeze has also been washed, cleaned and disinfected so that, when Ray appears a little later in his dressing gown, no evidence of the morning's small mishap remains, except for a rather unpleasant Alpine fragrance – which smells nothing like the Alps, as far as Carole is concerned, because she once went there on a skiing holiday, which mostly involved falling over on practice slopes. Carole never went skiing again.

'Jesus!' she hears Ray exclaim loudly. 'There's a dead cat in the sink.'

He has lifted Granny's lid and is looking inside, with an expression on his face that closely matches the one that Iona was wearing earlier.

'It's Granny, Ray. Not just a dead cat. *Our* dead cat.'

'I rather gathered that,' he replies. 'I didn't think we would have more than one dead cat in the house. We don't, do we? Please tell me that we don't.'

Carole chooses to ignore this attempt at levity. 'I stupidly turned off the deep freeze last night,' she admits. 'I just didn't realise that Granny would defrost so quickly.'

'Which she appears to have done rather successfully,' says Ray, putting the lid back on the cat's coffin and then washing his hands, saturating Granny with more water. 'Well, she always was a clever cat. No road sense, obviously, but very clever.'

'So, while you've been in bed on *my* birthday, I have cleaned and disinfected the floor and cleaned and disinfected the deep freeze.' It sounds accusatory, and Carole immediately relents. 'Sorry, that came out all wrong.'

'I was asleep,' he reminds her, 'otherwise I would have helped you in this noble endeavour. Happy birthday,' he adds, kissing her on the cheek.

Carole can't help but smile. 'I know, I know, although Iona will no doubt feel that the entire kitchen, if not the whole house, is now utterly contaminated. She doesn't like the idea of dead cat disease, although I doubt it's an actual disease.' She takes a deep breath, smelling strong disinfectant, and remembering how the Alps are supposed to smell. 'Your contribution to the proceedings is to dig a hole at the bottom

206

of the garden.' She points vaguely out the kitchen window.

'I rather thought that we were going to cremate the cat,' Ray says, putting on a serious face. 'After all, I know it's what she would have wanted.'

Carole opens a window to replace the Alps with East Lothian and looks at the wall clock. 'Christ! And I haven't even started on lunch. Where's Tim, by the way?'

Ray scratches his head. 'No idea, so I suspect that Iona has kidnapped him. I don't think the kitten had any chance of escape being too small to fight back. Meanwhile, I will go and get dressed and start on hole digging. It doesn't have to be six feet down, does it?'

'No, I don't suppose so,' she replies, not having given it much thought, and busies herself with peeling potatoes and preparing the lamb.

Carole then sets the dining room table, which she does every Sunday, without help from either Ray or Iona. It's just another chore that she's expected to do, she thinks, because it's part of her unwritten job description. Ray gets to jet off across continents, Iona gets an education, while she does everything else. It never used to feel like an unfair division of labour; it was just the way things were, or are.

The Gunns call it a dining room but it's no more than an L-shaped extension to their living room, and which Carole sometimes uses as her office. Not that she much needs an office to handle the household bills, or to keep up with some of her old university's research, but calling it her *office* makes her feel more important – and, in any case, she reminds herself, maybe I will soon be more than I am now and in proper need of an office. It's an exhilarating thought, remembering her last conversation with her old professor, and him saying in a (very) loud whisper that the job was as good as hers. Christ, and she still hasn't told Ray, and wonders again what he'll say.

On closer inspection, Granny's shoebox, now water and

cat juice saturated, is beyond being a serviceable coffin, unless she finds another watertight bag to put her in, which would seem undignified now that Granny has been released from the deep freeze. Carole hunts around in cupboards upstairs before finding another shoebox. This one is rather larger, presumably once containing a new pair of boots, and may require Ray to dig a larger hole.

Iona is back in the kitchen when Carole returns with the new coffin, and seems to have forgotten about the wet floor because she's eating toast and marmalade and spreading crumbs everywhere. 'Mum, do we have to have a dead cat in the sink?' she asks reasonably enough.

'Doesn't everybody have a dead cat in their sink?'

'Mum, please don't make jokes. They're never funny.'

It's something that Iona often tells her, although Carole does like to think that she has a sense of humour. She also likes to think that other people believe that she has a sense of humour. Sometimes, usually after a couple of glasses of wine, she tells jokes that people occasionally laugh at. 'No, of course we don't need to have *our* dead cat in the sink,' she says, trying to remind Iona that they've just lost a much-loved member of their family, but again wondering if going to all the fuss of a funeral is actually worth it. 'But first I'll have to get Granny all snug in her new box.'

'Line it with lots of kitchen roll, Mum. She'll still be leaking stuff.'

It's good advice and Carole does as she's told, lifts Granny into her new home (she's still quite stiff, so not entirely unthawed) and then puts the new coffin out on the lawn. Pleased with all this, Carole then disinfects the sink.

'When are Granny and Gramps arriving?' asks Iona.

'About twelve, I think,' replies Carole, 'and has anybody seen the cat?'

'She's on the lawn, Mum, where you've just put her.' Iona pulls a face which Carole wasn't supposed to see; the kind of face you pull in the company of a very old person who has just said something very silly.

'I meant our *new* cat.'

'He's on my bed,' replies Iona. 'He slept with me last night.' She says it triumphantly, having successfully purloined the family cat as *her* cat. On cue, Tim totters into the kitchen, perhaps attracted by the smell of toast and marmalade, and maybe realising that this room might be a source of food. Iona picks Tim up and deposits him in the litter tray where he promptly goes to sleep.

Carole points to Iona's plate. 'Did you know,' she says, 'that nobody really knows why marmalade is called marmalade?'

'No, Mum, but I suspect you're going to tell me something very interesting.' Iona has made it clear that she won't be remotely interested.

'Well, I think it's interesting. The story goes that, when Mary Queen of Scots was ill, her maid servants made her something sweet to eat. Something sweet, made from oranges. Having lived in France for most of her life, her maid servants were probably all French, so were no doubt quite good at doing things in the kitchen. The Scots would probably just have thrown the oranges at each other.'

'Mum!'

'Anyway, they'd made the concoction because Mary was ill, or *Marie malade*. Hence, marmalade.'

'What's *malade*?'

'Ill. Don't you do French in school?'

'No. Look, Mum, I know you were big into old stuff, but is there a point to this?'

Carole sighs, perhaps also frowning. 'No, darling, just trying to impart a small bit of wisdom.'

'It's Sunday morning, Mum,' Iona reminds her and chomps on another slice of toast.

She hears Ray come downstairs and then go out to the

209

garage. He reappears on the lawn carrying a spade and a sheet of plastic. She watches from the kitchen window as he first cuts out a square of grass at the back of their garden, which he sets to one side, and then digs out earth that he deposits on the tarpaulin. He then stretches and disappears back to the garage, leaving the spade propped up against a tree.

Carole has now switched on the oven, and consults her Delia Smith cookbook for cooking times. Although she's cooked roast lamb many, many times, it's comforting to have everything confirmed by an expert, and to have someone else to blame if it all goes horribly wrong, as it has done on several occasions. Carole has a soft spot for Delia, although she doesn't always follow her advice. For example, Delia's curry recipe requires, among other things, chilies, ginger, turmeric, cumin seeds, cardamom pods, fennel seeds and fenugreek. Carole's curry simply requires curry powder, and she has no idea what fenugreek is. But Carole has always found Delia's book helpful, if only to see how much time and money she's saving by not precisely following her recipes.

Carole now puts the lamb in the oven, having covered it in oil and sprigs of rosemary. Oddly, she can follow Delia's roast lamb advice, without the addition of weird or unnecessary ingredients. For some reason, for roast lamb, Delia wasn't able to come up with any fancy additions.

She closes the oven door with her foot and is just about to wash her hands in the newly-disinfected sink when, once again, she hears Iona scream, this time from upstairs, swiftly followed by her daughter clattering down the stairs.

'Mum, for God's sake!' she shouts from the kitchen door. 'The seagulls are eating Granny!'

This is not something that Carole had anticipated, as she heads full-tilt towards the French window in the living room and out into the garden. Sure enough, there are several seagulls gathered around Granny's new coffin, the top of which has been prised off. One seagull is perched on what must be Granny and is looking angrily at Carole, who waves her arms and makes loud, threatening noises and scares them all away. Two seagulls then sweep back to sit on the apex of a neighbouring roof and watch the proceedings with thwarted interest.

Carole checks that there is no visible damage to the cat, apart from it being dead, puts the top of the shoebox back on, takes the box into the garage, and clatters shut the over-and-under door. All in all, this is not shaping up to be the quiet funeral she had been planning, and she feels a little guilty about Granny and the now undignified start to her last day above ground.

She also remembers visiting Tim's grave and finding her own gravestone next to his and hopes that, when her time comes, she isn't pecked by seagulls and buried in a shoebox.

*

Her parents arrive soon afterwards, her mother smoking a cigarette which she has the good grace to extinguish before coming inside. Mary knows better than to step over the threshold of Carole's house smoking a cigarette.

Her father, Greg, is tall and rather stooped, with swept-back hair. When Carole was young, she thought his hair made him look like a film star like Gregory Peck, despite her Dad working as an accountant, and therefore not being glamorous in real life. He gives her a hug.

'You're looking well,' he says, which he tells her every time they meet, usually every Sunday, and even if Carole is *un*well. When she was in hospital as a child with appendicitis, he still told her she was looking well. An hour after giving birth to Iona, he said she was looking well. He would probably say that Granny was looking well, if just a little dead.

211

'I'm a bit frazzled, to be honest' replies Carole. 'It's been a tiring morning.'

'I expect it has been,' says her mother. 'What with all the funeral arrangements. Happy birthday, incidentally.'

She is, of course, joking about the funeral, but in a sarcastic way, which rather offends Carole, the only one of her family who had apparently *liked* the cat, and maybe only because she was the one who had chosen it from the cat rescue shelter.

'I really don't know why you're making such a big deal out of this,' continues her mother. 'It's just a cat. *Was* just a cat,' she adds for emphasis.

'I just thought it would be nice, that's all,' replies Carole.

'Anyway, we're here, so let's get on with it.'

They file through the house and out into the back garden, where Ray is leaning on his spade, looking rather hunky and rugged, thinks Carole, and who now fetches Granny from the garage and places her next to the hole. Mary has lit up another cigarette, offending Carole again, who thinks that some solemnity should be observed. Iona hovers in the background with her earphones on and nodding in time to the music.

'Is there an Order of Service?' asks Mary.

'Mum!'

'I'm just asking, Caro, that's all. I mean, are we to sing something jolly or *Abide With Me*?'

'Mum!'

'Or *You'll Never Walk Alone?*'

'Mum, she's a cat.'

'Was, Caro. How about *What's New Pussycat*?'

'Oh, for God's sake!' mutters Carole under the breath.

Inevitably the hole that Ray has dug is too small for the much-larger shoebox, and he has to get digging again. Carole's plan was then to lower Granny gently into her last resting place but, since the new hole is still rather small, the cat is instead unceremoniously dropped into her grave by Ray, who then has to press down on the shoebox lid with his foot. They all hear a small thud as Granny hits the bottom. The seagulls on the neighbour's roof look disappointed that perfectly good food is being thrown away.

Carole had imagined that they would have a moment of quiet contemplation for a small life taken from their family. But her mother is looking bored and is still smoking, Iona is still hovering with her earphones clamped in place, her father is fidgeting, and Ray is filling in the grave. He puts the clump of grass back in place and carefully treads it down, and deposits the left-over soil from the plastic sheet into a nearby flowerbed. Carole recalls her decision to plant something over the grave, something to mark the spot, and then remembers that she's ordered catmint from the garden centre.

'Is that it?' asks her mother. 'Christ, it's cold!' Without waiting for an answer, she heads back inside, followed by her Dad. Iona, Carole notices, is already inside. Ray carries his spade to the garage, passing his wife on the way, and gives her a quick kiss on the cheek.

'Well, that went well,' he says.

*

They sit in the living room after the funeral, drinking Cava, while Mary chatters on about her shop, and the new stock she's *acquired*, and how the shop is doing *amazingly* well, and about all her friends in Edinburgh who Carole has never met and has no desire ever to meet. Mary, however, thinks that her daughter should be interested in the fact that Ruth has just had a hip replacement operation, and is hobbling around *marvellously* well; that Dorothy and Peter have moved house (*at their age!*) and that Cath is leaving Vince, after twenty years of marriage, for her fitness instructor.

Carole has a momentary pang of sympathy for Cath who presumably now faces a lifetime of fitness regimes and healthy eating, and wonders if the woman has properly thought things through.

'God, it's been cold this week,' says Mary after she's run out acquaintances to regale them with. 'Anybody else think it's been cold? And it's supposed to be spring!'

'Enough to freeze the balls off a brass monkey,' agrees her husband.

'Greg, really!' Mary doesn't like smut of any kind.

'Did you know,' says Carole, 'that old warships in Nelson's time stored cannonballs on brass monkeys?' It was clear that nobody did, that nobody was much interested but that, being her birthday, everyone was far too polite to say anything. 'In very cold weather, the brass would contract, so that the indentations in which the cannonballs sat would become shallower. In freezing weather, they would fall off, and hence the expression.'

'So not rude after all,' says Mary.

'Not rude at all, Mum.'

'Well, I'm glad we got that sorted out. In which case, it's an expression you're allowed to use,' she says to her husband, 'but preferably without the explanation. Anyway, how has your week been, darling?' It takes Carole a few moments to realise that the question is aimed at her.

'Mum, I saw you two days ago, remember?'

'Oh yes, so you did. And what's become of my McGregor?'

'Actually, Mum, it's *my* McGregor now. You did give it to me.'

'Of course, of course. But one does get attached to one's acquisitions. What have you done with it?'

'It's in the spare bedroom, for our guests for enjoy,' says Carole, rather pleased that the first guests to see it will be her mum and dad who are staying the night. Between cooking and cleaning and rescuing Granny from seagulls, Carole has hung the picture up.

'It's gross,' says Iona, who is sitting on the floor by the unlit fire. In the hearth is a large bowl of plastic flowers. Carole doesn't see the point in real flowers, except to put on graves. The rest of them are grouped on chairs and sofas.

'It's a McGregor,' corrects Mary. 'Most certainly *not* gross. He's nearly had his pictures exhibited in the Royal Academy.'

'Just nearly?'

'He's an artist of great talent, Iona. An artist who has persevered in his craft despite many personal issues.'

'It's still gross,' says Iona. 'He's painted *our* kitchen table.'

'I'm sure he didn't,' says Carole, trying to sound bright and indicating to Ray that he should fill up everyone's glasses.

'McGregor is one of my most talented and gifted artists,' says Mary. Carole wonders what the difference is between *talented* and *gifted*. 'I'm sure his artwork will not only be something pleasing on the eye for many years to come but an astute investment, particularly when he does eventually have his pictures exhibited in the Royal Academy, which he's bound to do. Yes, indeed, most astute.' Mary seems certain of this, nodding at nobody in particular, and holding up her empty glass to Ray who is circulating with a newly-opened bottle of Cava.

'Granny, it's a mussel shell that's been painted on our kitchen table. If you want, I'll show you.'

'It's a work of art,' replies Mary. 'A depiction, I believe, of the fragility of life, and the indelible marks we leave behind.'

Carole had no idea that there was hidden meaning to her picture but, she supposes, a mussel doesn't live for very long while its shell lasts for thousands of years. What will she leave behind? she thinks. What indelible mark of hers will still be visible in a thousand years? Absolutely nothing, she decides. Then again, all a mussel does is cling to a rock. The mussel isn't remembered, only its shell.

'It's still gross,' says Iona.

'Don't be ridiculous!' Mary sounds quite cross that one of her masterpieces hasn't received the acclaim it deserves. 'He lives somewhere on Orkney and has to use a wheelchair. A car accident, I believe, when he was a child. He lost both his legs, poor man. Since then, he's never left Orkney, even to set foot on the mainland.'

Carole wonders how you can set foot on something if you don't have any feet but, sensibly, doesn't give voice to this thought. Instead it's Iona who says: 'Mum, tell her it was painted on our kitchen table.'

'A coincidence, Iona. Nothing more,' says Mary with finality.

'It even has the same wine stain and knife mark.' Iona looks angrily between Carole and her grandmother, and then stomps upstairs, returning a minute later with the picture held between two fingers, holding it in front of her, as if it smelled bad or might harbour germs. 'There!' she announces rather triumphantly and hands it to her grandmother.

'It's exquisite,' breathes Mary. 'Such brushstrokes, such sensitivity. A masterpiece in describing the very meaning of life.'

'It's creepy, that's what it is. Can't you see that it's our kitchen table? Come and look, if you don't believe me.'

'No need for that, Iona,' says Mary, 'I know what your kitchen table looks like, and this looks nothing like it.' She hands the picture onto Carole who looks at it carefully, and is relieved to see that the mussel shell is once again on a rather drab and unremarkable background. Gone is the wine stain and knife mark. Oddly, this doesn't surprise her, because she feels that everything is slipping back into place, and that

216

a new normality is taking shape; a new normality without the sentimentality of old lucky charms, or other people's love tokens.

'It's not our table,' says Carole and hands it onto Iona, who also now studies it.

'This is getting way creepier,' says Iona.

Twenty-one

At lunch, Ray carves, as usual, and Carole passes round the vegetables, as usual, and, as usual, Iona sits and does nothing, although she's not wearing her earphones, probably reluctantly. The mussel shell picture has been consigned to the dining room sideboard and Iona casts occasional and accusatory glances at it. She still clearly can't quite believe the evidence of her own eyes, and that the key to all wisdom hasn't opened any useful Pandora's box.

Carole's mum tries to find out what subjects at school Iona is enjoying, with limited success as Iona has one eye on the mussel shell picture and the other on her phone, clearly eager to burn one of them and tap away on the other. But it's a convivial lunch, with Ray making sure that everyone's glass is filled, and that anyone who wants a second helping gets one. Carole looks round the table with quiet satisfaction, happy that everything is well cooked and that everyone is enjoying themselves. This birthday, she decides, will be considered a success, unlike some other birthdays when the roast had to go back into the oven, or emerged from the oven black and smouldering (although that only happened once, many years ago, and the Chinese carry-out had been delicious).

Mary turns to her daughter. 'Carole, this is yummy.'

'Half price in Tesco, Mum. I did tell you.'

'Well, Ray, how was New York?' asks her father, changing the subject, in case the price of lamb in Tesco might precipitate a lengthy conversation about supermarkets or the price of food, obliging Ray to give a shorthand version of a very unproductive week on the other side of the Atlantic.

'At least you get to travel,' says her father. 'I never got to travel anywhere. Maybe just to Glasgow or Aberdeen. That was the furthest I got, although I once went to York. Stupid of me because my meeting was in Newcastle. Fell asleep on the train, didn't I! Mind you, my client was very understanding, and I made sure to get off in Edinburgh on the way back. Didn't want to end up in Inverness by mistake!'

Everyone just nods, unwilling to say anything that might trigger any more accountancy anecdotes which, to be fair, Carole's father rarely indulges in, knowing fine well that accountancy anecdotes are never interesting.

'Actually,' she says, to change the subject, 'I have a bit of news,' and looks nervously across the table at her husband, who still knows nothing of her potential new career. *Why haven't I told him?* she thinks. *It's the first thing I should have told him.*

Even Iona is looking at her expectantly, having always had a mother who never has any bits of news, or none that are remotely newsworthy or interesting, and certainly never funny.

'I bumped into my old professor in North Berwick last week,' she begins, 'and he told me that my old faculty has a vacancy. A lecturer vacancy, to be precise. He encouraged me to apply.'

'And did you?' asks Mary.

'After some thought, yes I did.'

'Well, bravo!' says Ray, who is looking pleased for her, as well as a little bit miffed.

Carole wishes that she'd told him earlier. 'Sorry, Ray, I should have said something.'

'Well, you managed to keep that a secret,' he says, 'and that's a first. Maybe I'll now have to track down Juan and have it out with him, man to man.'

'Whatever are you talking about, Ray?' asks Mary.

219

'A private joke, sorry.'

'Mum, you haven't done a proper job for yonks,' pipes up Iona, not trying to be unkind but merely pointing out the obvious. To Iona, Carole must seem ancient, or simply someone only equipped to do the shopping, dusting, cleaning, cooking and, rather badly, organise cat funerals. But Iona does seem, at least temporarily, to have forgotten about the mussel picture.

'Maybe not,' agrees Carole, 'but I also bumped into him again in Edinburgh yesterday.'

'You seem to have done rather a lot of bumping this week,' says her mother, finally laying her cutlery down on a clean plate. She dabs her mouth with a paper napkin and picks up her wine glass.

'So?' asks her father.

'Well, he said that the job is as good as mine.'

'Bravo some more!' says Ray, and Carole smiles.

'Of course, I have to go for an interview. Probably next month. So, I may not actually *get* the job.'

'Of course, you will,' says her mother.

'He told me not to dribble or talk gibberish.'

'Oh dear,' says Iona, again probably not unkindly.

'Well, what do you all think?' Carole asks.

'It's what you were always made for,' says Ray quickly, before anyone else can butt in. 'You know that as well as I do.'

'When you were at university,' says her father, 'you used to come home at weekends or for the holidays' – he takes a leisurely sip of wine, before continuing – 'and you would utterly bore your mum and me with your archaeological stories.'

'Well?' says Mary. 'What's that supposed to mean?'

'What I'm saying is that we haven't been bored by any of Carole's stories for a long time. In fact, far too long.' He turns his gaze from his wife to his daughter. 'So, go get some more stories to bore us with.'

'Thanks, Dad,' says Carole, feeling a tear well in her eye, maybe because of too much mint sauce.

'If you get the job,' says Iona, still clearly unconvinced about her mother's abilities, and therefore about her job prospects, 'does that mean you won't be able to take me to piano lessons?'

Carole hadn't given this any thought. 'I suppose not,' she agrees. 'But maybe we could find someone more local to teach you. Dr Cruz is perhaps a little too far away.'

'But it would mean that the house is empty when I get back from school?'

'Most probably, yes,' says Carole.

'Cool!' says Iona, looking happier than she's done all day.

*

Carole ponders what this week has taught her. That the past is never quite lost? That the past shapes who we are now, and who we could be? She supposes that's close enough to the truth, although she still has no idea how the madnesses could have happened. Divine intervention? But she's not a believer, and doesn't think that speaking in a woman's voice through a sentient sat nav would be His style. If the Bible is anything to go by, He much prefers thunder claps, burning bushes or writing things down on tablets of stone. Then who or what? But she also knows that it's a question she's unlikely to find an answer to. Things happen, end of story, and it's probably the same whether those things are ordinary or extraordinary, explicable or inexplicable. At least, she hopes that it's the end of the story, looking nervously at the mussel shell picture.

But has she been changed? Yes, she knows that she has. She's reaching forwards with a new purpose; to hopefully go back to what she's qualified for and was good at. Going

221

back to the future. She's also rediscovered that she loves her husband and that, even at her age, she can make new choices, because that's what life is all about. Making choices, and then hoping that they're the right ones, or simply accepting it if they're the wrong ones. She smiles: she's happy, and looks round the table; at her daughter surreptitiously tapping on her phone under the table, and at her husband, and at her parents. After Iona's illness, she couldn't bear the thought of having more children and having to go through any more protracted illnesses. They'd been planning for three, maybe four children, at least one of each, but that was quietly shelved. She can't now remember whether she and Ray had talked about it, or if it was something that had been quietly accepted.

'Dear God! You've got another one,' says Mary, who has spotted the kitten sitting uncertainly in the doorway.

'A present from Ray,' explains Carole, realising that the new cat hasn't been mentioned. 'Well, we're kind of used to having a cat about the place. If nothing else, he'll scare the mice away,' she jokes, catching a warning glance from Iona.

'And what's the little fella's name?' asks her Dad.

Carole bites her lip. 'Tim,' she says, and looks at her mother who seems merely amused.

'Tom?' says her Dad. 'As in Tom and Jerry?'

'No, Dad, Tim. We thought that it might be a nice way of remembering …' She trails off, unsure if remembering the other Tim is a good idea or not.

'Why not,' says her mother in a small voice and smiles a little sadly. 'Maybe, an appropriate name. It's always good to remember, Carole.'

The kitten looks at everyone with big unblinking eyes and then hobbles off to sit under an armchair.

Carole tops everybody's glass up and there is a toast to Carole's birthday. It's a day with a ritual familiarity to it, honed over many years, because Carole's birthday is always celebrated on the Sunday closest to it, when her parents will be there. Carole is a little unclear when or why this tradition started, but it means that everybody knows precisely when it's time for her to open presents, or eat lunch, or fall asleep. It's a bit like Christmas, she thinks, but without silly hats or Brussels sprouts, which she hates and Ray loves. But the familiarity pleases Carole; that it's a day when everything is planned, and that nobody needs to be reminded what to do next. She supposes that other families also have their set rituals, practiced and polished to perfection over the years.

Next, once glasses have been replenished, comes present opening. Iona has given her a gift card for their local shopping centre, no doubt purchased by Ray, but which she's pleased about because it means that she won't have the chore of returning something that she doesn't like, and offending Iona in the bargain.

'Please don't tell me it's lovely,' says Iona.

'It's very kind of you, and *very* practical,' says Carole, navigating around the table to give her daughter a hug and a kiss.

'So, what will you buy?' persists Iona.

Carole looks at the gift card and the amount she can spend. Probably not very much, she thinks. 'I will buy something special, to remember who gave it to me,' she replies, which seems to satisfy Iona.

Ray hands her a small oblong box. 'Here's my gift, although I now feel incredibly stupid about it.'

Inside the box is a silver Luckenbooth brooch, two hearts intertwined, surrounded by Celtic knots and with a blue sapphire in its centre. She puts a hand to her mouth, momentarily beyond words. It's almost exactly like her old brooch, but new.

'I figured,' continues Ray, 'that, since I first met you, I'd never seen you wear your old brooch and that you must have lost it. Quite why I got that idea I don't know. In a dream, maybe,' he shrugs and scratches his head. 'So, I bought you a replacement. That was a mission of mine a couple of weeks ago.'

She shakes her head. 'Ray, it's stunning.'

She runs her fingers across it, across the delicate Celtic knots, tracing the outline of each heart. It's also heavy, and not from a tawdry tourist shop. On the box is a fancy jeweller's name that even Carole has heard of so it must have cost a fortune.

'Then I saw you wearing the brooch again yesterday, and realised that you hadn't lost the old one.' Ray holds up his hands, looking sheepish. 'If you like, you can always change it. I've still got the receipt. Get something that you do want.'

'But I do want it,' she says, and reaches for his hand and squeezes it. Despite herself, she's started to cry and has to dab at her eyes with her napkin.

'You didn't cry over my gift card,' says Iona, reaching for Carole's brooch and peering at it suspiciously. 'Please don't tell me that it's two mussel shells having sex?' she asks in a low voice.

'It's two hearts, darling. It's called a Luckenbooth and it's traditionally Scottish. They were made in Edinburgh and they're a symbol of love.'

'Christ!' says Iona, quickly handing the brooch back and looking a little sick.

Carole pins the brooch to the front of her dress and, as with the old one, runs her fingers around it, again feeling tears on her cheeks. To compose herself, Carole goes to the kitchen to fetch biscuits and cheese, and to make sure that the oven has been switched off and, if not, that their kitchen hasn't caught fire.

*

But she's also thinking about the day before because, after

224

throwing the mussel shell into the sea and visiting her brother's grave, she had one last task to perform. She had to give back something that wasn't hers. It had been a sudden realisation, a rush of understanding that there are gifts you keep and other things you can only borrow. Like children, which you can never keep. She had finally understood when her old Luckenbooth brooch had materialised again, gleaming and intact, and pinned to her chest: a reminder that, even across centuries, love is an eternal bond, but not hers to borrow. She'd walked from the beach and driven to her old home outside North Berwick. This time, it had a car parked in the small driveway and a wisp of smoke was blowing from a chimney. But the garden was still unkempt and the window frames still needed painting. It took her a while to remember that it had only been a few days since she was last there.

She had pulled onto the grass verge, switched off the engine, and walked to the new bridge. She'd stood, hands on the balustrade, and looked towards the town and over it to the sea. A cruise liner was headed upstream towards Edinburgh; an oil tanker was headed towards the open sea. Between the shoreline and the ships was the Bass Rock, painted white by millennia of seabirds.

She'd then clambered down to the small stream, remembering other journeys; sometimes alone, sometimes with Tim. Neither of them ever told their parents about their secret place in the woods. It was a solemn promise they'd made; the clearing would always be theirs, and nobody else's. She'd climbed slowly through the trees, her feet crackling on small branches underfoot. It was quiet in the wood, just as she remembered, except for muted birdsong high above. In places it was nearly dark, with branches intertwining although, looking up, she could see sunlight and, looking down, a patchwork of shadows at her feet.

225

'Penny for them?'

Ray has appeared at the doorway and is clutching a large envelope.

'Sorry, I was crying.' She dabs her eyes with a tea towel.

'The brooch isn't that bad, is it?'

She shakes her head, smiling through her tears. 'It's perfect, Ray.'

'I've also got you something else,' he says, holding out a large envelope. 'Actually, for both of us, so it's not really a birthday present.'

'That sounds like a guilt offering.'

'No, nothing like that,' he says, and hands her the envelope.

She opens it with a mixture of excitement and trepidation; unexpected gifts from Ray are, well, unexpected, or were, until yesterday and today. Inside is a brochure with a picture of a big, posh house and it takes her a moment to realise that she's seen this photograph before, and a few more moments to remember that she last saw it on Ray's computer.

'I thought we could go away for a few days next week,' he says. 'Just the two of us.'

'The two of us?' she echoes, still looking at the picture on the brochure.

'I've organised for Iona to stay over with Julie. Don't worry,' he says, 'it's all organised with Julie's parents. They would be delighted, or so they said, to have Iona for a couple of days. Quite how delighted I don't know, but that's what they said. Anyway, whatever they *really* feel, they agreed to the idea.' Julie is Iona's best friend, and the hockey team's star goal scorer.

Carole is now flicking through pages. The hotel, it would seem, had just about everything that Carole could wish for, mainly a bar and restaurant, and a lot of things that she doesn't wish for. She will never venture into the sauna, having never ventured into a sauna before, and who goes swimming when it's not boiling hot? But it's an indoor swimming pool, and presumably heated, so she just might decide to live dangerously again. There's also a spa offering a full range of *pampering treatments*, so Carole might try some of those, whatever they might be.

'I saw you looking at this a while ago on your computer,' she says. 'I thought you might be planning an assignation with someone else.'

'Good Lord! Why on earth would I do that?'

'I dunno. Angst, maybe. Sorry.'

'You could always go with your friend Juan.'

'He's Spanish, Ray, and doesn't speak very good English.'

'Do you have to speak English to enjoy a luxury hotel?'

For some reason, more tears have leaked down her cheeks. 'I'll let you in on a secret, Ray. Juan doesn't really exist.' She smiles, rips off a bit of kitchen roll, and again dries her tears. She hasn't cried this like in, well, years and years. 'But I really thought that Samantha or Jane or Karen, or whatever she was called, might exist.'

'Why on earth would I want to go out for hamburger when I can have steak at home?'

'That, Ray, is a very flattering but very odd thing to say.'

'It wasn't me who said it,' he admits. 'Paul Newman, the actor, said it about his wife Joanne Woodward.'

'Then it's a very nice thing to say,' says Carole, who liked *Butch Cassidy and the Sundance Kid*, and gives Ray a hug, and a smoochy kiss.

'God!' says Iona who has come into the kitchen with an empty glass. 'What's with all the lovey-dovey stuff?' and marches back to the dining room, glass unfilled.

'The hotel looks great, and the brooch is lovely. You couldn't have given me anything nicer.'

'Except that you already have one.'

'But not one that you've given me. That, Ray, is the important thing.'

She holds him tight and they kiss again.

'Christ!' says an outraged voice. 'Could I please just get a can of Coke?'

'Bah! Humbug!' replies Ray in his best Dickensian voice.

Twenty-two

They sit over cheese and biscuits and a bottle of port is handed around, all part of the birthday ritual although nobody much likes port and everyone is too full to tackle any cheese. Everyone, it would appear, has eaten far too much roast lamb to have any room for anything except more wine.

Iona, who has been slurping Coke from the can, spots Tim limping from underneath the armchair. She pushes back her chair, picks him up, and without asking walks round the table to put the kitten on her grandmother's lap.

'So, here's the new addition to the family,' says Mary. 'Nice to meet you, Tim. It's actually quite cute.'

'He, Granny,' corrects Iona. 'It's a boy cat.'

'Of course, of course.' Mary pets the cat affectionately for a few moments, then screeches loudly. 'The bloody thing has just peed on me!'

Iona is back immediately to remove the kitten from Mary's lap and heads from the room, with the cat held securely in both hands. They all hear Iona admonish the kitten (*naughty puss!*) and then a scrunch as Tim is abruptly deposited into his litter tray.

'Bloody hell and damnation!' says Mary very loudly. 'I hope this isn't going to become another bloody tradition!'

'Christ!' mutters Carole. 'Language, language.'

'It's only a kitten,' says Ray, looking to his wife for support. 'Probably only a very little wee.'

'Come on, Mum,' says Carole standing up. 'Let's get you cleaned up.'

Mother and daughter head towards the kitchen, with Mary delicately holding out the front of her dress with two fingers.

'The last time this happened, I had to give my dress to a charity shop,' she says, 'and I'd rather keep this one, thank you very much!'

But soon peace once more prevails, with Mary placated with a large glass of brandy, although she keeps looking at the floor in case Tim has decided that her dress is now an alternative litter tray. Carole stacks plates and is about to carry them to the kitchen when Iona picks them up and does this task for her. Carole follows her into the kitchen to find Iona rinsing the plates under the hot tap, and then loading them into the dishwasher.

'Well, this is a first,' says Carole. 'Thank you.'

'It's the other half of my birthday present,' Iona replies. 'I have decided to be useful, sometimes. But only sometimes,' she warns.

There is unfortunately one last birthday tradition to complete, started by Iona some years previously, and endured by the rest of the family ever since. The Yes/No game, where someone, usually Iona, introduces the bare bones of a puzzle and it's up to everyone else to ask questions, with the only response allowed from the questioner being either a Yes or a No, until the puzzle is solved. But it's also a game that everyone does enjoy, or pretends to enjoy, because it marks the end of the birthday formalities, and the point when they can totter to chairs and sofas and watch whatever is on TV. Carole's dad is usually the first to fall asleep, then Ray, then Carole's mother. In previous years, it's only been Carole and Iona who have stayed awake, and sometimes only Iona.

'Right,' says Iona, 'I'll start.'

Everybody nods, glad to be starting the game because, the sooner they start it, the sooner it will be over.

'A man lives on the 22nd storey of a building. Every

morning he gets into the lift and presses the button for the ground floor. Then he goes to work. Every evening he comes home, but only ever presses the 12th floor button, and then walks up the stairs to the 22nd storey. Why?'

'He wants the exercise?' (Carole.)

'No.'

'The button for the floor he lives on doesn't work?' (Carole's dad.)

'No.'

'Is where he works important?' (Carole's mum.)

'No.' Iona is grinning like a Cheshire cat.

'Is he deranged?' (Ray.)

'What's deranged?'

'Mad.' (Ray again.)

'Ah, no.'

'Is his job important to this?' (Carole's mum.)

'Mary, you've just asked that.' (Carole's dad.)

'I'm asking it in a slightly different way, that's all.'

'Still no.'

'Okay,' says Ray, pouring more brandy into his glass and handing the bottle onto Carole's dad. 'We give up.'

'He's a midget,' says Iona, all teeth and laughing eyes. 'He can't reach up to the button for the 22nd floor.'

'He could jump,' says Mary in a practical voice. 'Midgets can jump, can't they?'

'Or he could carry a walking stick, or something,' says Ray. 'Something to poke the button with.'

'Or he could simply wait for someone else to come along, and ask them to press the right button. If the building he lives in has so many floors, I's bound to be a busy lift. I don't suppose he'd have to wait long,' says Carole.

'Mum, that's not really the point,' says Iona.

'All we're doing is suggesting ways around the poor man's predicament, that's all,' says Mary.

'It's just a game, Granny. The midget doesn't actually

exist.'

'Of course, of course,' says Carole's mum, also now pouring brandy into her glass and looking a little glassy-eyed.

*

The day before hadn't therefore just been about disposing of a mussel shell or revisiting her brother's grave, because Ray had seen her wearing the Luckenbooth in the pub where they'd met. For the second time they'd met, she reminds herself; or maybe a different version of the first time. Her broken brooch was trying to tell her something; to remind her that not all possessions are there to be kept. It was therefore a day about making amends; atoning for something that she shouldn't have done. She'd gone back to her childhood clearing in the woods and, as always, she'd found the small clearing easily enough, and she'd sat against an oak tree for a while, her mind full of jumbled memories, of the possibility of magic, and whether a sorcerer made this place. She only sort of believed in magic when she'd first discovered the clearing, although she did worry a little bit about witches and wizards; now, of course, she absolutely knows that magic exists and that, maybe, it's always around us, but we have to look for it. Maybe, without knowing it, it's what she had been looking for, a magic jigsaw piece to fit herself together, and Carole has always been good at finding things.

Then she took out her trowel and carefully dug a hole in the centre of the clearing. It was quite hard work cutting through the ground elder, but she set about her task slowly and methodically, placing the earth in a neat pile beside the hole. When it was quite deep, she took off her brooch and dropped it into the hole, then covered it over again. She patted it flat with her hands and then her feet, so that

232

virtually no trace of excavation remained.

There are some things that are meant to be found, she thought, and others that are meant to remain unfound, because she now knew that her brooch couldn't have been lost accidentally. It couldn't have become snagged on a tree branch, or simply fallen off by mistake. It had been carefully buried at the precise centre of the circle and that, long ago, a courting couple had also considered the circle as their special place.

The old brooch was, for her, now more than silver and sapphire; it was also about loss as well as love. One of the young lovers would have buried it when that love was broken. Carole knows, or thinks she knows, that they spent a lifetime together, but that he was eventually lost to her. Maybe war, or disease, or maybe – she hopes – old age. It would have been the woman who buried the Luckenbooth; a too-sentimental act for a man to do, she thought. She imagined her with white hair under a bonnet, a little stooped with age, with long skirts to her ankles, digging in the spot where Carole had been digging. Like her, she had probably been crying when she dug her small hole. Two women separated by three hundred years or more. Carole was in a place that was once *their* place and, who knows, may have become someone else's place after that, before becoming Carole's secret place. She had no right to keep what was once their symbol of love. It had been theirs, but never hers. Search for me, she thinks, but sometimes don't find me.

'I'm sorry,' said Carole to the earth at her feet and to the trees that surrounded her, and the trees rustled and whispered in reply, and Carole could almost hear them saying *thank you*.

*

'I've got another one,' announces Iona, to everyone's private

233

disappointment. Carole's mum yawns loudly, one hand across her mouth, looking wistfully at the living room sofa which is her traditional after-lunch spot. The rest of the family try to look vaguely interested.

'A man gets up and goes to work, and is immediately fired. Why?'

'Is this the midget again?' (Carole's mum.)

'No.' Iona looks a little cross.

'Well, does he live in a tower block?' (Carole's mum, again.)

'Granny, what's that got to do with anything?' Then remembering the rules, Iona says, 'No.'

'Was he rude to his boss?' (Ray, who does seem to be taking the game seriously.)

'No.'

'Had he done a bad bit of work?' (Carole.)

'No.'

'Had he been rude to someone?' (Ray is still trying to take things seriously, but Carole can see that he'd much rather be on the sofa and dozing off.)

'Had he groped someone's bottom?' (Carole's dad.)

'Dad!' Carole is rather shocked that her father could have asked such a thing.

'Well, it's what happened in my day,' he replies. 'Can't get away with doing things like that now.'

'And when you were young it *was* okay, is that what you're saying?' asks Mary. 'Is that the kind of thing you used to get up to?'

'No of course not, but there was some leeway, as it were. I'm just saying that definitions of what are right and wrong in the workplace seem to have changed,' he replies. 'There wasn't such a thing as sexual harassment in my day. Some of the better-looking girls got their bottoms pinched regularly, and nobody seemed to mind.'

'The girls getting their bottoms pinched probably did,'

says Carole, coming to the defence of women everywhere.

'Well, things have certainly changed for the better in that department,' says Mary.

'No,' says Iona, finally able to give an answer, although nobody can now remember what the question was.

'Did he stab someone?' asks Ray.

'Dad, that's just being stupid!'

'No, it's not. It's a perfectly reasonable question.'

Iona sighs. 'Then the answer is no.'

'Then, did he fight with someone.

'No.'

'Shoot someone?'

'Dad, please! No!'

A short silence descends as everyone tries to think of other questions to ask, although the obvious, and unobvious, questions seem to have already been asked.

'We give in,' says Ray, speaking for the whole family.

'Because he'd forgotten to put on any clothes,' says Iona, and squeals with laughter.

Carole's mum sighs. 'But that's ridiculous. Someone would have told him before he got to work. I know I would if I saw someone naked walking down the street.'

'Do you see many naked men?' asks Iona.

'Not as many as I would like,' she replies. 'Anyway, how can you forget to get dressed?'

'Mary, it's just a game,' points out Ray.

Carole's dad, whose eyes have been closed for a few moments, wakes up with a small start. 'So, he didn't grope somebody's bottom?'

'He'd have known that he hadn't put on any clothes,' continues Mary. 'For a start, he'd have been cold.'

'Oh, for God's sake!' says Iona. 'But it does mean that I've won twice,' and can't keep a note of triumph from her voice.

'Stupid game,' mutters Mary, under her breath, but loudly

enough for everyone to hear. 'Anyway, I'd have thought that not putting on clothes would be a sign of mental illness. His boss should have been more understanding.'

'Let's not play anymore,' says Iona.

'Well, if you say so, sweetie,' says Mary, winking at her husband. 'Nearly time to rest my eyes, I think.'

But Carole is temporarily elsewhere, back in the wooded clearing, watching an old woman cry, burying her love token in a place where it would never be found. Then she's transported to the far north of Scotland, back to another place of timeless mystery, with rolling waves around her, and seabirds screeching above. The Stenness stones stand as witnesses to history, having seen millennia of generations come and go, and Carole realises that she hasn't been back to Orkney since her mad visit when Iona was ill. Has it been so long? she asks herself, remembering a landscape that won't have changed since ancient times; the same waves, the same seabirds, and the same melancholy solitude.

Carole realises how much she now wants to go back, to stand again at the centre of what had once been *her* circle, to feel herself made complete in a place of safety and sanctuary. That's what her stones have always meant to her: a place without judgement where nothing bad can happen. She also now knows something else. She may not understand *how* her madnesses came about, but she now knows *why*. Search for me. Find me. Treasure me. The exhortation in her dream, perhaps also in the stone circle: to keep looking and find the axe-head, which she did the next day. But it was more than that, she now knows. Me, me, me: a subconscious entreaty to always be true to herself, and not lose sight of who she was, is, and could be. Mentally, she walks to Odin's stone and puts her hand through the hole and feels Ray's hand in hers.

Carole snaps out of her reverie, holding Ray's hand. 'I have a toast,' she announces, and raises her glass with her free hand. 'To birthdays!'

Everyone raises their glass and repeats the words.

'God bless us all! Every one of us!' adds Ray, back to his Dickensian voice, which simply makes him sound like a deranged (aka mad) country bumpkin.

'And to many more yet to come!' says Mary.

Carole realises that she's still holding onto Ray's hand and is now also holding hands with her mother on her other side. Mary is holding onto her husband's hand, who has taken hold of Iona's. Iona's other hand is in Ray's. She's reminded of a séance, and half expects Ray to start speaking in tongues.

But it's also the power of the circle, Carole thinks. In a circle there is nowhere to hide; within it, we are all equal because a circle is infinite, without beginning or end.

'In which case,' says Carole, tears welling in her eyes, and extricating her hand from her mother's. 'Here's to everyone!' and dutifully everyone raises their glass once again.

Carole looks around the table. Everyone is smiling, and Ray is squeezing her hand. Iona is also smiling, and looking happily at her phone. Her parents are also smiling, but anxious to be off to the living room and go to sleep, and Tim is looking out from under an armchair with a look of alarm on his face and, being unused to so much noise, perhaps wondering if remaining in the animal shelter might not have been the better option.

It's only Carole, slightly less inebriated than the rest of them, except Iona whose total concentration is now on her phone, hears Alexa, for the very last time, add her contribution.

You have finally reached your destination.

Twenty-three

(Extract from The Daily Express, 23rd July)

Lost Treasure Found on Orkney

A Neolithic treasure trove 'of immense value and international significance' has been discovered on Orkney by a team from the University of Edinburgh.

The stunning find includes gold and silver jewellery, as well as ceremonial and household artefacts that 'will rewrite our understanding of our ancient history,' according to Professor Keith Bridges from the university's archaeology department.

The priceless collection, made some 5,000 years ago, was found near to what remains of the Stenness stone circle, one of several stone circles on the island group.

'Of course, some of us have long suspected that there might have been a Neolithic treasure trove at the site, and it's wonderful that my suspicions have been proved correct,' said Professor Bridges.

Little remains of the Stenness circle, although it's believed to be among Europe's first man-made structures, and probably predates Stonehenge by at least five hundred years.

The artefacts are being transported to Edinburgh university for restoration and dating, and are likely to go on public display later this year.

There are also plans to take the treasure trove on a

travelling exhibition so that the whole country has an opportunity to see it.

A spokesman for the National Museum of Scotland said that a new gallery would be opened as soon as possible, entirely dedicated to the Stenness treasure.

'The important thing in archaeology is to keep looking, otherwise you'll never find anything,' said Dr Carole Gunn from the university's archaeology department, who led the expedition.

'It's also important that we understand our past because it's the past that shapes who we are today, and who we can become tomorrow,' she said.

Acknowledgements

With thanks to my editor Katie McCune and assistant editors Mia Attwooll and Eilidh Harrower who turned my words into a book.

About the author

Charlie Laidlaw is a PR consultant, teaches creative writing, and lives in East Lothian. He is a graduate of the University of Edinburgh and was previously a national newspaper journalist and defence intelligence analyst. He has lived in London and Edinburgh, and is married with two children, to whom this book is dedicated. His other novels are *The Things We Learn When We're Dead, The Space Between Time, Being Alert!* and *Love Potions and Other Calamities.*

W: www.charlielaidlawauthor.com

T: @claidlawauthor

F: @charlielaidlawauthor

Other Titles from Ringwood

All titles are available from the Ringwood website in both print and ebook format, as well as from usual outlets.

www.ringwoodpublishing.com
mail@ringwoodpublishing.com

Not the Life Imagined
Anne Pettigrew

A darkly humorous, thought-provoking story of Scottish medical students in the sixties, a time of changing social and sexual mores. None of the teenagers starting at Glasgow University in 1967 live the life they imagine.

In *Not the Life Imagined*, retired medic Anne Pettigrew tells a tale of ambition and prejudice that provides a humorous and compelling insight into the complex dynamics of the NHS fifty years ago.

ISBN: 978-1-901514-70-4
£9.99

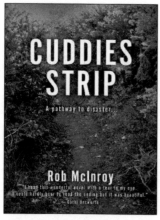

Cuddies Strip
Rob McInroy

Cuddies Strip is based on a true crime and faithfully follows the investigation and subsequent trial but it also examines the mores of the times and the insensitive treatment of women in a male-dominated society.

It is a highly absorbing period piece from 1930s Scotland, with strong contemporary resonances: both about the nature and responsiveness of police services and the ingrained misogyny of the whole criminal justice system.

ISBN: 978-1-901514-88-9
£9.99

Inference
Stephanie McDonald

Natalie Byron had a happy life in Glasgow. Or at least, she thought she did. The morning after a date, Natalie wakes up inside a strange house, in a strange bed, sleeping next to a man named Jamie who claims he is her boyfriend. Outside the window are rugged cliffs surrounded by endless sea.

Fearing she's been kidnapped, Natalie flees. When everyone around her insists that her life in Glasgow is nothing but a delusion, Natalie begins to doubt her own sanity.

But there is one thing Natalie is sure of. She needs to get off this island.

ISBN: 978-1-901514-68-1
£9.99

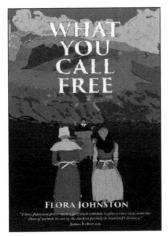

ISBN: 978-1-901514-96-4
£9.99

What You Call Free
Flora Johnston

Scotland, 1687.

Pregnant and betrayed, eighteen-year-old Jonet believes nothing could be worse than her weekly public humiliation in sackcloth. Desperate to escape, she takes refuge among an outlawed group of religious dissidents. Here, Widow Helen offers friendship and understanding, but her beliefs have already seen her imprisoned once.

This extraordinary tale of love and loss, struggle and sacrifice, autonomy and entrapment, urges us to consider what it means to be free and who can be free – if freedom exists at all.